HAWTHORNE FAMILY SERIES
VOLUME I

DELANEY DIAMOND

HAWTHORNE FAMILY SERIES: VOLUME I

Copyright © 2013 Delaney Diamond

THE TEMPTATION OF A GOOD MAN

by Delaney Diamond

A HARD MAN TO LOVE

by Delaney Diamond

Print Formatting by IRONHORSE Formatting

ISBN: 1-940636-02-7
ISBN-13: 978-1-940636-02-3

Delaney Diamond
Atlanta, Georgia

CONTENTS

THE TEMPTATION
OF A GOOD MAN

CHAPTER ONE

"You're young. It's okay to have fun every once in a while."

Those were the words Celeste Burton's mother had spoken about thirty minutes ago as she pushed her through the front door of their two-bedroom apartment.

Celeste knew that on a cerebral level, but it didn't lessen the guilt, even if she did have reason to celebrate. Tonight she turned thirty, and her mother had stuffed some cash from her secret stash into her palm and pushed her through the door with a "Now get out of here and have some fun for a change!"

Celeste scanned the crowded space of Avery's Juke Joint. Weekend nights always brought out an eclectic crowd of professionals. Customers dined at the bistro tables, hovered around the bar talking, and a number of them had created their own dance floor in front of the stage where a live band played popular funk and blues hits.

Despite its name, the establishment bore little resemblance to the ramshackle structures African-Americans used to visit to relax and socialize after a hard week of work. The renovated building had once been a retail store. It boasted high ceilings, flat-screen televisions, and framed contemporary paintings in a kaleidoscope of colors and geometric shapes. The large paneled windows faced Peachtree Street, one of Atlanta's busiest roadways. Gyrating bodies moved in time to the music, and all around her people laughed, sipped on colorful drinks, and looked like they were having a good time. Her eyes searched the room for the familiar faces of her friends, Janet and Gwen.

Someone jostled her from behind. "Excuse me," a contrite male said.

Instantly attracted to the whiskey-warm tone, Celeste turned her head to see if the face matched the sexy voice. A pair of espresso-colored eyes captured hers, sending a jolt of awareness through her body. A neatly trimmed beard, sideburns, and a mustache shadowed his face.

"No problem," Celeste mumbled.

His warm gaze raked her from head to toe, lingering for a couple of heartbeats on her bare shoulders. The muscles in her belly clenched in reaction, and her heart skipped a beat at his bold perusal.

Surprised by her intense, immediate attraction to a complete stranger, she took a deep breath as another bump captured her attention and forced her to face forward. When she righted herself and looked back over her shoulder toward the sexy-voiced man, all she could see was his retreating back. She stifled a confusing sense of disappointment.

Craning her neck, Celeste finally spotted her girlfriends and two men standing at a table across the room, near one of the windows. Janet waved wildly, and Celeste grinned, waving back. She began to wind her way through the crowded dining area.

As she neared where her friends sat on stools around one of the bistro tables, she couldn't help but notice they'd hit the jackpot tonight. Both men were good-looking and well dressed.

Janet gave her a big hug. "Happy birthday, Celeste!"

She was always in a good mood and seldom without a smile. Celeste bent down to her petite friend for a hug.

"Happy birthday," Gwen repeated, only she didn't offer a hug. She remained seated and with one gulp drained the martini glass filled with green liquid.

"Looks like the party started without me," Celeste remarked, raising an eyebrow. Gwen was the party animal of the trio. By the looks of it, she hadn't waited for Celeste to start having a good time.

The dark-skinned man chuckled and stuck out his hand. "I'm Lucas. Lucas Baylor. This is my buddy, Xander Dixon."

Xander was shorter than Lucas, with lighter skin. He was lean and wiry in contrast to Lucas's thicker, more muscular build. Celeste took notice of Xander's wedding ring when she shook both men's hands.

"I hope you don't mind," Xander said, "but your friends were nice enough to invite us to share the table with them. Happy birthday, by the way."

"You don't mind, do you, Celeste?" Janet asked, still grinning from ear to ear.

"No, not at all."

That wasn't entirely true. Normally she wouldn't mind, but it was her birthday, and she had hoped to spend it with her girlfriends. Instead, they'd invited two men to join them, and she felt like the third wheel at her own celebration.

"Oh!" Xander exclaimed, looking past Celeste. "Look who finally showed up. Dr. Roarke Hawthorne!"

"Tenured professor at UGA!" Lucas added.

"Booyah!" both men said in unison.

Celeste turned her head to see what all the excitement was about and looked right into the dark brown eyes of the least professorial-looking man she'd ever seen. The man with The Voice. For six years she'd taken classes part-time, working toward a bachelor's degree. If he'd been one of her professors, she would have never gotten any work done in class.

He nodded as he stepped past her, and the sleeve of his purple long-sleeved shirt brushed her forearm, raising the hairs and making her skin tingle. She tried not to stare, but it was hard not to because of his smooth skin and the heart-stopping smile stretched across his full lips.

"Sorry I'm late," he said. "I hope my no-good friends have been treating you ladies well?" His words indicated he was speaking to all three of them, but his gaze remained on her. "And I sort of met you a second ago, didn't I?"

The nervous fluttering in her stomach made it almost impossible for her to get out the simple words, "Yes, we bumped into each other."

"We were about to order another round of drinks," Lucas said, gesturing for the waitress to come over.

Introductions were made, drinks ordered, and then Xander clapped his friend on the back. "Well, how does it feel?" he asked.

Roarke seemed to lapse into deep thought and stared down at the small round table they were all crowded around like sardines in a can. "It feels…amazing. I can finally relax. There's nothing like job security."

"What do you teach?" Gwen asked.

When his attention shifted to address her friend, Celeste studied him. She figured him to be a couple of inches over six feet. Attractive, with skin the color of a chocolate

Hershey kiss, a man like Roarke didn't go unnoticed, not even in a crowd. A charcoal gray vest stretched over his broad torso and a multicolored tie with a predominant shade of purple.

"I teach physics at the University of Georgia in Athens. This week I received my tenure confirmation, so I drove all the way from Athens to come celebrate with my buddies."

"It's not that far. It's barely an hour," Lucas said. "And you should frame the letter."

"Don't be modest," Xander chimed, patting his buddy on the back. "*Dr.* Hawthorne is an astrophysicist. He wrote a popular article for the *Journal of Applied Physics* about...What was it again?"

"The statistical anomaly—"

"Yeah, yeah, whatever. Don't show off. You know that science mumbo jumbo is over our heads."

"You asked!" Roarke laughed. "Don't be modest; don't show off. I can't win with these guys." He gestured with his thumb and returned his eyes to Celeste. She felt as if he spoke only to her. An invisible cord pulled her deeper under his spell.

"You're the black Stephen Hawking. I smell a Nobel Prize," Lucas said.

"Whoa, let's not get carried away." Roarke held up his hands to his friend in protest. They were large, masculine hands with long, slender fingers, which could undoubtedly offer all sorts of pleasure.

Celeste swallowed, shocked at the thought that zipped through her mind. Why was she thinking about the pleasure this man's hands could offer?

"There he goes being modest again," Lucas said. "Your research was groundbreaking. We should take out a full-page ad in the paper so everyone knows what you accomplished."

"One day we'll say we knew him when." Xander sniffed and wiped a nonexistent tear. "Don't forget the little people."

"What are you even doing here?" Roarke asked him. "Your wife let you out to play tonight?" His attention turned to Lucas. "How many times has she called him?"

Lucas held up two fingers. Just then, Xander lifted his phone from his pocket. He smiled sheepishly. "I gotta take this."

Lucas held up three fingers. Roarke groaned, and they both rolled their eyes as Xander slinked off to a corner with the phone pressed to his ear.

"Come on, Lucas, let's dance," Gwen announced in a loud voice. She moved her shoulders in time to the music. Celeste wondered how many drinks she'd had already.

"I'd be happy to do the honors." Lucas helped Gwen down from the stool. "You, too," he said to Janet, whose head bopped in time to the beat.

She stopped her movements. "Oh, I can't. I'm engaged." Holding her hand upright, she showed him the ring. Every time an opportunity arose to mention her engagement, she took it.

"What does your engagement have to do with anything? I just want to dance, and it's obvious you do, too."

"Well…" Janet seemed uncertain, frowning at Celeste.

Celeste waved her away in an effort to ease her conscience. "I'll be fine. Go dance."

"Are you sure you can handle those ladies by yourself?" Roarke called as the three walked away. Without turning around, Lucas shot him the finger and squeezed his way through the crowd with both women.

With her friends gone, Celeste racked her brain for something witty and interesting to say. She glanced at

Roarke and found him watching her. His gaze didn't waver, and she shifted uneasily from one foot to the next.

"Your wife must be proud."

She smothered a groan of embarrassment. Did the comment sound as bad as she imagined? She didn't want to seem like she was coming on to him. He stood with his forearm on the high table and his left hand tucked into his pants pocket, making it impossible to see if he wore a ring or not.

Not that it mattered. *I didn't come here to pick up a man.* Considering her history with men and the drama in her life, she had no interest in finding a man right now.

"I'm not married."

A tingle of satisfaction replaced the embarrassment and piqued her curiosity. Good-looking and educated but no wife?

"How about you?" he asked.

"No, I'm not married."

Divorced, but that was another story.

"In a relationship?"

His lips stretched into an innocuous smile. She suspected her answer to the question would determine how the rest of the evening went. The safe answer would be to say yes. She could tell him she was involved, and then he'd probably leave her alone, which was what she really wanted. But, she didn't want to lie, and all of a sudden, she didn't want to be safe.

"No."

The change in him was subtle, but she saw it nonetheless. There was a shift in his eyes, and then he crossed his arms on the tabletop and leaned forward, offering his undivided attention. "Thanks to my loudmouthed friends, you know why we came out tonight. What brought you ladies out?"

"It's my birthday."

He raised his eyebrows. "Well, happy birthday. I'm not even going to ask your age because I know better."

"Smart man." They both laughed. The tension in her shoulders lessened. "So...astrophysicist? I don't meet one every day. How did that happen?"

"You really want to know?"

"Yes, I really do."

"I'll give you the short version. My mother bought a telescope for my tenth birthday, and ever since then I've been fascinated by astronomy. I became obsessed. At night, I would get up after I should have been asleep, pull aside the curtains, and watch the stars. I was in awe of the universe and amazed by its beauty. As I got older, I wanted to know more.

"I studied ancient civilizations, their take on astronomy and its relevance in guiding their everyday lives. I read every book I could get my hands on about Galileo. Imagine, we now see him as the father of astronomy and physics, but in the early part of the seventeenth century, they placed him under house arrest because he dared to contradict the geocentric view at the time that the earth was the center of the universe. He argued that it was the sun, and scientists back then—" He stopped, then grinned ruefully. "I got carried away. Boring, right?"

"No, not at all." Boring was the last thing she thought of him. He spoke so passionately about the subject, she practically felt his excitement. She could imagine him behaving the same way as a child. She'd never thought much about astrophysics, but she definitely wanted to know more now. "I think it's kind of...interesting."

He groaned and, making air quotes with his hands, repeated, "Interesting?"

Celeste nodded. "In a good way."

"Years ago it wasn't in a 'good way.' I wasn't the most popular kid in school, and I wore the Coke-bottle-lens glasses to match."

"You wear glasses?"

"No. Thank God for laser eye surgery. And puberty." They both chuckled.

Especially puberty.

"You guys kind of screwed up the whole Pluto thing, didn't you?" Celeste teased. "In elementary school I learned Pluto was a planet, now it's not. I'm so disillusioned."

Roarke hung his head. "No one cares about the 999,999 things we get correct," he said in a sorrowful voice. "Only the one thing we get wrong. Scientists are human, too."

Xander returned to the table. "Where is everybody?"

"Lucas took my friends onto the dance floor."

Xander glanced from one to the other. "You know, I think I'll go help him out." He winked.

"He's real subtle, isn't he?" Roarke shook his head. "Okay, so what's your story?"

Celeste shrugged. "There's not much to tell. I recently graduated from Georgia Tech with a degree in public policy."

"My younger brother and sister graduated from there. Congratulations."

"Thanks. Now I need to find a job." She took a deep breath. "And I have a six-year-old daughter. My world revolves around her." She liked to mention her daughter up front, which caused some men to run in the opposite direction. She watched his reaction, but he didn't flinch.

"I understand."

The vehemence with which he said the words prompted Celeste to ask, "Do you have kids?"

"No, but I raised my younger brother and sister from the time I was eighteen. I tell them all the time they're my kids."

"What happened to your parents, if you don't mind my asking?"

The immediate transformation in his disposition made her regret the question. The smile on his lips evaporated, and his face became shuttered. Even though she'd tried to tread carefully, her question had obviously been too personal and made him uncomfortable.

"They're both dead."

"I'm sorry. I—"

"There's nothing to be sorry about. You didn't know, and they died a long time ago." He seemed to force himself back into a lighthearted mood. "Are you having fun on your birthday?"

She pretended not to notice the abrupt change in conversation. "I haven't been here long, but…" She let her voice trail off. "Well, to be honest, this isn't what I wanted to do tonight. I would much rather go somewhere quiet and listen to a small ensemble play jazz or something."

"Really? I wouldn't mind doing the same thing." He edged closer, and her skin warmed to his nearness. His voice lowered to a warm purr. "Xander and Lucas got me a room at the Ritz-Carlton for the night and invited me here. Since they're paying for everything, I thought I'd better stick around, but…I think you and I may be victims of meddling friends. Am I right?"

Celeste nodded. His conspiratorial tone made her curious.

A speculative look came into his eyes. "You know, there's a spot around the corner. They serve tapas and have a small band that plays jazz. Would you like to check it out?"

She hesitated. What did she know about him? He seemed harmless, but looks could be deceiving. The battle scars crisscrossed all over her heart served as a reminder.

He leaned closer. Their eyes locked, and she held her breath against the attraction that crackled across the short distance between them. His direct gaze and flirtatious half smile caused tiny pinpricks of heat to surface along the back of her neck.

"I'm one of the good guys. I promise."

A good guy. Did they really exist? After years of disappointment, she had dismissed the thought of finding one, treating the idea like an urban legend, or a unicorn or some other mythical creature.

Nonetheless, here was a man who claimed to be good, and the spicy scent of his cologne made him smell delicious. Real delicious. The manly fragrance coupled with the inviting sound of his voice made her second-guess herself. Maybe, just this once, she was correct in her assessment.

"What about our friends?" she asked.

"They're welcome to come, too."

That wasn't what he was offering, and they both knew it. He knew she was attracted to him, and he observed her with unabashed interest.

Her mother's words repeated in her head. "You're young. It's okay to have fun every once in a while."

This could turn out to be a harmless flirtation. She wouldn't go anywhere alone with him. They would be walking down a public street to their next destination, a public restaurant. She made a decision to shift into fun mode and closed the door on anything less.

"Okay. Let's go."

CHAPTER TWO

Roarke felt a twinge of guilt at ditching his friends, but all he wanted to do was go somewhere quieter where he could further engage Celeste in conversation. He couldn't believe his luck when he walked up to the table and saw the caramel-skinned beauty he'd bumped into near the door.

Her friends protested when they told them they planned to leave, but in the end, they offered to meet up later. When they stepped out of Avery's Juke Joint, the cool breeze of late spring whispered over them and stirred the naturally curly tendrils of her shoulder-length hair.

Cars drove by at a slow crawl. Retail stores, condominium high-rises, and restaurants lined either side of the street. Men and women dressed in their weekend best passed by on the sidewalk.

"This way," Roarke said.

"How do you know about this place?"

"Just because I live in Athens doesn't mean I don't know what's going on in the big city," he joked. He directed her down a side street toward the open door of Tito's Lounge. "The drive's not bad, so I come to Atlanta every so often to take a break, but I don't get to do it much." What an understatement. He'd kept a busy schedule for as long as he could remember.

Tito's Lounge, located in the lower level of a three-story building, was already filled with patrons anxious to see the night's live performer. As they approached, the buzz of conversation spilled from the open door and filled the air outside the cozy space.

Celeste preceded him into the lounge, and he took the opportunity to rest his hand against the small of her back, as if to guide her through the door. Truth be told, he'd wanted to find an excuse to touch her. Warmth suffused his palm, and he kept his hand in place, as if it belonged there. He enjoyed the curve of her back through the gold dress, and he wondered what it would be like if he touched her bare skin.

She glanced at him. They stood almost eye to eye. Her thick eyebrows looked like they'd been carefully applied with the expert stroke of a painter's brush. Her lips parted and closed, as if she were about to say something but changed her mind. He knew she felt the same awareness. It hovered between them.

He watched as her lashes lowered toward her high cheekbones in a demure fashion. As if she were bashful and didn't know how hot she was. As if she didn't know she was wearing the hell out of that little gold strapless dress, which, combined with those red heels with the ankle strap, made it look as if her legs went on for miles.

"All the tables in the main area are already reserved," the host said. "But you're welcome to relax in the back. You won't see the musicians, but you can still hear the music."

Roarke turned his attention to Celeste to make sure she was fine with the arrangement, and she nodded. The host guided them into the partially enclosed lounge, which consisted of leather couches along three walls and a few coffee tables directly in front of them. Red rosebud-shaped candleholders made of glass sat on each table. The flickering light of the small candles inside each one formed a luminescent glow that bounced off the crimson-painted walls.

Black-and-white sketches of jazz greats like Dizzy Gillespie, Thelonious Monk, and Louis Armstrong hung on the walls. Exposed pipes on the low ceiling gave the place a rustic look. Only one other couple sat in the lounge, on the opposite side of the room from where Celeste and Roarke lowered themselves. The couple was huddled together and talking softly.

"This is nice, Roarke. Much more my style than Avery's."

The husky inflection of her voice made him want to ask her all kinds of questions just to hear her talk. His name sounded like an invitation on her lips, and he wondered what it would sound like when she sobbed it on her back with him buried inside her.

He couldn't remember having such an intense, immediate attraction to a woman before. In his effort to earn tenure, he'd been busy, with no time to do any serious dating, particularly in the last couple of years. In addition to his teaching requirements, he'd stayed occupied with research, writing, and filling his service requirements. With that chapter closed, he would be able to relax and enjoy the fruits of his labor.

Ready to jump back into the driver's seat and control the direction his life took, the idea of settling down retained a prominent place in his mind. At thirty-three years old, thoughts of marriage and starting a family plagued him. It didn't help his younger sister was getting married in a week.

"It's one of those hidden gems you selfishly hope other people don't discover."

She sat with her long legs crossed over each other at the knees. With her height, she could have been a model. On second thought, no. Other than small breasts, she didn't have a model's shape. No way a body so thick and curvy could fit into a size-one dress without busting the seams.

They ordered drinks and a couple of appetizers, and Roarke settled back against the seat. They chatted for some time, even after the band took the stage in the next room. He felt at ease with Celeste, and conversation flowed without effort between them.

He learned she lived with her mother and daughter in a two-bedroom apartment in Decatur. She told him she waited tables, but didn't mention where she worked, choosing to hedge over the information. When he inquired about her daughter's father, she would only say they were divorced.

He couldn't fathom why anyone would let Celeste go, but some men didn't appreciate the good women in their lives. His own father had suffered from the grass-is-greener syndrome, destroying their family and eventually causing him and his younger siblings to be parentless.

Roarke leaned forward and took a sip of his drink of choice—rum and Coke—managing to keep one eye trained on Celeste the entire time. When he sat back again, he asked, "Do you have any pictures of Arianna?"

"Of course." She beamed with parental pride and pulled a digital picture keychain from her purse. After clicking the slide show option, images of a cute, brown-faced little girl at different ages glided across the small screen.

"She's adorable," he said honestly. The last photo drifted into place, showing Arianna smiling into the camera in front of a birthday cake with six candles on it.

"She's the best thing that ever happened to me." Heartfelt emotion filled her voice and eyes.

"She has a beautiful name. What made you decide on Arianna?"

"Actually, my mom named her. She thinks names are very important, and she wanted Arianna to have a special name. I went along with it when she told me what the name meant."

"It means 'holy one,' right?"

Her face showed her surprise. "Yes, that's right."

He chuckled. "The etymology of names is kind of a hobby of mine."

"Really?" She looked skeptical.

"What, you doubt me? Pick almost any name, and I can give you the origin and the meaning."

"No way."

"I'm serious. Pick one. Make it good."

She screwed up her face into the cutest little scowl, exaggerating her efforts at concentration. "How about...Celeste?"

He spread his palms wide. "Come on—too easy. Give me a harder one."

She put a hand on her hip. "You don't know, do you?"

He cast an incredulous look in her direction, unable to believe she'd challenged him. "What? Are you questioning me, my skills, and my honesty?"

She cast her gaze upward toward the ceiling as if to think about it. "Umm..." Her gaze lowered again. "Yes."

"Do *you* even know what your name means?"

"Of course!" Her indignation was adorable.

"All right, then. It would have been a shame for a man whose life centers around astronomy to not know this one. The name Celeste is derived from Latin. It means 'from the heavens.' *Heavenly.*" He couldn't take his eyes off of her, and he shouldn't have edged closer.

The smile on her face made a downward slide. Her throat muscles worked a slow swallow. "Correct," she said.

"I know." Roarke rested his elbow on top of the back of the sofa and let his forefinger play with a lock of her hair. She didn't move away. The back of his hand lightly grazed more of the fine strands. With Herculean strength he resisted the urge to grab a handful. "So what do I get?" he asked.

"I don't—I don't know what you mean."

"You challenged me, and I won. Don't I get something?"

"You want a prize?"

"Yes."

A look of uncertainty crossed her face, but after a few seconds, she offered, "How about a hug?"

"A hug is nice, but I'd rather have a kiss." At her look of alarm, he amended his request. "On the cheek."

Her brow furrowed in an indication of distrust. "You're not going to do that thing where you turn at the last minute so I end up kissing you on the mouth, are you?"

Not a bad idea. "No, I'm not. I'm one of the good guys, remember?"

"Good guys don't coerce kisses from women they just met," Celeste pointed out.

Undeterred, one corner of his mouth lifted into a half smile. "Actually, they do."

The pink tip of her tongue peeked out to moisten her lips. His mouth went dry as he watched the fleeting movement. In slow motion she leaned forward and pressed her mouth to his cheek. His jaw hardened on impact, and warmth spread along the side of his face. The light fragrance of her perfume—peaches? apricots?—invaded his nostrils and dismantled his resolve to remain impassive.

He couldn't resist holding her in place, smashing the soft curls against the back of her head. He heard the sudden inhalation of her breath as he brushed his hair-roughened cheek against the silky-smooth softness of hers.

"That wasn't so bad, was it?" he asked in a thick voice.

He'd tried to sound nonchalant, as if they were having a normal conversation, but there was nothing normal about his attraction to her. He dipped his head and pressed a quick kiss to the underside of her jaw. She shivered, and she reached out and sank her fingers into his upper arm. The warmth of her touch sent his heart rate escalating at a dangerous pace.

With his hand securely at the nape of her neck, his gaze locked with hers. She'd roused something in him. A powerful, consuming need that made him question the workings of his normally logical brain, now clouded in a befuddling haze of lust.

Her wild-eyed stare signaled her own confusion. "No, it wasn't," she whispered.

At first he had no idea what she was talking about, but then he realized she'd answered his rhetorical question.

When his phone beeped, Roarke broke eye contact, and the moment was lost. Aggravated, he glanced at the screen and read the text from Lucas: *Ladies leaving. Me and Xander heading out. U coming?*

He showed the screen to Celeste. "What do you want to do?"

Her tongue drifted over her lips again, and he gritted his teeth against the reactionary tightening in his crotch. She picked up her purse from the coffee table. "I should probably go, too."

Roarke placed his hand on her wrist, and she froze. "Or you could stay."

She stared down at his hand, and several moments passed before she spoke again. "That's not a good idea."

"Why not?" He wasn't ready for her to leave. He would rebut every single objection until he convinced her otherwise.

"I don't know you."

"So stay, and get to know me. I'll answer all your questions."

"You know that's not what I mean."

Roarke ran his thumb back and forth over the velvet skin of her wrist. "I'm asking you to stay a while longer. Aren't you having a good time?"

"Yes, but—"

"But what?" He smiled. "You said earlier you seldom take time out for yourself. It's your birthday, and it's not even midnight yet. Are you telling me you're ready to go home already?"

"No, but I could catch my friends and see if they want to go somewhere else."

Roarke shrugged. "Or we could stay, listen to music, and talk some more. If you're worried about your safety, what could I possibly do to you here?"

"I'm not worried about my safety."

"Then what is it?" He knew exactly what it was. The sexual tension between them was so thick only a machete could cut through it. If she were half as attracted to him as he was to her, it was certainly cause for concern.

Her face displayed how she struggled with the decision to remain with him. Up until the last few minutes, he had been a perfect gentleman. Had he come on too strong and now she was backing off?

She expelled a breath. "Okay, I'll stay."

The overwhelming satisfaction he felt made him want to jump up and pump his fist. Instead, he texted a response to his friend.

CHAPTER THREE

Over an hour later, Celeste and Roarke stepped out into the temperate night. A mist of rain sprinkled down on them as they moved with brisk steps down the sidewalk, toward the public garage, to Roarke's car. She'd told him she could take the train back to the station where she'd left her vehicle, but he insisted on giving her a ride.

Deep down, she was happy about it. She didn't want the night to end, and she wished she could think of a reason to prolong the time in his company. He'd been considerate all evening, refusing to let her pay for anything and reminding her it was her birthday. They'd chitchatted about everything, from politics to religion, from world affairs to current events on U.S. soil. His breadth of knowledge of each topic they tackled amazed her.

A loud boom of thunder clapped overhead, and the surrounding buildings rattled an answer.

"Wow, that was loud," Celeste murmured, looking up at the sky.

"Yeah, it—damn!"

As if someone turned on a celestial faucet, rain rushed down on them in a torrent as lightning flitted across the sky in a jagged arch. Celeste squealed, hunching her shoulders in vain to protect herself from the heavy droplets.

"Come on!"

Roarke took hold of her hand, and they jogged to the shelter of a jewelry store's entryway. The deluge imprisoned them behind a curtain of water. They hovered in the doorway for protection, only a few feet from the downpour, pressed against each other as the wind whipped the rain into a wild frenzy. Roarke provided a shield with his body, his back to the street to prevent the wild sprays from reaching her.

They stood there, clinging to each other, when reality slowly set in. Their bodies were pressed into a corner. The grumble of thunder and the splatter of raindrops created a symphony of sound that caused Celeste to melt against him, as if her bones had abandoned her body.

"Typical Georgia weather," Roarke murmured, his breath stirring the damp hair on her head.

She felt the stealthy motion of his hand creep up her left side and come to rest below the curve of her breast. Desire flooded her body, making her wet and hungry within seconds in anticipation of his next move.

"I've lived here all my life, and I'm still not used to it."

She barely recognized the husky tremor of her own voice. She'd clearly lost the battle to sound casual. In the darkened corner, she was surrounded by the sharp citrus scent of his cologne. The gentle scratch of Roarke's facial hair brushed the skin of her cheek. When his tongue snaked to the corner of her mouth, she struggled to regulate her breathing, and her eyelids lowered in acceptance.

They'd danced around it all night, but each smile, each word, each touch had been leading up to this moment. His hand pressed her lower back so her hips became glued to his. Pressure built between her legs to an almost unbearable, nuclear level.

Then he kissed her. The hungry assault of his lips pulled a moan from her as she looped her arms around his neck and received his ardor with enthusiasm. The sharp flavor of rum and the sweetness of Coke danced across her palate. His sneaky thumb inched higher and rubbed the erect nipple of one breast, sending a dart of pleasure to settle between her legs.

His mouth continued to glide over hers, soft but firm. His tongue made sweeping movements, thrusting in and out in a seductive motion that had her mindless with burning need, scattering her earlier reservations. All she could do was moan and run her fingers over the dark curls on his head.

Roarke shifted, and the next thing she knew, her back was against the cool glass of the jewelry store door, her dress hiked high up on her thighs so he could lift her leg and position himself more intimately against her. The hard bulge he pressed between her legs made her tremble with the realization of a need so basic it permeated every cell of her body.

She couldn't think around the hunger clawing at her loins. She wanted him desperately and increased the fervency of her kisses, letting her tongue duel with his, and her teeth nip at his mouth. All the while, his thumb continued its relentless movement across the now rock-hard nipple of her breast, her thong wet with moisture at the ceaseless torture.

He pulled down a corner of her dress and released the puckered nipple to the night air. Lowering his head, his mouth became a salve to the swollen, achy flesh. With the soothing warmth of his mouth and the slow-motion stroke of his moist tongue, he eased the sting of the nipple's arousal.

She trembled, arching into him, resting the back of her head against the glass, aching as his hips gyrated in circles against hers. She listened to his groans, endured the pleasurable sucking motion of his lips and the continuous swirl of his tongue.

"Get a room!" someone yelled, but the words seemed to come from far away. They did nothing to curtail the hunger flaring through her like a firestorm.

Celeste couldn't hold back any longer. She bit down on her lower lip, but it was to no avail. He had her pinned against the glass, one leg in the air, her breast in his mouth, his erection grinding against her in a ruthless rhythm she couldn't fight against. Her tightly wound body exploded, and she cried out as the orgasm tore through her, violently pumping her hips to achieve maximum pleasure.

He released her nipple and whispered in her ear, "Yeah, baby, that's it. Let it go."

Another violent spasm rocked deep within her, and she trembled, grabbing at him as their hips glided against each other through the barrier of too many clothes. A deep, shuddering breath escaped her lungs as the remains of ecstasy eased away.

She was shaken, and her mind fried. The depth of feeling that overtook her had moved with the power of a freight train, making her feel helpless and vulnerable. Embarrassed, she avoided his gaze.

He pulled the dress back over her bared breast and then caressed the fullness of her lower lip with his thumb. "I've been wanting to get you off all night."

"Well, you certainly did a good job," she replied, her voice still shaky. She finally mustered the nerve to look at him. "What took you so long?"

"I needed to be sure you were open to it," he replied with a grin. He released her leg but didn't step back. They remained as close to each other as Siamese twins, and she could feel the hard length of his unsatisfied need. The nonstop beat of the rain continued around them. "We should probably get you someplace warm, where you can dry off. You're all wet." He stroked the underside of her jaw with his knuckles, and a shiver of pleasure traveled across her skin. Everything he did turned her on.

The rawness of his voice and the hunger in his eyes revealed much more to his invitation. She knew what he offered, though he didn't say the words. The unspoken question dangled in the night air between them. That she even considered going with him showed the state of her mind. This was not the behavior of a mature thirty-year-old. Instead, she felt the unfettered irresponsibility of youth, the reckless abandon that came with the acknowledgement tonight was hers to enjoy however she chose.

"Yes, I'm all wet."

The raunchy flirtation caused a flame to flare to life in his eyes. "I guess I'll have to lick you dry."

His words almost made her knees buckle. The idea that she was in over her head rattled through her brain, but she didn't want to think about the consequences or repercussions of her actions. She wanted to taste what it was like to be uninhibited. For so long she'd walked a straight and narrow path to ensure the best for herself and her daughter. Tonight she wanted to know pleasure, and she knew without a doubt she would experience even more of it with Roarke.

"I don't think that's possible," she whispered.

"I'd like to try."

They made haste through the rain. The doorman at the Ritz-Carlton swung open the door at their approach. In the elevator, Roarke hungrily seized her mouth again, dragging her close and letting his hands rove possessively over her hips and buttocks, singeing her lips with hot kisses until the elevator chime notified them of the arrival on his floor.

At the door to his room, he inserted the thin card into the slot, and the lock clicked. He turned to her, giving her a look as if to say, *Are you sure?* In answer, Celeste pushed down on the handle and led the way inside.

It was all happening so fast, but she didn't want to stop. To tell him she'd never done anything like this before would be so cliché. So when he grabbed her from behind, she leaned into his warm embrace. He marched her to a spot in the room where he could flick a switch and illuminate the space in lamplight.

"You're so damn sexy." He uttered the words in a low tone, at the same time reaching for the zipper beneath her arm.

His insistent erection pressed against the cleft of her butt cheeks, and she rested her head on his shoulder. He shoved the dress down and turned her in a circle to face him. For a moment, her earlier boldness diminished as she stood there in only a red thong and red heels. Then she saw the lust smoldering in his dark eyes and endured his inspection, standing straight and letting her breasts jut proudly from her chest.

"Sexy," he said again before backing her against the wall. With strokes of his tongue, he licked the sheen of rainwater from her skin, traveling up her arm and switching to mini-kisses across her shoulder. He settled into the crook of her neck, where his kisses became more arduous and demanding. When his fingers hooked in the thin elastic strips at her hips and shoved the thong down her thighs, her entire body flushed with expectation.

She watched him lower to his knees, and she stepped out of the satin panties.

"Let me see if I can dry you off."

The rasp of his voice scraped across her nerve endings before he ran his long fingers up her damp calves, past the back of her knees to hold her thighs apart. He pressed his mouth to the juncture of her thighs, and his tongue began an in-depth exploration of the delicate folds.

Celeste gasped loudly at the firm pressure of his soft lips, acute arousal winding its way through her as she watched him from her view above and heard the sounds his lips made as he continued with his pleasure-giving task. His fingers tightened on her thighs, keeping her open to the degree he wanted. Clutching his dark head, she rolled her hips against his face in a mindless grasp toward a climax.

Her body grew taut as he continued his vain attempt to lick her dry, every cell attuned to the thrust and twirl of his tongue and the pressure of kisses from his full lips. She barreled toward an orgasm. Another one, so soon after the first. A hoarse cry of satisfaction burst from her lungs as a tidal wave of pleasure overtook her body and left her weak and sagging against the wall.

Roarke rose to his full height and watched the labored rise and fall of her perfect little breasts. He started unbuttoning his vest. "I'm just getting started." Her eyes widened. "Keep on the heels," he said with a roguish grin.

When he'd stripped out of his clothes, they moved onto the bed, where he dragged her down on top of him. He ran his hands up and down the length of her back, molding her soft contours to his harder frame, caressing her hips and thick thighs. He kissed her deeply before rolling her over so she lay beneath him.

He retrieved a condom from his pants.

"Roarke," Celeste whispered, "if I don't...come again, it's because I can't come—"

"You've never been with me," he said with confidence. He took two pillows and settled them under her hips, then braced himself on one arm. Her beauty enthralled him, and he felt like he was losing himself in her sweet brown eyes. "There's a science to this." As he spoke, he caressed her skin, loving how her body arched into his touch. The smoothest silk couldn't match the sensation of her soft skin under his fingers. "Eighty percent of women have an orgasm through oral stimulation. Only twenty-five percent through penetration." He hovered his lips only a hair's breadth above hers. "Most men don't take the time to get to know a woman's body the way they should." He tweaked the brown nipple of one breast, following up with a gentle massage, enjoying the contortion of her face at the pleasure.

"Every woman is different," he continued. Even though he tried to speak in clinical terms, the husky heat of his voice betrayed his aroused state. Her moaning was starting to drive him crazy. "But every woman has a G-spot."

"I thought that was a myth," she said in a soft, shaky voice. Her delicate fingers reached up to caress the back of his neck.

"It's not a myth." He dipped his head and kissed her. She clung tighter to him. "I'm about to make you come so hard they'll hear you for miles."

She was halfway there already before his muscular thighs splayed her legs apart. When he pushed into her, he filled her, the muscles stretching to tighten around his wide shaft. Through the use of long, controlled strokes, the tension slowly unfurled inside of her, taking her back down the now familiar path of sensual madness.

His mouth closed over the ignored breast, and his teeth nibbled at her hardened nipple, sending a shock of electricity through her system. Relentless, he targeted the other one, sucking the turgid flesh, opening his mouth wide over the areola as if he wanted to take the entire mound into his mouth.

She spiraled toward inevitable release as his heated hand palmed her breast, kneading its softness and shaping it with his hands. His touch was gentle, yet firm, a formula perfectly calculated to drive her out of her mind. As his mouth continued the delicious sucking motion, his fingers tweaked the hardened nipple of the other breast.

A gasp broke from her lips, and she lifted her hips from the pillows toward him. Roarke angled his body and hit something deep inside her, made her beg in a hoarse whisper for the final thrust that would give her what she craved.

"Hold on to me," he whispered roughly.

She couldn't think. She could only feel, and she was burning up, hot, desperate. She kept her eyes closed, wrapping her arms around him as he instructed, lifting toward him with each downward stroke, clinging to him harder as their bodies moved faster. Faster.

She screamed. Loud. Curling her fingers into the sweat-dampened skin of his back. It was a cry of fulfillment. She knew for sure they must have heard her in the room next door. She'd never experienced an orgasm from penetration before, and her foggy brain fought to comprehend what had happened. Her body shuddered and seemed to break apart from too much sensation.

Several hard pumps of his hips later, spasms rippled through Roarke. With a groan, he drew back and slammed into her one more time, his spine stiffening as his body emptied. With a heavy breath, he collapsed on top of her.

Floating back down to Earth, a thought gripped Celeste.

Roarke was almost too good to be true. Good-looking, smart, a great conversationalist, and an affectionate, masterful lover.

She moaned as he pulled her into a tight embrace.

A foolish woman could easily find herself thinking she was already falling in love with him.

CHAPTER FOUR

After she dug some hairpins from the bottom of her purse, Celeste combed her fingers through her hair and brought what order she could to it by pinning it back. Her overly bright eyes stared back at her in the bathroom mirror.

What a night.

A smile graced her lips and her body warmed from the memories.

She'd lowered her inhibitions and thrown herself full throttle into the best sex ever. Since Roarke only had three condoms, they'd found creative ways to enjoy each other throughout the night. She'd done things with him—and ice cubes—she hadn't done with her own husband. After a glorious night spent in his arms, she didn't regret taking a chance.

Now what? She didn't know the protocol for a one-night stand. Should she wake him or just leave?

Celeste flicked off the light and walked lightly on bare feet into the dark room. With the heavy curtains still drawn, she could barely see Roarke's sleeping form under the covers. The white sheet sat enticingly low on his hips, revealing the muscles of his taut stomach.

Indecision weighed heavy on her mind as she hovered a few feet from the bed. She wanted to lean down and kiss his cheek, but it might wake him. Or better yet, slide beneath the sheets and feel his arms lock around her again, but she couldn't. She'd already slept late and lingered in the bed too long listening to his even breathing.

Besides, she should be honest with herself and take a hard look at what had taken place. She'd spent the night with a man she met for the first time last night. They'd had a good time, but bottom line, she should go. This was a one-night stand and nothing more, and she had to get rid of any latent expectations.

Accept it's over, get out, go home, and go to work.

A few more moments passed.

Maybe…What if…?

Celeste shook her head to clear it of her wistful ruminations. What was she thinking? Whatever emotional connection she thought they shared was assuredly one-sided. If she stuck around until he awoke, the situation would become awkward. She should leave while she still had her dignity intact and pretend the night meant as little to her as it undoubtedly meant to him.

A heavy knot like a stone weight filled her chest. Afraid of spending too much time evaluating her emotional state, she picked up her shoes and moved quietly to the door.

Outside in the bright morning sun, she walked briskly toward the metro station. Their time together didn't end how she'd wanted, but it had still been memorable in a way she'd never imagined when she left home last night.

With a crooked smile, she made a silent admission.

Best. Birthday. Ever.

****

"Derrick's here," Gwen said as Celeste hustled to the beverage stand in the main dining room of Sig's Cigar Bar & Restaurant. Derrick Hoffman, her friend and regular customer, never came in on Saturdays, but his visit was a pleasant surprise. She expected the usual large tip.

She'd been running late for her shift but managed to get there on time, change into her uniform, and clock in with a minute to spare. Management stressed the importance of the hostesses (as they were called) to be clocked in on time without fail and ready to work each shift. That included having their hair pulled back into a neat ponytail and being dressed in their uniform, which consisted of black pumps, a black miniskirt, and a white tank top. Gwen had convinced both her and Janet to apply for positions at Sig's, and despite her initial doubts, the job turned out to be a good choice. It was still a struggle, but thanks to Sig's, she could support her mother and her young daughter.

The weekend tip money alone was worth it, and they made even more during the playoffs because more men came in to imbibe expensive liquor with their friends while they talked trash to each other. All the hostesses knew the tighter their clothes and the more they flirted, the more money they could make. The regulars were generous, and security taught the newcomers real fast what was and wasn't allowed.

"How'd it go with that guy last night?" Gwen asked as Janet walked up. "Did you have sex?"

"Don't be shy. Ask the tough questions," Janet said dryly. She folded her arms across her chest and gave Celeste an inquisitive look. "Did you?"

"She can't look at us, so that means yes!" Gwen crowed. "Details, details! What did the *professor* teach you?"

Celeste's cheeks flushed with heat. "I don't want to talk about it."

"Oh, come on," Gwen wailed. "I didn't get any last night. I thought maybe I had a shot with Lucas, but I kept hinting all night, and he didn't even ask for my number before he and the married guy ran off." She rolled her eyes in disgust.

"Do you have to get laid *every* time we go out?" Janet asked.

Gwen shoved her and then returned her attention to Celeste. "Please, just tell me one thing." Gwen clasped her hands together as if she were about to say a prayer. "Please tell me that tall, sexy man was good."

Celeste bit the corner of her lower lip. "Amazing," she admitted in a low voice.

The other two women squealed. Celeste waved her hands for them to shush. "I'm not telling you anything else. I can't believe I even did it." She covered her eyes with her hand.

"So you had sex with a hot guy the first time you met him. Please, that's nothing."

"Yeah, Gwen does it all the time." Janet hopped out of reach before Gwen could hit her. "Are you going to see him again?"

"Um, not exactly." Celeste hesitated. "He was asleep when I left."

"*You* left *him*?" Gwen looked at her as if she'd grown two heads and then lifted her hand above her head for a high five. "Pretty good for a first-timer. Don't leave me hanging with your bad self."

"Gwen…"

"Come on."

Reluctantly, Celeste slapped her palm against Gwen's.

Janet shook her head at Gwen. "What's the latest on your ex?" she asked Celeste. "Did he come through this time?"

"What do you think? More empty promises, as always. He swore he would send the money last week so I could send Arianna to science camp, but of course he never did. It doesn't matter to him that I'm struggling to take care of his daughter. He doesn't care she can't have the experiences the other kids do because I can't afford to give them to her by myself." Anytime she talked about her ex-husband, a downtrodden feeling crushed her spirits.

"At least you didn't mention it to her, so she won't be disappointed," Janet said, her voice filled with sympathy.

"I've learned my lesson. I don't believe anything he says."

Celeste tried to think about her ex-husband as little as possible. After their divorce, he'd put enough distance between him and her and their two-year-old daughter as possible, traveling northwest to Washington and disappearing as if he'd never been a part of their lives.

After a few months, he resurfaced and began a ritual of calling every few months. The minute she mentioned child support, he became as scarce as rain in the desert. Two years passed, and she didn't even know if he was dead or alive. He didn't call to check on Arianna, nor did he provide any gifts for her birthday or Christmas. Not even a card.

"Arianna is six years old, and she hasn't seen him in four years," Celeste said. "What kind of man bails on his kid like that?"

"The same kind of man who started back calling you a year ago but doesn't offer any kind of financial help," Gwen said dryly. "That's no real surprise, though, is it?

When you were married he never had any money, and what little he did earn he spent it on partying and other women."

Gwen's blunt words cut through her. Thinking it was the right thing to do, she had tried to work through the broken marriage to her philandering husband, even going to couples counseling. In the end, she realized he didn't want a normal marriage. She left him, taking the most valuable thing that had come out of their relationship—their daughter.

Within a few years after the collapse of her marriage, Celeste locked away her adolescent dreams of finding love. She'd kissed so many toads on her way to finding a prince, she didn't believe in princes anymore.

She scrimped and saved, going to school part-time so she could find a better job than waiting tables. Despite the hardship of being a single parent, she wouldn't change her circumstances. She didn't regret having Arianna, but she did wish she'd been more prudent in her choice of husbands. It broke her heart whenever Arianna asked about her father, and she grew tired of making excuses for his absence and unfulfilled promises.

Janet gave her back a comforting rub. "Everything will work out. You'll see."

Celeste swallowed down the lump in her throat. Some days she didn't know if she was coming or going, and last night had been such a change of pace, several times this morning she'd wondered if she had imagined the entire night.

"I better go," she said. She poured a glass of water with little ice and two lemons, the way Derrick liked.

"I would do him in a minute," Gwen murmured, looking over at the booth where Derrick sat.

"Word is you already have," Janet said.

"I wish."

Celeste kept her head down to hide her amusement. Listening to the two of them go at it often made her laugh.

She made her way over to the booth where Derrick Hoffman sat. The atmosphere of the club was high on pretension, but it allowed for relaxation with its dim lights, mahogany walls, leather couches, and private rooms.

Some of the other women developed sexual relationships with their regular customers, thinking they could catch themselves a rich husband. The relationships usually fizzled out after a short period.

Most of the other hostesses had regulars, but none quite like Derrick Hoffman. He dressed like money, smelled like money, and drove one of only eighty Ferrari SA Aperta convertibles in the world—screaming money. They met at Georgia Tech over a year ago, where he'd been earning a master's in international logistics. They became friends, and before long he was a regular at the cigar bar.

Despite their friendship, she knew very little about his immediate family. His mother and biological father died in a plane crash, and he never talked about his siblings, a sister and two brothers. She sensed he didn't get along with his brothers at all, but he must have a slightly better relationship with his younger sister because he mentioned her on occasion.

"Hi there, lady," Derrick said when she walked up. He lowered his cigar and stood up. "How was your birthday?"

"Good. You should have come." Celeste returned the hug he gave her.

He sat back in the seat, and she dropped down into the booth next to him. "Did you go to Avery's Juke Joint as planned?" As usual, his wavy black hair was combed and brushed to perfection. His skin, the color of Caribbean sand, looked as clear and spotless as if he'd had a facial.

Celeste nodded. "We didn't stay long. We ended up going to a small jazz spot named Tito's Lounge." She purposely avoided mentioning Roarke.

Even though she considered Derrick a friend, she wasn't exactly comfortable talking to him about her one-night stand. It was private. The idyllic night had come and gone, and she would treasure the memory. She ignored the way her heart contracted in her chest, as if cruel fingers curled around it and squeezed.

"Tito's Lounge? Never heard of it. But I'm glad you enjoyed yourself even though I couldn't grace you with my presence."

Celeste smiled knowingly. "Right, you were probably with a woman."

He ignored her, but his upturned lips hinted at the accuracy of her comment. "You have plans next weekend?"

"Yes, actually," Celeste answered in a nasal French accent, "I'm off to Paris for dinner and a dress fitting."

"Don't get smart." Derrick took a puff on the cigar and blew the smoke away from her.

"I have to work. You know I hardly ever take time off."

"I have a wedding to go to, and I need a date."

"Who's getting married?"

"My younger sister. The wedding is taking place on St. Simons Island, at the family's property. Last time I attended a family event, there was a bit of a ruckus, so I need everything to go smoothly next weekend."

"I don't know," Celeste hedged. "How can I help?"

"The woman who was supposed to attend as my plus one canceled on me. I need someone who's poised, attractive, and knows me well enough to carry off being my companion, and who won't embarrass me. Consider it your belated birthday present—an all-expenses-paid trip to St.

Simons Island. We'll fly down on Friday and come back on Monday."

It sounded too good to be true. There had to be a catch.

"There's no catch," he said, reading her mind. "I need a date, that's all."

She sighed. "It sounds enticing, but I can't afford to take off a whole weekend."

"What if I pay you whatever you would make here if you stayed at work?"

Celeste frowned at him. "You must really need a date. Besides, I can't ask you to do that."

"Why not? You know I can afford it. And since I missed your birthday celebration, this way I can make it up to you." He fiddled with the cigar. "But, it's more than that. You'll be doing me a favor. I'm tired of being the black sheep of the family, and I need to make a good impression."

Perplexed by the thread of bitterness running through his words, Celeste asked, "What is it with you and your family?"

"Don't you worry your pretty little head about a thing. I need to know I can count on you to come with me and be on your best behavior. How about it?"

The idea tempted Celeste. "What about sleeping arrangements?"

"You want to sleep in my bed?" Derrick asked with a sly smile. Even though they had a platonic relationship, he was prone to flirting from time to time.

"*No,*" Celeste responded.

He shrugged, as if he couldn't resist asking. "You'll have your own room." His mouth twisted into a remorseful smile. "The older folks don't approve of us younger folks sleeping in the same room unless we're married."

Celeste propped her chin on her fist. "Okay, assuming I agree to this crazy plan, you're saying I don't have to come out the pocket for anything? Just show up?"

Derrick nodded. "Just show up."

"Are we taking the private plane?"

"Yes."

"Oh, goodie! I've never been in a private plane before."

"Yeah, it's convenient, and there are perks to having one."

"I bet," Celeste said dryly. She rose from the seat. "If Phineas found out what you do with his plane…" She shook her head. Phineas Hoffman was Derrick's stepfather and the only father he'd known since the age of four. The one or two times he'd mentioned his biological father, he always called him The Sperm Donor.

"Is it my fault so many ladies want to be inducted into the Mile High Club?" He grinned, not even bothering to try to look innocent.

"You're a mess." Celeste pulled out her pad and pen. "You want the usual, or are you going to try something different on the menu this time?"

"The usual," he replied. "So we're on for next weekend?"

"Yes, sounds like fun. I could use a vacation. Thanks, Derrick."

They discussed the specifics before Celeste returned to the beverage stand to punch in the order.

In front of the computer, her thoughts drifted to Roarke and the hotel room. She inhaled a shaky breath. The man was sexy, no doubt about it, and he knew his way around a woman's body. He must have made all A's in anatomy. She smiled to herself at the silly thought.

There was no point in thinking about Roarke. Professor Hawthorne would go back to Athens and academic life and forget all about her. She'd still be pining away for him, as if something more special than great sex had taken place. Sure, he made her feel beautiful and more special than she had in a long time, but so what? And so what if she felt comfortable in his company and enjoyed talking to him? More than likely, he was a charmer, like her ex. He'd driven into Atlanta to have a good time, and he'd found it with her.

She should be ashamed of her behavior, but she wasn't. Her fingers shook slightly as she punched in the order, her mind wandering back to the way Roarke had kissed his way down her stomach and the sensation created by the short hairs on his face as his lips traversed the sensitive skin of her lower abdomen.

She would never forget him or last night.

She let her gaze rest on Derrick. She wasn't completely at ease with the idea of pretending to be his girlfriend, but it would be nice to get away for a few days. She couldn't remember the last time she took a vacation, and it wasn't as if she could afford one on her own. Derrick's offer appealed to her, although she had concerns about navigating the minefield of problems she suspected existed between him and his siblings.

Someone sat down in her section. Taking a deep breath, she brushed aside her reservations and went to greet him.

Enough with the negative thoughts. What could possibly go wrong?

CHAPTER FIVE

Roarke pulled up outside his family's two-story house on St. Simons Island, the largest of the four Golden Isles that stretched along the state of Georgia's southern coast. Not too far away he could hear the roar of the ocean.

A manicured lawn and moss-covered trees surrounded the yellow house with green shutters, in his family for generations. As the story went, his paternal great-grandfather, Joseph Hawthorne, had been the loyal manservant of a plantation owner who'd fallen on hard times. He'd lost everything, including his health.

Roarke's great-grandfather remained at his side and took care of him until his death. In return, the owner left this house on the beach to him. Though dilapidated and in a state of disrepair at the time, Joseph worked constantly on it for years to bring the house back to its former splendor. Since then, it had been placed in a trust and was available as a vacation home for Hawthorne family members. Individual photos of Joseph, his wife, and photos of their descendants, hung on the interior walls.

Roarke stepped out of the vehicle and took a deep breath, inhaling the distinctive smell of sand and the saltiness of the Atlantic Ocean. Beyond the lawn, the property dipped to a sandy beach and sparkling water. Though he'd been born and raised in Atlanta, whenever he came down to the island, he felt more at home. Perhaps because his favorite memories from childhood stemmed from this place, where summer vacations with cousins and siblings were spent enjoying cookouts, riding bikes, swimming, fishing, and getting into mischief.

"Roarke!"

He raised his head from bending over the opened trunk of the car to see his little sister, Cassidy, bolt down the steps of the house toward him. Not so little anymore. He had to stop thinking of her like that. Cassidy was getting married tomorrow. The sun glinted off the blonde highlights in her sleek, short bob.

She hopped into his arms. "Thank God you're here!" she said in a dramatic voice.

Uh-oh.

His younger brother, Matthew, followed more slowly. He was an inch taller than Roarke and filled with bulky muscle from his days as a linebacker playing college football. "Get ready for the drama," he warned with a roll of his eyes.

Cassidy dropped onto her heels and ignored Matthew's comment. A breathless flurry of words rushed from her mouth. "You're not going to believe this. I can't get in touch with the wedding planner. She should have been here at eight o'clock this morning. Eight, Roarke. It's now"— she glanced at her watch—"eight thirty. Eight thirty. Where is she? What if something happened to her? What am I going to do? I don't—"

"Cassidy." If he didn't stop her now, she would have a complete meltdown. Her behavior was partially his fault. He became her legal guardian at the age of eighteen. As the only girl and the youngest, he'd always given in to her theatrics and tried to fix all her problems, and she expected him to do the same right now. He steeled himself for the pre-wedding melodrama and tried to defuse the situation. He placed a hand on either side of her face. "Calm. Down."

Cassidy took several deep, quivering breaths. "I'm sorry. I'm just so nervous. Everything has to be perfect." She gnawed the corner of her upper lip.

"No, it doesn't," Roarke said, keeping his voice calm and steady. "Even if it's not, it'll be fine. Got it?" She continued to gnaw on her lip and nodded her head. At least he was getting through to her. "The wedding's not until tomorrow night. Give it another thirty minutes, and if Sheila doesn't call or isn't here by then, we'll call her, okay?"

Cassidy nodded vigorously. Crisis averted.

"Thank you for everything, Roarke."

Cassidy wrapped her arms around his torso and pressed her cheek to his chest. He enveloped her in his arms. Her words of gratitude were about more than today. Everyone said he'd sacrificed so much, but he never saw it that way.

After his father passed away in a plane crash and it was discovered his lover was on the same flight, their mother withdrew into herself and within months died of a heart attack. Older family members insisted she died of a broken heart.

Roarke hadn't taken the time to analyze the whys and wherefores. With his younger siblings now orphans, and as the oldest, he'd felt a responsibility to do what he could to make sure they remained emotionally healthy. The original plan had been to have them move in with family since his first year at MIT would soon start. Instead, Cassidy and Matthew begged to be with their older brother. He rented an apartment, and the two moved up to Massachusetts to live with him. At the age of eighteen, he became a full-time student and the legal guardian of his younger siblings.

"You're welcome, princess. I'm just happy we found someone who would put up with you."

She smiled up at him. "Me, too."

****

Breakfast consisted of Roarke's pecan pancakes and Matthew's "famous" loaded omelets filled with cheese, sausage, ham, and sautéed onions, green peppers, and mushrooms. Matthew and Cassidy sat at the breakfast bar, while Roarke stood on the opposite side.

Matthew mussed his sister's hair. "I can't believe you tricked poor Antonio into marrying you."

Cassidy smoothed her hair back into place and cut her eyes at her older brother. "I didn't trick him. He *loves* me."

"Yeah, until he realizes you have no intention of learning how to cook."

"Did you miss the part where I said he loves me?"

"You know how those island men are." Matthew shoveled food into his mouth.

"I know all you care about is feeding your face, but Antonio's not the same. Besides," Cassidy smirked, "he's not concerned about my cooking in the kitchen. It's my cooking in the—"

"Whoa, whoa!" Matthew dropped his fork. "Slow your roll. I'm not trying to hear that."

"Please keep any cooking outside of the kitchen to yourself," Roarke added.

Cassidy shook her head. "The two of you are ridiculous. How many times have I listened to you brag about your conquests? I'm *twenty-three*. I'm getting married. It's not like I'm still a virgin. I—"

"Cass!"

"I feel nauseous. Seriously, stop. *Keep it to yourself.*" Roarke spoke past a mouthful of eggs. "You're our little sister. I don't want to think about you doing those things."

Cassidy sighed. "Freaking double standard," she muttered. "You two"—she stabbed the air with her fork for emphasis—"are living in a dream world. You have sex with everything that moves." She looked pointedly at Matthew, who shrugged. "Yet you want to think there are still virgins out there waiting for you to deflower them."

"I hold no such illusions," Roarke said. "And I don't sleep with everything that moves."

"Me, either—to the first part."

"Good, because you'll be really disappointed. The only virgin I know is Lorena, and that's because her father's kept her under lock and key for the past twenty-five years. I feel sorry for her. I'm surprised he let her out of his sight to be my maid of honor."

"Lorena's a virgin?"

Both Roarke and Cassidy turned to Matthew. Roarke noted the heightened interest in his voice. "Why are you so interested?" Cassidy asked.

"I'm not. I'm...surprised, that's all." Matthew picked up his glass of milk and took a large swallow. He became captivated by the food on his plate.

Roarke suspected there was more behind his brother's outburst, but Cassidy seemed satisfied and directed her attention to him. "It's about time *you* get married and start having a family. You know Aunt Iris is going to mention it when she sees you this weekend."

Roarke hated having to field questions about his love life, but he resigned himself to its inevitability. He'd been too busy to date seriously, but if he had his way, his love life would be different. The image of Celeste's face floated across his mind's eye.

The shock of waking up to an empty hotel room still stuck in his craw. One night hadn't been enough. He couldn't forget her, but apparently, she'd forgotten him. After a full week since their night at the Ritz-Carlton, he still couldn't conceive of a reasonable explanation for why she'd left the way she did. He thought they had hit it off.

"I'm a grown man," he said to his sister. "Don't worry about me. I'll deal with Aunt Iris and anybody else who asks questions. One wedding at a time. Let's get you married first."

He forced the last forkful of pancake into his mouth, although he didn't feel much like eating anymore. He'd finally swallowed his pride and contacted Lucas and Xander a couple of days ago to find out if either had obtained contact information for the other women. He thought he could reach out to her through one of her friends, but no such luck.

He couldn't understand why she left without a word. It didn't make sense, as if he'd imagined the passion they shared. He racked his brain in an effort to figure out what had gone wrong. Even worse, he thought about their night together over and over, the torture of it making his body clench in sexual frustration.

"Uh-oh, here comes trouble. It's your brother," Matthew said in a low voice.

Immersed in his thoughts, Roarke completely missed the red sports car parking outside the house.

"Be nice," Cassidy said, smacking the back of Matthew's hand. "He's your brother, too."

"He's our half brother, and you know as well as I do whenever he's around, trouble's close behind. Why'd you invite him?"

"Because he's our brother," Roarke said in a firm voice before Cassidy could respond. "He's not at fault for what our father and his mother did. Try to be nice for a change."

"That's not why I dislike him, and you know it. He's a bastard," Matthew grumbled. "And I don't mean it in the biological sense. I don't know why you bother. He hates you. He thinks it's your fault he didn't have our father in his life."

"We're here for a wedding, okay? It's all about Cassidy and Antonio this weekend and making sure the guests have a good time. I'm sure we can get through the weekend without going at each other's throats for once."

Roarke took his empty glass to the refrigerator for more juice.

Matthew continued with his play-by-play. "She's out of the car. She's tall, like the last one, but at least she doesn't look as slutty. Maybe she won't hit on you and cause a big mess like his last girlfriend did New Year's Eve weekend."

Roarke and Derrick had almost come to blows when Derrick's most recent female companion ended up in Roarke's room after too many drinks.

"Cut it out, Matt," Roarke said over his shoulder. "Let's keep the peace this weekend. Do not bring that up." He poured himself some juice.

Despite being brothers, a complicated history of enmity existed between Roarke, Matthew, and Derrick. Derrick didn't like Roarke, and Matthew, ever loyal to the brother who'd taken care of him, didn't like Derrick.

When Roarke's mother found out about the child born from the affair between her husband and Derrick's mother,

THE TEMPTATION OF A GOOD MAN

she gave him an ultimatum. He'd chosen to remain in his marriage.

Derrick's mother married a wealthy older man, but at some point the affair resumed. According to the passenger manifest, they sat next to each other in the plane crash that took their lives.

Hidden behind the freezer door as he added ice to his juice, Roarke heard the door open and his sister say, "Hi, Derrick." She'd always reached out to him, and Derrick got along with her.

Roarke closed the door and was about to lift the glass to his lips when he halted.

Celeste? What in the world...?

It couldn't be her.

He listened in disbelief as Derrick introduced her as his girlfriend. She smiled politely at his siblings, and when she finally looked at him, the light of recognition ignited in her eyes. The smile froze on her face, and her eyes widened. Even with her scared-rabbit appearance, she took his breath away. Her naturally curly hair was pinned into a ball at her nape. The style highlighted her prominent cheekbones and the strength of her jawline. She wore a pair of khaki shorts and a loose-fitting white blouse with tiny buttons down the front. The sandals on her feet showed off her red-painted toenails.

"And this is my other brother, Roarke," Derrick was saying, but Roarke could hardly hear the words. In fact, he could barely breathe.

Someone must have sucker punched him in the jaw. How else to explain the ringing in his ears as he watched the woman whose memory tortured him day and night—the woman he'd spent the night making love to—stand next to his brother as he professed they were a couple.

"Do you two know each other?" Derrick asked.

Celeste recovered first. "Oh, sort of. We met at Avery's Juke Joint last week." She smiled up at Derrick, and rabid jealousy uncoiled in Roarke's belly. She faced him again. "He and his friends hung out at our table for a while. Small world."

Fear filled her eyes, pleading with him to remain silent about the night they'd spent together.

"I agree," Roarke managed. "Small world."

Like a rewinding movie reel, his brain replayed in graphic detail their night together. Their damp bodies intertwined, her thick thighs clenched around his waist, her mouth drifting down over his chest and flicking his hard nipples with her moist tongue.

He could see the faint impression of her untethered breasts beneath the blouse, and his body quickened to life.

He needed to stop thinking about her in that way.

To avoid crushing the glass, Roarke set the juice on the breakfast bar and shoved his hands into the pockets of his slacks. The last thing he wanted to do was get a hard-on for her in front of his family.

"How long have you two been together?" He maintained a nonchalant tone to his voice. He dreaded the answer to the question, but it was essential that he know.

"How long has it been, babe?" Derrick asked, slipping his arm around Celeste's shoulders. He proceeded to answer the question himself. "We met over a year ago, but we've been together for a few months."

A few months. The words cut through him like shrapnel.

No wonder she left the way she did. He'd been a one-night stand, a passing fling for her before she returned to her relationship with his brother. His gaze shifted to where Derrick rubbed his palm up and down Celeste's bare arm—the same arm he'd licked rainwater from. His neck muscles worked to dispel the slow burn creeping across his throat.

He was usually a good judge of people, so he couldn't understand how he'd missed her dishonesty. Had he really been so enthralled by her physical appearance he missed the cues to her lack of character? To think he'd entertained the thought of pursuing her and a lasting relationship. It infuriated him and made him question his own common sense.

There hadn't been any signs...well, yes, one. A huge, glaring sign he'd chosen to ignore. She'd left him without a word, not even a note. She'd never intended for their night together to be anything more than sex. She'd made a fool out of him.

The flow of conversation continued between the others, and Roarke felt an upsurge in his body temperature as he watched her smile and chat with his brothers and sister.

He despised cheaters and cheating. She'd used him, and in the worst way possible. She'd made him a party to the one thing that was anathema to him.

His gaze held fast to her face. With the moment past, she now bore the look of someone with a clear conscience, as if their night together never occurred.

He couldn't stand the sight of her.

CHAPTER SIX

After Derrick brought in the luggage from the car, he left Celeste and went into town. She should have gone with him, but she didn't think she'd be good company.

Her hammering heart pushed blood through her veins so fast she felt light-headed. She rested her head against the cool glass of the window in the room where she would spend three nights. Her bedroom, situated between Cassidy's and Roarke's, should have been the maid of honor's room, but Cassidy insisted on giving it to her because there would be no other rooms available once the rest of the family arrived. The bride-to-be also quickly pointed out her aunt and grandmother would not approve of anyone sleeping in the same bed unless they were married, just as Derrick had said.

Celeste opened her eyes and stared out at the rolling blue waves, wishing she could enjoy the tranquil beach scene before her. She couldn't. Not with her insides turned upside down at the god-awful situation in which she found herself. Roarke and Derrick were brothers!

Derrick's lighter-colored skin and narrower nose were products of his white mother. The only true resemblance she saw between both men was in their height and strong jaw. Otherwise, no one would ever suspect they were brothers.

Her so-called vacation could potentially turn into a big mess. She didn't know if she could successfully carry through this weekend charade with Roarke here.

A knock on the door interrupted her thoughts. On leaden feet, Celeste made her way across the thick carpet, past the four-post bed and antique dresser.

When she opened the door, her stomach felt as if it dropped ten stories. Roarke stood there, his face lacking the warmth to which she'd grown accustomed during their brief time together. His cold gaze met hers, rooting her to the spot.

"What are you doing here?" she asked.

"What do you think I'm doing here?" he responded. "Are you going to let me in?"

"It's not a good idea." An invisible fist squeezed tightly at her throat. These were not the type of circumstances under which she wanted to see him again.

His face hardened, and his voice turned raw. "You think I don't know that?"

He didn't move, waiting, until she stepped aside and allowed him in.

Once inside, he stood with his back to her after she closed the door. Conflicted, her emotions vacillated between happiness and trepidation. She had cradled the memories of their night together like a secret cache she could bring out and enjoy whenever she needed a boost. She'd thought about him often and had longed to see him again. But not like this. Not with the accusatory look in his eyes.

He faced her. "What did my brother tell you about our relationship?"

"Not much." She stood with her hands clasped in front of her, not sure what to do with them, not sure what to do with her entire body, really, because of the surreal situation. She wanted to touch him, to run her hands over a muscular chest she'd grown to know well, to fall into his arms and hear his easy laughter once more instead of the angry diatribe she feared he would soon direct at her.

"Probably because we don't have much of one."

Easy to figure out. "Why not?"

"Ask my brother." A sarcastic laugh and shake of his head followed. "You—you're a piece of work. You deserve an Oscar for your performance last week. I asked you, point-blank, if you were in a relationship, and you said no." His angry eyes raked her from head to toe, filled with nothing approaching the seductive warmth from Friday night. Her fingers tightened around each other. "People like you make me sick. You run around satisfying your own physical lusts, and to hell with everyone else and how it affects them."

Shocked, Celeste said, "No, that's not what happened. I'm not the kind of person you think I am. I—"

"Don't bother with your explanation. Do you really think I give a damn?"

She sucked a painful breath into compressed lungs. "No, I'm sure you don't. Are you going to tell him?"

With a bark of bitter laughter, Roarke shook his head in disgust. "Is that all you can think about? How much longer can you continue the lie so my brother doesn't know the kind of woman you truly are? Don't worry, I won't say a word. I won't let anything ruin my sister's wedding, and I won't let you forge a deeper rift between Derrick and me.

As far as I'm concerned, what happened between us never took place."

Their night together had been excellent, earth-shattering. Unlike him, she couldn't pretend it never happened. She'd gone to the university's Web site to read his bio, and after Googling him, she found links to articles he'd written about astronomy and physics. She couldn't get him out of her mind and had lost count of the number of times she'd pulled up his online image.

"Thank you."

"I'm not doing it for you!" The words seemed to be torn from him, and his anger made her insides quiver in distress. He advanced on her and stopped a few paces away. "How did it work? You planned to seduce a man, and I happened to be the fool who came along and walked right into your trap? Ensnared by the high heels, the short little dress, and the sexy voice..."—he swallowed hard—"the sexy voice that makes a man wonder what it sounds like when you're screaming his name? Derrick and I don't get along, but he doesn't deserve this. Did you think about him even once when you were clawing my back at the hotel?"

His harsh words stung since nothing could be further from the truth. She'd donned the clothes to be attractive, yes, but he suggested behavior far more salacious than she'd intended. Celeste hadn't been out trolling for sex, and she resented the charge that she had been.

"Did you really want me thinking about him while I was having sex with you?" she shot back. Her taunt was like brandishing a red flag at an angry bull. A muscle in his jaw pulsed, and his nostrils flared. She half expected to see smoke drift below his nose. Before he could speak, she continued. "We're both adults, and we both got what we wanted."

"So, what, you were just looking for a good time? It could have been Lucas, or even Xander, right? He's married, but that probably doesn't matter to someone like you."

"I don't sleep with married men. For the record, we were two consenting adults, and it was one night."

"It wasn't just one night!" He looked about to explode. "It was *all* night. We couldn't get enough of each other, or did you forget that part?"

She couldn't forget, and every word he said was true. "No," she responded in a small voice.

They'd made love with the ease and familiarity of people who'd been lovers for years. He knew where to touch and where to kiss, zeroing in on each spot as if he'd received a map to all her erogenous zones ahead of time.

Her skin warmed at the thought. Being so close to the hard body she'd spent the night wrapped around tested her nerves.

"If you haven't forgotten, do you think I have? When I look at you, all I see is you naked, under me, over me...and you're my brother's girlfriend! I don't sleep with another man's woman, no matter how seductive she thinks she is."

Celeste closed her eyes against the sensual mental picture his words conjured. The brief moment allowed her to catch her breath and modulate her voice to an even tone. "What happened between us is my problem, not yours. But for the record, I did not set out to seduce you or anyone else. If you recall, you suggested we leave Avery's and go somewhere else. When I tried to leave, *you* asked me to stay."

"So it's my fault?"

"No one is at fault here. I—"

"Are you serious?" His eyebrows arrowed down in disbelief. "Do you really think you haven't done anything wrong by deceiving me and my brother?" He laughed without humor. "Derrick sure can pick 'em, but I can't even blame him this time. You don't look anything like the kind of woman you really are. You even had me fooled. Poor guy thinks he's found a good one this time, except he found someone sneaky enough to hide who she really is. The kind of woman who'll open her legs for any man she picks up at a club and go back to his room for hot sex like a cheap hooker."

Jaw slackened, her mouth fell open in shocked anger. The sting of his words couldn't have hurt more if he'd actually hit her. In one sentence he sullied the time she'd spent in his arms, turned it into something tawdry, and insulted her at the same time. She swung at him in defensive anger. The slap landed so hard her palm stung in protest from the force. His head barely moved, as if he'd anticipated the blow and braced himself before it landed.

"You..." Celeste stopped. To her chagrin, her voice shook; her body became rigid. She collected herself before proceeding. "You're no saint. It takes two, doesn't it? What does that make you for taking me, a woman you'd just met, back to your hotel room?"

The sardonic smile and the way his eyes traveled up and down her body were just as crushing as his next words. "A man who knows an easy lay when he sees one."

She brought up her other hand even quicker than the first time, determined to land another blow, but he didn't let her. As he reared back, his hand came up with whiplike speed and captured her wrist. "No way," he bit out. "You only get one."

Celeste tugged, but his grip only tightened. "You have no right to talk to me like that. You don't know anything about me."

"I know enough. I know you're an amazing actress and a liar, and I'm sorry I ever laid eyes on you."

Hurt, Celeste struck back. "Well, you're right," she said with a flippant inflection to her voice. "I'm a fantastic actress."

He knew right away what she was referring to, and his eyes narrowed on her face. She raised one brow in a mocking salute to his ego.

"Is that right?" he asked slowly.

His grip on her wrist tightened, and she pressed her lips together to prevent a cringe of discomfort. "Yes," she confirmed.

Then she realized what she'd done. She'd unwittingly issued him a challenge. His gaze lowered to her mouth, and her heart redoubled its efforts. A prickly sensation skittered across her chest and tightened her nipples. She gave her wrist a sudden jerk, but his warm clasp didn't budge.

"You may be a liar and a cheat, but you're not that good of an actress," he said with conviction. "There's no way you could've faked it every time. In fact"—a thoughtful look entered his eyes, and alarm pumped through her veins—"you didn't fake it even once."

Lust flickered in his eyes, and for tense moments they stared at each other, lost in the memories of heated whispers and tangled sheets. Then, as suddenly as he'd grabbed her, he dropped her arm like a hot coal.

"Derrick doesn't deserve to be lied to and made a fool of." He stepped around her toward the door.

Celeste grabbed his forearm to stall his exit. "Wait, please."

"Celeste, I can't do this."

She slipped between him and the door. She couldn't be the reason for a confrontation between the two brothers, and she couldn't bear the humiliation of Derrick finding out she'd slept with his brother the first night they met. "Please don't say anything to Derrick. I'll stay out of your way. I promise. You won't even know I'm here."

He looked down at her hand, and she followed his gaze to where her fingers wrapped around his arm. She withdrew them with haste. When her eyes found his again, desire shimmied down her spine at the hunger she saw in his.

"That's not what I meant," he said, his voice thick and low. "I can't be near you. You're too much of a temptation. Maybe you can stay away from me, but I don't know if I can keep my hands off of you." He slammed his palms against the door above her shoulders.

Celeste jumped, her eyes widening in shock. Shaken, she pressed back against the hard door to distance herself from him. They were too close, and the instinctive movement did little to protect her from the heat of sexual frustration emanating from his pores.

His chest rose and fell with each deep breath, and a storm brewed in his dark brown eyes. *"What are you doing to me?"*

The tortured question needed no answer. Even if she'd been obliged to respond, he seized her mouth before she could, and his tongue thrust between her lips. The muscular, dark cords of his arms encircled her waist and held her against his body, crushing her soft curves into each hard contour of his.

Celeste took the brutal assault without hesitation, savored it, moaning as she reveled in the power and passion of the kiss. She thrilled to the rough scrape of denim between her thighs when he pushed her legs apart with his knee and lifted her off the floor by sinking his fingers into her fleshy bottom.

Her arms locked behind his neck as their frantic kisses continued unabated, even while he walked with her to the bed. When her back touched the mattress, he lifted his head and focused on the tiny buttons of her blouse, which gave his fingers pause. Before she guessed his intention, he yanked the edges apart, sending a rush of unadulterated excitement crashing through her, while white buttons scattered across the bed and onto the floor.

Celeste whimpered and lifted her torso toward him. He dragged his palm down the valley between her breasts before lowering his head to devour them—licking, sucking, nibbling, creating an ache in her loins so acute it became a physical pain. Each caress of his mouth sent shivers down the length of her body to the tips of her toes.

One hand caressed the soft flesh of her breast, a massage that forced her to arch her back at an even sharper angle, giving him all he wanted, trying to assuage the hunger racing through her at breakneck speed. The only sounds she dared issue from her lips were muted noises of pleasure for fear someone else in the house would hear them.

Celeste pulled at Roarke's shirt, tugging it up so her hands could glide across the warm skin of his back. His deep-throated groan encouraged her. With utmost pleasure, she continued her exploration, enjoying how the muscles rippled beneath her touch.

"You feel so good." His fingers burrowed under the leg of her shorts and found their way under the crotch of her panties to the plump flesh between her legs. "You can't fake this," he breathed against the underside of her breasts, swiping his thumb through the moisture.

Her body jerked from the intimate contact as the fire between them burned out of control. Her legs fell wider apart to make room for another finger to join the thumb between her legs. She wanted his hands, his mouth, and his tongue to cover every inch of flesh—flesh that had yearned for him during the longest week of her life.

"Roarke," she moaned.

The sound of her own voice resonated in the room like breaking glass, jolted her senses, and dragged her back from the edge of full surrender.

She recalled his harsh words. He wanted her, but he despised her at the same time and had accused her of being easy.

Finally having a moment of clarity, Celeste pushed against Roarke to free herself from his hypnotizing touch. "Stop." She shoved away his hand, but his mouth continued to relentlessly suck her breast as if he couldn't stop. "Roarke, please," she begged in a breathless struggle. She shoved hard against his shoulders, forcing him to finally relinquish the throbbing nipple and roll off of her, onto his feet.

Standing beside the bed, he appeared shocked, maybe even a little disoriented. He scrubbed the back of his hand across his lips. In turn, she grasped her ruined shirt together with trembling hands, her body still in shock, trying to right itself after such a sensual ambush. Under the weight of his confused stare, she sat up, still clutching the edges of her shirt in a belated demonstration of modesty.

What the hell is wrong with me?

With his heart thundering in his chest, Roarke stared at the slender fingers of Celeste's hands clutching her shirt together. He'd done that—attacked her like a wild animal, starving for a taste of silky brown flesh, desperate for a chance to wrap his lips around the sweetest nipples he'd ever had the pleasure of sucking.

"I'm sorry," he said. She didn't move or make a sound, only stared down at her legs.

He was too close to the fire. He stepped back in an effort to recapture his sound judgment. His erection pressed insistently against his fly, anxious to break free of his jeans and find its way back to her. Because, heaven help him, he couldn't rid his mind of how it felt to lie between those beautiful long legs.

What the hell is wrong with me?

He shouldn't want her. How could he, when he knew she was a liar and a cheat? When Derrick, his own brother, had brought her here, making her off-limits?

Because her arousal brought him pleasure. He enjoyed getting her off, hearing her pant for him, hungry in pursuit of an orgasm. He wanted to be the one to give it to her. The only one.

"Stay away from me," he rasped, his chest tight with the difficulty it took to breathe.

In that moment, her pretty brown eyes rose to his face, and the look she sent him spoke volumes, told him what he already knew—he'd made an unfair statement. *He* came to *her* room, and he initiated the kiss. But in his defense, she'd touched him, and the simple, harmless act had been his undoing. Her touch rendered him helpless, bound by his thoughts and reduced to base instinct, like a dog in heat.

He needed to think.

Roarke spun on his heels and jetted out without another word. In his room, he closed the door, swallowing down the guilt and self-hatred.

He was scum. No, he was the slimy material under the belly of scum.

The realization their night together had been a one-time occurrence, never to be repeated because she was in a relationship, should have been enough to keep him in check. Not so. Instead, all he could think about was getting her under him, flat on her back. Without even trying, she had him and his morals tied up in knots.

He ran his hand down his face and caught a whiff of her arousal on his fingers, and as impossible as it seemed, his body hardened even more. He stared at his hand as if seeing it for the first time. Resisting the urge to run his fingers under his nose to enjoy her scent again, he went back out into the hallway to the bathroom.

He pumped out the hand soap in large globs, avoiding his own gaze in the mirror.

He wasn't his father.

Several times he washed his hands, giving them a rough scrub to eradicate any trace of what he'd done.

I'm not my father.

Grinding his teeth, Roarke finally faced himself in the mirror above the sink and didn't like what he saw. He didn't pursue women in relationships, and cheating was never an option. All his life he'd stuck to those principles.

Until today.

Today, he and his morals had been blown to bits by a stick of dynamite named Celeste Burton.

CHAPTER SEVEN

"What are you doing up here?" Derrick asked, coming into Celeste's room. "More of the family arrived a while ago. Come on downstairs, and I'll introduce you."

Celeste greeted Derrick's words with the best smile she could manage. After a quick shower and change, she'd hid in the room for as long as she could. When he came to get her, she accepted she couldn't stay there forever and let her mind dwell on the confrontation with Roarke. She would do her best to steer clear of him for the rest of the weekend, which was no easy task staying one door down in the same house. At the very least, she would avoid being alone with him again.

"Derrick, what's the deal with you and Roarke?" Saying his name made the apex of her thighs pulse.

His gaze narrowed. "Why?"

Feigning nonchalance, Celeste shrugged. "Just wondering. I know your relationship with your family isn't the best, and especially with your older brother."

Derrick paused for a minute, then closed the bedroom door.

"I did bring you into the middle of all this, so I may as well tell you some of what happened. You'll get a better understanding of my relationship with my family." He took a deep breath. "You already know the Hawthornes are my half siblings. We have the same father."

Celeste nodded. She remained silent and watched an emotion similar to pain flit across Derrick's face.

"The Sperm Donor had an affair with my mother while married to Roarke's mother, and then, surprise!" He lifted his arms wide. "I came along. Roarke's my older brother by three months."

"Derrick…" Her heart ached for him. She saw the hurt in his eyes, even though he tried to make light of the situation with sarcasm. "But why is there so much animosity between you and Roarke?"

"That's easy to explain. The Donor's wife made him choose. His mistress and his bastard son or his wife and his legitimate son. He chose his wife and son."

"Derrick, I'm so sorry—"

"Don't feel sorry for me." The words came out harsh, but she knew the anger wasn't directed at her. "I'm fine. I didn't need him anyway. For years I never knew this side of my family. After he passed away, they reached out to me. As for staying away from my mother—well, he didn't keep the promise he made, and neither did she. Neither one of them cared about the people they could hurt. They died together in a plane crash the year I turned eighteen. Even though he continued to screw my mother for who knows how long, not once"—his entire body tensed and the bitterness became even more apparent—"*not once* did my *father* come to see me. And Roarke Hawthorne Jr. looks exactly like him."

He spewed the last sentence past thinned lips. Hatred filled his eyes. Roarke, with their father's name and looks, had benefited from having his father in his life growing up.

"Roarke Hawthorne, Mr. Perfect," he continued, "always playing the role of peacemaker, sacrificing, raising his brother and sister while in college." His mirthless laugh filled the room. "Gimme a break. It's all an act."

Derrick couldn't seem to stop now he'd started, and Celeste hesitated to interrupt him. The anger and loathing directed toward Roarke were clearly unjustified, but he couldn't see it. Inside, he remained the little kid whose father chose another over him, and who'd lost out on the father-son relationship.

"He plays this role like he's holier than thou, but he's as slimy as our father. The family spent New Year's Eve here at the house. I brought a woman with me, and we stayed at one of the nearby hotels. Guess who wound up drunk in Roarke's room one night after we spent the day here?"

She thought it was a rhetorical question, but he waited for her to answer. "Your date?"

"Bingo!" Derrick said bitterly. "You win the prize. He lured her up to his room to take advantage of her in her drunken state."

"How do you know—"

"I know. I'd been looking all over for her, and then I heard her laughter through the door of his bedroom. I found them together in his bed, Celeste. She told me everything, although he tried to deny it. Stay away from him. I'm surprised he didn't try to get you into bed when he met you at Avery's last week. Obviously, he can't resist a pretty face, and I wouldn't put it past him to try to seduce you, too."

Celeste tried to dismiss Derrick's words, but she couldn't.

Not only did he try, he succeeded. Her stomach twisted painfully. She hated the thought that Derrick's words contained any truth and she'd been a simple notch on Roarke's bedpost. Even though she'd had similar thoughts, hearing Derrick voice them was crushing.

"Have the two of you ever gotten along or been close?"

"Never. And we never will."

The situation between Derrick and Roarke was worse than Celeste imagined. She couldn't tell Derrick about her and Roarke now. Not only would it hurt him, it would only serve to further feed the flame of hatred he held for his brother.

What would even be the point of telling Derrick? Roarke had made it clear what he thought of her. He wanted her for sex, and that was all. The thought cut deep, scraped the walls of her heart and wounded her feelings.

Nonetheless, her thoughts and feelings didn't matter. Her friend was hurting. Years of rejection had spread and eaten away at him like an ulcer, coloring his perception of the truth. She sympathized with Derrick's predicament, but his pride left no room for her pity.

"Now you understand why my relationship with my dear brother isn't all that great."

"Yes." She watched as his breathing slowed to normal. "What about Phineas? Hasn't he been a good father to you?"

"Phineas is an old white man who was unfortunate enough to fall in love, but smart enough to realize you can buy anything with money, including a young wife. When The Sperm Donor relinquished all paternal rights, my mother made Phineas adopt me, and he got stuck playing stepfather to her half-black son." With a wry twist to his lips, he added, "Unfortunately for him, we came as a package deal."

Abruptly, as if he suddenly realized he'd said too much, Derrick turned to the door and swung it open. "Let's get out of here."

Before they walked out, Celeste reached out and pulled him into a hug. He went rigid, but she held on until his stiffened body loosened in her arms. He held her for a brief moment and then released, letting his arms hang loosely at his sides.

Looking deeply into his eyes, she whispered, "You have to let go of this anger you have inside. It's not healthy."

As luck would have it, Roarke appeared in the hallway at that moment, and her stomach plummeted. He paused, and their gazes locked over Derrick's shoulder. The power of his stare rocked her insides. She could only imagine how the scene appeared, confirming every contemptible thought about her, so soon after their heated tryst.

Too quick for her to decipher the look he cast in her direction, his face became a shuttered mask so swiftly she thought she imagined it.

"Hey," Derrick said in a stiff voice, glancing over his shoulder at Roarke. Celeste lowered her arms, and he looped his arm around her back. "More family's arrived."

"Yeah," Roarke said, staring down the hall. He didn't look at her. He didn't look at either of them. "Cassidy told me. Everyone's on the back porch."

He walked away, and they followed behind.

Moments later, they joined the family downstairs. There, Celeste met three other people staying in the house: Aunt Iris, a tall, dark-skinned woman who stood behind the wheelchair of an older woman everyone called Granny, and their Uncle Reese, who was in the process of prepping a couple of grills for the meat and vegetables on a table nearby. She was also introduced to a few cousins staying in one of the hotels with their children.

With the sun high in the sky and the waves crashing nearby, Celeste relaxed into the southern comfort of the beach house with a twinge of envy. The Hawthorne family sipped lemonade and sweet tea and munched on snacks as they waited for Uncle Reese to "do his thing" on the grill.

A couple of hours later, with the groom, additional guests, and a few neighbors present, the large group ate the bounty of food, seated on the back porch and gathered around folded tables on the lawn. The Hawthornes were a big, loving family and made her feel welcome. She thought how nice it would be for her daughter Arianna to experience the love and camaraderie of a large family in such an idyllic location.

Because of the number of people at the house, she managed to keep her distance from Roarke easily enough, though she couldn't resist looking at him from time to time.

After a stomach full of chicken, ribs, rolls, sides, and dessert, Celeste sat next to Matthew on the porch swing. She surveyed the group and listened with interest to their conversation. Roarke leaned against one of the white posts, and Cassidy stood next to him, her arm wound around his and her head resting below the top of his shoulder.

Roarke's Aunt Iris asked him about marriage and children, and Celeste couldn't help listening attentively to hear what he had to say. The sting of jealousy ran through her at the thought of Roarke married with children. He deflected his aunt's question by pointing out Cassidy was getting married tomorrow.

"Hey, don't shift the focus off you to me!"

"Thanks for having my back." He slipped his arm around his sister's neck in a mock headlock.

The playful banter between the two continued. Cassidy's obvious adoration for her older brother directly conflicted with Derrick's assessment of Roarke. In fact, from her observation, Roarke was well regarded by everyone.

Could it all be an act?

It was possible. Hadn't her own husband fooled her into thinking he was a loving, giving person interested in a monogamous relationship, when all along he'd been "giving" his loving to as many women as he could during their marriage?

She wondered if the old adage had merit in Roarke's case: If it seems too good to be true, then it probably is. Still, how much of what Derrick said about Roarke was truth and how much misconstrued because of jealousy?

CHAPTER EIGHT

Celeste awoke the next morning feeling groggy. Stressed over the previous day's events, she'd hardly slept a wink. After a somewhat revitalizing cup of coffee, she inquired about Derrick's whereabouts and found out he'd already left for the day. No one knew when he would return. When she called his cell phone, it went straight to voice mail, and that's when she decided to go exploring on her own.

In Pier Village, the center of activity, she would find quaint shops and restaurants. It wasn't too far, and the walk would be good exercise. She made up an excuse for why she couldn't stay for breakfast, but the truth was, she didn't want to sit through the meal with Roarke.

As she left the house, she heard the wedding planner bark orders across the yard in the middle of a cyclone of activity. A local spa unloaded a couple of massage tables and other items from the back of a van. The bride and her wedding party would have massages, facials, and other services to help them get ready. When she returned, no doubt delivery trucks would be all over the yard as the setup for the wedding continued.

The ceremony would take place outside in front of over three hundred guests, the majority of whom were Cassidy's family and friends, and they would move into the tent for the reception. The groom, Antonio Vega, was an Afro-Latino from Puerto Rico. Most of his family still lived there. His immediate family, which included Lorena, the maid of honor, his brothers, and parents, would be in attendance, along with others who resided stateside.

Her own wedding hadn't been such a grand event. Short on cash, she and her ex arranged a small ceremony in his mother's living room, and they never got around to a honeymoon. Despite the lack of a fairy-tale beginning, Celeste had been happy because at the time she thought she was marrying the man who would remain her husband until death separated them. She'd been too naïve to see the signs at the time, and the example of her parents' successful marriage before her father's death had distorted her views on marriage and partnership.

She laughed to herself. What a difference a year could make. Before long she suspected her husband of cheating, and a short time later found the evidence.

With sunglasses on and her hair pulled back into a braided chignon secured into a neat knot at the nape, Celeste started toward town. Five minutes into her walk, a black car slowed beside her, and the owner honked the horn. Roarke sat in the driver's seat and rolled the window down.

"Need a lift?" The mirrored shades he wore blocked her ability to see his eyes.

"I'm going down to the village. I don't mind walking," Celeste replied. Despite the barrier of steel between them, her pulse began a thunderous race at his presence. Sitting in the car with him was not a good idea.

"Hop in," he said, popping the lock. "There's no point in walking when you can ride."

Except when the person you accepted the ride from was a man you were insanely attracted to, and the word "ride" sent your mind off in an X-rated direction.

"Thanks," Celeste mumbled once she settled into the passenger seat.

Inside the car, she became even more aware of him. Her senses drew to him like metal splinters to a powerful magnet. Her skin prickled from sitting so close, and her nostrils captured the morning freshness of soap and his distinctive aftershave.

"Do you have any particular place in mind?" Roarke asked as he shifted the car into gear.

"No. I planned to eat breakfast first and then map out a plan for the day."

"I'm going to eat breakfast, too. I'm headed to the 4th of May Deli on Mallery Street. They have good food. You should try their seafood omelet. They use local shrimp and crab. If you have a hearty appetite, add a short stack of pancakes."

Celeste glanced sideways at him. "Sounds delicious, but...do you think it's a good idea?"

"What?"

"You know what."

"For us to spend time together?"

"Yes. After yesterday, I'm not so sure..." Celeste knotted her fingers in her lap.

Roarke turned his head toward her and then back to the street. "Yesterday shouldn't have happened," he agreed in a slow, careful voice. His grip tightened on the steering wheel. "Again, I apologize. I was out of line for what I did and said. Today is a new day. As you pointed out yesterday, we're both adults. We're only having breakfast, but if you prefer, I could sit at a different table."

She would *prefer* not to have to be so close to him and suffer through this hands-off policy. "That won't be necessary," Celeste said. "I'm sure we can tolerate each other through a short breakfast."

The planes of his face set into hard lines, but he didn't say another word until after he parked the car and they entered the deli.

Once they'd ordered, Roarke made an obvious effort to generate conversation between them. "Are you doing one of the tours?"

Celeste nodded.

Seated across from her with his sunglasses off and wearing a dark blue shirt with jeans, he bore the casual air of a summer vacationer. Trying to crush the fluttering of her heart at how attractive he looked in the casual clothes, she lowered her gaze. She spread a brochure and map she'd lifted from an information box at the airport on the table.

"There are so many choices, though."

"One place you definitely want to visit is the lighthouse. It's a historic landmark, and it would be a shame for you to leave without seeing it."

Celeste sighed. "I should've planned this better. I don't know where to begin, and I won't be here a long time."

"We could rent a golf cart to get around in. A lot of visitors like the pace and convenience."

Celeste raised her eyebrow. "We?"

A look of puzzlement, then realization dawned on his face. "Oh, I did say 'we,' didn't I?" When he laughed, his face softened. Warmth replaced the frost present in his eyes since yesterday.

"Are you offering to be my tour guide?" she asked with a tilt of her head, bolstered by his sudden approachability.

He leaned back in the chair, and seconds slowly ticked by until she almost felt the need to squirm. "I do know this island like the back of my hand." Two more heartbeats before he continued. "Yes, I'm offering to be your tour guide, if you need one." A small smile touched his lips.

Elation filled her, and she was ill-prepared to prevent it from showing. Derrick warned her to stay away from Roarke, but Derrick had gone off somewhere and left her to fend for herself. What better way to enjoy her sightseeing excursion than with her own personal guide?

"Thank you," Celeste said, her lids drifting downward, a smile playing across her lips.

They would only be touring the island, but she felt like a lottery winner. He'd used the word "we." He wanted to spend time with her, and her heart rejoiced in it.

Across the table, Roarke couldn't smother the warm sensation rising in his chest. She'd done that thing, where she lowered her long lashes in a bashful manner. And smiled, sending shards of pleasure straight to his gut.

Thinking he could evade her, he had decided to skip breakfast and his Aunt Iris's flaky buttermilk biscuits. Instead, here he sat face-to-face with the same person he'd been trying to avoid. The greatest temptation he'd ever experienced in his life.

He knew better. He shouldn't have offered to join her for breakfast, and he definitely shouldn't have offered to be her guide when he understood the danger she presented. Every thought over the past week had been about finding her and getting an explanation for her desertion. Now he had it, how despicable was he to still want to spend time with her?

Yesterday evening, at the family cookout, he'd been happy when she left to go inside early. Yet watching her long-legged stride and retreating back served to torment him, too, because he'd wanted nothing more than to follow her into the house and release the pervasive tension blanketing his body the best way he knew how.

Right now he wanted to reach across the table to touch the pale toffee of her soft skin. Why even put himself in a position to be tortured by a woman he couldn't have?

Because of late he'd become a glutton for punishment, and even though he couldn't have her, he willingly accepted whatever he could get. One solitary day. Not even the whole day, because they had to return to the house this afternoon to get ready for the wedding. Five hours? Six?

He couldn't turn it down.

They didn't have a reservation but were still fortunate enough to get a golf cart. Using a leisurely pace, Roarke took the morning to cover the historic sites of the island. They toured the ruins of Fort Frederica, built in 1736 and a stronghold for the English when they fought the Spanish in 1742. They drove by the Avenue of Oaks, once the entrance to an antebellum plantation named Retreat Plantation, but now the entrance to the Sea Island Golf Club.

At St. Simons Lighthouse, they watched a short film about the structure and then proceeded to climb the 129 cast iron steps. Celeste huffed her way to the top behind Roarke.

"Wimp," he teased.

"We just climbed one hundred and twenty-nine steps. Not twenty-nine. One hundred and twenty-nine. I'm allowed to feel tired."

They stepped out onto the metal gallery that encircled the top of the tower. They were the only ones at the top.

From there Celeste could see the stunning view of the coastline and the grounds below. "Beautiful," she breathed.

"Was it worth it?"

She smiled up at him. "Definitely."

His lips turned up at the corners. The smile traveled all the way up into his eyes. He'd tucked his sunglasses into his pocket, giving her the luxury of viewing his entire face. Calling him handsome didn't do him justice. Warmth radiated from her chest, and she quickly glanced away to hide her thoughts and stunt the growth of warm feelings.

"Look." Roarke pointed out toward the water. Something moved out there.

"What is that?" There was more than one.

"Dolphins," he replied.

Celeste watched the gray objects playing in the waves. "Wow," she whispered.

From the corner of her eye, she saw his gaze shift back to her. "You're lucky. Not everyone gets to see them."

She did feel lucky, standing next him. Even though their excursion around the island wasn't complete, she already knew she wouldn't forget this day and the pleasure of his company.

Midday, they took a stroll along the waterfront before heading over to Barbara Jean's, a popular casual dining spot on the island. Roarke assured Celeste everything on the menu was delicious, but she couldn't decide on what to eat. He took charge and ordered dirty rice and she-crab soup to start, added the famous crab cakes, and they shared a couple of seafood platters between them.

When he ordered dessert, Celeste waved him off, stating she didn't have room for another bite. But when the Chocolate "Stuff" showed up, she couldn't resist dipping the extra spoon the waitress brought into the sinfully delicious bowl of chocolate goodness topped by fresh whipped cream.

After lunch he took her to St. Simons Pier and the historic King and Prince Beach & Golf Resort, perhaps the most famous lodging on the island and itself a historic landmark. Before too much time passed, they went to the village to shop, and Celeste purchased items for herself, her mother, and her daughter.

Roarke hated seeing the day come to a close, but they had to return to the house. Silence pervaded the car on the ride back. He wondered if the same gloominess filled her the way it did him.

"Thank you for taking the time to show me around today."

"No problem." He used the clipped tones as a defense mechanism. If he didn't shield himself now, the pain would be much worse when she walked away from him at the house, and tenfold worse when he saw her with Derrick later.

Derrick. He hadn't given his brother a thought the entire time he was with Celeste. Had she thought about him?

When they pulled up, he saw lots of cars, which meant the house would be full of guests.

They exited the vehicle in silence, and at the bottom of the stairs leading up to the porch, Derrick made an appearance from inside. He was frowning, and his lips were thinned in a line of anger.

"Well, well," he said. "Why am I not surprised?"

Roarke ignored the dripping sarcasm. "You finally decided to show up?" he asked.

Celeste walked slowly up the steps ahead of him. When the three of them stood on the porch, Derrick put his arm around Celeste's shoulders and drew her close. "You never quit, do you? Did you decide to come to the wedding without a date so you could take what's mine?"

"Derrick!" Celeste said in a stricken voice.

Roarke eyed his brother's hand on Celeste's shoulder and clenched his fists to resist the urge to knock it off. "I won't even dignify that with an answer."

"Stay away from her." Derrick's voice practically seethed venom.

"Maybe if you were a little more attentive, didn't leave her alone for long periods while you disappear for hours on end, you wouldn't be so worried."

"Are you threatening me?" Derrick stepped toward Roarke.

"Derrick, stop it!" Celeste grabbed his arm. She stared at him in disbelief. "Let's go."

"You can't have everything you want. Get your own woman, Roarke," Derrick said with a point of his finger. "Stay away from mine. I'm not telling you again."

Celeste tugged on Derrick's arm and dragged him inside.

Roarke didn't have any right to be jealous. The unfounded sentiment traveled through him, conjoined with anger, as he watched them walk away. He wanted to snarl, to roar, to claim her as his own, but that was the problem. She wasn't.

Somehow, because they'd spent the day together, his brain had been tricked into thinking she was.

Celeste turned on Derrick with an angry whisper. "I'm your pretend girlfriend, remember? What is wrong with you?" she demanded. They stood facing each other in his room.

"Me? What about you? What was that about?" Derrick gestured violently. "I told you to stay away from him, and you run off alone for hours?"

"I couldn't find you. I called your phone, and you didn't answer."

"I was busy." His gaze narrowed. "What were you two doing?"

"Nothing!" Celeste's cheeks flooded with guilty heat. She'd spent a lovely day with Roarke, but now it had been spoiled because of the deception she'd agreed to. Realizing her answer wouldn't satisfy him, she added, "All Roarke did was take me on a tour of the island."

"I could have taken you on a tour of the island."

"When, Derrick? I couldn't find you, remember?"

"You could've waited."

"For how long?" Celeste swallowed to calm down. "You told me you didn't want me to embarrass you, but I don't want to be embarrassed, either. I'm supposed to be your girlfriend, but I couldn't find you anywhere. The minute we got here yesterday, you disappeared to go into the village. Then you left again first thing this morning. If I didn't know better, I'd think you have a woman here."

Derrick's body tensed before he averted his eyes.

"*Do you?*"

"That's none of your business!"

"It is my business. If you have a girlfriend, why didn't you invite her to the wedding instead of me?"

"I never said I have a girlfriend."

"You didn't deny it, either!" Derrick was hiding something from her. Then it dawned on her. "I'm a decoy, aren't I? You're seeing someone else, but for some reason you can't or won't bring her around your family. You're embarrassed, or—"

"I'm not embarrassed." Derrick cut her off in a deceptively soft voice. "And you're not a decoy. I brought you here because the person I wanted to bring couldn't make it. That's all you need to know. You're getting an all-expenses-paid weekend vacation, plus wages. You don't get to ask questions."

This couldn't continue. She was stressed and upset, and Derrick did a good job of making her feel guilty for the precious hours she had spent with Roarke. She'd only been there a day, and she was already falling apart. Another day and a half would have men in white coats dropping by to haul her off.

"It doesn't feel like a vacation," she said. "This was a bad idea. You're obsessed with hating your brother, and it puts me in an awkward position."

"You can tough it out for one more day," Derrick said without sympathy. "We have an agreement. Stick to the plan."

He slammed the door as he left the room.

What had she gotten herself into?

Celeste recollected the anger in Roarke's face. The harsh lines had returned, a terrible end to an otherwise glorious day spent in his company. Once again he'd spoiled her, refusing to let her pay for anything and explaining the history of the island like a true guide would do. His memory amazed her.

She smothered a sigh of what could have been. She savored the short time they'd spent together and wished she could have devised a plausible excuse to remain in his company. For just a little longer. It was almost as if…

No. Celeste shook her head. Her heart stopped working midpump.

She wasn't…falling in love with him? With a hard swallow, she sank onto the bed.

No.

Those were the thoughts of a madwoman. Pure insanity. The men in white coats really would come for her now.

She barely knew him. But even as she thought it, she recognized the untruth. Images flooded her mind: their long night of conversation at Tito's Lounge, where she not only found out about his love of jazz, but many other details about his life; the amiable breakfast this morning; him in the golf cart next to her, pointing out landmarks, answering questions, and visiting places he was probably bored of visiting—but doing it anyway—just so he could show her around; sitting across from her at lunch and sharing food off each other's plate; the wild groping in her room yesterday; and their insatiable lovemaking that night at the Ritz.

Celeste buried her face in her hands.

No! she screamed silently.

She didn't want to fall for him, to care about him, but her heart had other ideas. She could never face him and his disdain for her now. It would hurt too much.

In less than two days she would be gone, never to see him again. The painful thought forced a choked sob to escape her throat.

CHAPTER NINE

Celeste went to her room before Derrick returned, and she remained there until a few minutes before the commencement of the wedding ceremony. She and Derrick sat next to each other on white-covered chairs with red sashes. Pink and red rose petals were sprinkled on the white aisle runner leading up to the decorated wedding arch where the minister, the groom, and the wedding party stood.

The sounds of a solo saxophone drifted on the air as Roarke escorted his sister down the aisle. The dark suit and tie enhanced the power of his height and build, drawing her eyes to him instead of the radiant bride.

Despite mentally scolding herself not to dwell on what could have been, she wondered what it would be like to be the woman in his life. In truth, she already knew. A man like Roarke would spoil his woman. She had experienced a sample of it today. Perhaps it was because of the romantic nature of the wedding ceremony, but she knew without a doubt, if he loved her, and she could spend the rest of her life with him, she could look forward to a lifetime of unselfish thoughtfulness and kindness. Words she'd never known in a relationship before.

The wedding planner had timed the event perfectly, so that the burnished orange glow of the setting sun adorned the sky as the bride and groom kissed and the minister announced them to the audience. Afterward, all the attendees except the couple and the wedding party moved to the clear-top tent. Later in the evening, the starry sky would be visible through the ceiling.

No expense had been spared for the nuptials. A bartender mixed drinks, and servers glided around the room with pre-dinner hors d'oeuvres. A band played modern hits on a stage in front of a white dance floor. Lights looped along the ceiling, and red flowers in white vases decorated the tabletops.

"Rum and Coke."

The words made Celeste's breath hitch as she stood in front of the bartender, waiting for a glass of wine. He must be directly behind her. She could almost feel the heat from him, warm, like the sound of his voice. Other guests flanked her, but she was only aware of Roarke.

"Are you okay?" he asked close to her ear. She felt the brush of his breath along the back of her neck, exposed by the updo hairstyle.

"Why wouldn't I be?" she murmured over her shoulder, but never looked at him.

She couldn't. She worried the extent of her feelings would show in her eyes. Her body hummed with the need for even the smallest bit of contact from him. She wanted to lean back into his embrace and have him nuzzle her neck, letting the hairs on his face graze her skin.

"Because of what happened this afternoon. I don't want to create problems between you and Derrick."

"Don't worry about it. We're fine."

What did these other people order? Celeste thought impatiently. If the bartender would hurry up and pour her drink, she'd be on her way.

She heard Roarke exchange greetings with someone, then silence.

The bartender handed her drink over the shoulder of the woman in front of her. Quickly, Celeste turned to escape, but he stood right behind her, and she bumped into the solid wall of his chest. Brought up short, wine spilled over the top of the glass onto her fingers.

Staring at his tie, she said, "Excuse me."

"You can't look at me now?"

She tightened her clasp on the stem of the glass to steady the shaking of her hand. She stared down into the clear liquid.

"I enjoyed the tour today…but we both know…"

"Know what?"

"We shouldn't have."

"Nothing happened. It was perfectly innocent."

"I know."

"Is that the problem?" His voice had dropped even lower, caressing her senses. The people around them seemed to disappear, as if she and Roarke were the only two people standing there.

Celeste swallowed with difficulty. He didn't have any idea how much torture he inflicted with his words and close proximity. She needed to get away from him. She finally looked into eyes. His stared intently into hers.

"What are you thinking about?" he asked.

The temptation to bare her soul and spill the secret about how much she wanted him, cared for him, weighed on Celeste. Her heart was beating at an unsteady pace, and she felt the ridiculous need to cry.

"I think you need to leave me alone and let me pass," she said.

She couldn't think of another time in her life when the words she spoke had been such a painful contradiction to what she felt. For a moment she regretted them when she saw the transformation in him. His face tensed just before he stepped aside to let her by.

Roarke stood against the wall, watching the guests circulate as they waited for the wedding party. He'd taken the requisite pictures before the ceremony, but the photographer wanted a few more of the bride and groom now that night was falling.

Actually, he wasn't watching the guests. He watched Celeste.

Someone clapped him on the shoulder. "Hey, Roarke, how's it going?"

"Just fine, Uncle Reese. How about yourself?"

"Good, good. You did a fine job with little Miss Cassidy. She grew up to be a mighty fine young woman. I'm proud of you." He winked and moved on.

Uncle Reese's words put a nick in Roarke's conscience. He wouldn't be very proud of Roarke if he knew how hot with lust he was for another man's woman. He'd barely resisted the urge to drop kisses along the back of her neck, or move the strap of the sleeveless dress she wore out of the way so he could run his tongue along her shoulder.

He swallowed some of his drink.

This obsession with her wasn't healthy. The last thing he should do is watch her, wishing she were his date instead of his brother's. Ever since he saw them together after the trek around the island, he'd been unable to avoid the truth: the jealousy and rage inside him had more to do with his heart than his groin.

Yes, he wanted her. His lust-addled brain imagined a repeat of their all-night lovemaking at the Ritz. But more than lust drove him; he enjoyed her company. He wanted to spend time with her and took pleasure in making her laugh just as much as making her come.

Even though he knew she had cheated, he had fallen for her. It had to be the least intelligent thing he'd ever done in his life.

There might be a slight chance she had feelings for him, but she acted as if she didn't want to look him in the eye. Something must have happened between her and Derrick to cause such a reaction. Or maybe she regretted the day they'd spent together.

Maybe he should challenge Derrick to a duel. The thought made him laugh.

"What's so funny?" Matthew asked as he walked up.

"Nothing," Roarke replied.

"You're going to bore a hole into the back of her head if you keep staring at her like that."

Roarke paused the drink halfway to his mouth. "Who?"

"Is he pretending he doesn't know what you're talking about?" Xander asked. He and Lucas walked up on Roarke's other side. Both men attended the wedding as guests, but Xander owned a bakery. He'd given the four-tier white cake with red and pink roses, and the groom's *tres leches* cake, as wedding gifts.

"Yes," Matthew answered. To Roarke he said, "You're not doing a good job of hiding how you feel about her, bro."

Damn. Was he that obvious? "She's with Derrick," Roarke said.

"And was with you last week," Lucas pointed out.

"Doesn't matter."

"Then why can't you take your eyes off of her?"

Roarke drained his glass. Apparently, he was that obvious.

"I know your grandmother and Aunt Iris aren't allowing them to stay in the same room, are they?" Xander asked.

"No," Roarke answered. "She has her own room. The one Lorena was supposed to have. Lorena and Cassidy are sharing a room."

"In the same bed?" Lucas asked.

Roarke nodded.

"Am I wrong for being a little turned on by that?" Three sets of eyes turned to Lucas. "I'm kidding, I'm kidding."

Celeste stood in a corner, talking to one of the other guests.

"What are you going to do?" Xander asked, following his line of vision.

"He's going to forget about her," Lucas answered. "Look, she's in a relationship and didn't tell you. Worse, it's with your own brother. Do you really need another reason for Derrick to hate you? I know you like her, but those are the facts. You might as well hook up with one of these lovely, single Georgia peaches just waiting to have a wedding story to tell their girlfriends when they return home. Make sure you mention you're *Dr.* Roarke Hawthorne when you introduce yourself. Women love titles."

Matthew nodded his agreement. "Weddings are the perfect opportunity to get laid."

Xander shook his head Lucas. "I can't believe they pay you to give advice. Not every man is trying to see how many women he can nail before he dies."

"Says the man who married his high school sweetheart and hasn't had sex with another woman since then," Lucas said.

"I'm happily married."

"Good for you. Not everyone wants that particular noose around his neck." Lucas wrapped his fingers around his own throat in a mock choking gesture.

"Why didn't you hook up with Celeste's friend—what was her name...Gwen?"

"Too aggressive. I like my women a little more docile."

Matthew laughed. "Maybe you should invite her to one of your workshops."

Lucas stroked his chin thoughtfully. "Hmm...maybe I should."

Lucas wrote a successful relationship blog called *Why He Won't Marry You* and an advice column in a national magazine. Occasionally, his speaking engagements took him on tour across the country. Men idolized him, but angry women viewed him as a pariah.

"Guys, I appreciate your efforts to cheer me up," Roarke said sarcastically, "but I'm fine. Pretty soon she'll be gone, and what happened will be behind us."

Matthew turned his eyes on his brother. "Until she shows up at another event with Derrick."

The same thought had crossed Roarke's mind. If this relationship lasted between her and Derrick, she would be at other family functions, and he would have to pretend not to care. His chest tightened.

"I may have my father's name, but I'm nothing like him. She and Derrick are a couple. She's with the man she wants to be with, and whatever the attraction was between us, nothing can be done about it now."

As he said the words, he recollected her face, and the way she wouldn't even look at him. There was no doubt in his mind something had changed. But what?

Minutes later, the wedding planner announced the bridesmaids and groomsmen, who came in and took their places on either side of the entrance.

Lots of cheering and loud clapping filled the space when she said, "Mr. and Mrs. Antonio Vega!"

The group of ten walked down the middle of the tent to the dance floor. All of a sudden, the beginning strains of a recorded version of Michael Jackson's "Thriller" came through the speakers. The guests looked around in surprise at the action taking place up front. The wedding party moved in zombie formation, getting into position.

"No, she didn't! That's my sister!" Matthew hollered.

The music picked up, and the group started the choreographed dance. For the next four minutes, Roarke watched in awe the precision of the zombielike movements, pelvic thrusts, and sweeping arm gestures. They shimmied across the floor, and the more they danced, the more the audience became excited.

Anyone who had been seated was on his or her feet, and thunderous applause greeted the end of the routine. Cassidy's beaming face turned toward her brother. Roarke smiled at his little sister. With a heavy heart, he realized this was the last time she would turn to him, seeking his approval. He gave her the thumbs-up just before her husband swept her up into his arms.

****

Last night, Celeste read her daughter a bedtime story over the phone. Tonight, because of the wedding festivities, Arianna was already asleep when she called.

Celeste's mother gave her a rundown of Arianna's day and told her that her ex-husband had called. He promised

Arianna he would come get her so she could spend the summer with him in Washington.

"With what money?" Celeste demanded. "Why would he tell her such a thing when he knows he's not going to do it?"

"I know, honey, but I thought I'd warn you. She's already excited, and she chattered about it from the minute she hung up the phone. She drew one of her little pictures and hung it on the refrigerator. She said it's a picture of you, her, and her daddy in Washington."

Tears pricked behind Celeste's eyes. "All right," she said, feeling defeated. "I'll handle it."

"Don't let it bother you too much, honey. How's your little trip going?"

"It's going."

"Is everything okay?"

Celeste almost caved at the worried tone of her mother's voice. Sadness came over her.

"I'm fine. I have a lot on my mind. Kiss my baby for me, okay?"

She needed to confide in someone, but she couldn't tell her mother she'd fallen hard for a man who thought she was a cheater and who also thought she was involved with his brother. Even if she'd had any chance of developing a budding romance with him, she'd blown it by making the mistake of coming here under false pretenses. She didn't dare dream he had stronger feelings for her besides the undeniable physical attraction between them. If she thought for one second he did, she would have a talk with Derrick to end the deception.

When she hit "end" on her cell phone, Celeste plopped onto her back across the bed.

As vacations went, this was not a good one.

She rolled onto her side. One full day to go. She would leave this picturesque location and go back to the stark reality of her life, having to prevent any damage her ex could cause to her daughter by not following through on his promise.

"Jerk!" she said softly, squeezing her eyes against the tears. She would tell him off as soon as she could. She didn't have the energy right now.

Hours later, Celeste still hadn't fallen asleep. Her mind raced with thoughts of Roarke, her ex, and her daughter. Feeling restless, she rolled out of bed and slipped on a pair of shorts and an oversized shirt.

Maybe a walk on the beach would help. She could wade into the water, a pleasure she hadn't indulged in since she'd come here.

Barefoot, Celeste tiptoed down the stairs. The quiet of the house made her move carefully so as not to make a sound and disturb anyone in the household. She eased out the back door and made her way off the porch onto the grass.

Stretching her arms high above her head, she gazed up at the star-filled night. So many stars. An ocean breeze mussed her loose hair and cooled her skin.

Movement at the corner of her eye caused her to turn sharply. Roarke stood there, hidden in the shadows. He wore only a pair of jeans, his broad chest bare, his chocolate skin gleaming in the moonlight. Raw masculinity oozed from every pore.

"I didn't know anyone was out here. I'll go—"

"Don't leave on my account."

CHAPTER TEN

"We're supposed to stay away from each other." Funny she had to keep reminding him of that. The message wouldn't register in his brain.

The porch light shone down on her like a spotlight, showing off her bare legs in a pair of shorts and an oversized shirt that hung seductively off one shoulder.

"I think there's enough space out here to keep us far enough apart from each other. Don't you?"

If he answered his own question, the answer would be no. The yawning expanse of the Grand Canyon didn't provide enough space to keep him a safe distance from this woman.

"I guess." Celeste grew silent, and Roarke returned his attention to the black water. It rolled up to the seashore, the lulling sound almost hypnotic. "I couldn't sleep," he heard her say, "so I came out here to get my feet wet."

He held up his bare foot and showed jeans rolled up to his calves. "Same here." That was only half the truth. Yes, he couldn't sleep, but he'd come outside because inside the house, he couldn't stop thinking about her, knowing she slept but a few feet away.

A smile tugged at the corners of her mouth, and he smiled back. Easy. He knew better than to get too relaxed. The minute he let his guard down, he'd be doing something foolish and impulsive. And hypocritical.

He should have let her walk back into the house as she'd intended. Avoidance would be the best way to keep the wild attraction at bay, but he didn't want to avoid her. He'd watched her descend the stairs and stretch her arms above her head to ease her tense muscles.

At the same time, taunting thoughts dared him to step behind her and remove the oversized shirt, which didn't hide anything, only tempted. They encouraged him to push her down on the grass and quench his thirst for her. A thirst so deeply ingrained in him, it seemed to be part of his DNA. The day spent in her company had only been bearable because being in public created a buffer, forcing him to behave with a grain of common decency.

Celeste lifted her eyes heavenward and showed off the graceful line of her neck. "I hope this isn't a stupid question," she said, lowering her gaze back to him, "but I've always wondered, why does it seem as if there are more stars in places like this? In Atlanta, I hardly ever see them. Someone told me once it's because of the lights in the city. Is that true?"

"It's not a stupid question, and yes, it's true. The reason we can't see the stars in cities is because of light pollution. Light pollution happens when naturally occurring light levels are altered by artificial light. The light from signs, streetlights, et cetera shine directly upward and obscure the stars, making them difficult to see in larger cities. It's also a pain for astronomers, because it limits our ability to make good observations."

She listened with rapt attention. "I can see how much you love what you do."

"I can't deny it. I do." He hooked his thumb in a loop of his jeans. "Being able to escape into my own world, into the stars, helped me through some difficult periods in my life."

"Derrick told me about your parents." She appeared hesitant, as if she wanted to gauge if she'd said too much.

"So now you know the whole sordid story. Did he tell you my mother died soon after our father did? Supposedly of a heart attack, but...well, we think her heart was broken from losing my father and finding out he was with his mistress when he died. The actions of two people hurt a lot of other people."

"How did you handle all of it?" she asked quietly.

"To be honest, I didn't think about it much. I grieved, but not for long. I had to take care of my brother and sister, and my first semester at MIT was about to start. I couldn't let what happened to our parents keep us from moving forward. The pain of my parents' deaths and the chaos afterward slowed me down for a bit, but we were alive, and our whole lives stretched ahead of us. Our only option was to move forward."

Celeste bowed her head, and he watched as she drew shapes in the grass with her toe. "I don't think parents fully understand how their actions affect their children. I'm conscious of what I do and what I say to Arianna. I wish her father—I wish her father was as considerate. It's hard sometimes, but I promised myself I'd never say a bad word about him in her presence, and I haven't. It's his loss he doesn't have a better relationship with his daughter. She wants to see him so much, but he's always too busy, and he never comes through to help me out like he says he will."

The dull tone of her voice called out to his protective instincts. He took a step toward her and stopped. The need to shield her from pain rushed through him, but it wasn't his place. He balled his hands into fists, fighting the urge.

"You shouldn't have to do it alone," he said, anger and frustration hardening his voice.

Celeste looked up at him, an embarrassed expression on her face. "I didn't mean to drop my personal problems on you. I'm upset because I spoke to my mother tonight and found out my ex made more promises he knows he won't keep. I wanted to send Arianna to science camp this summer, but I won't be able to. He couldn't come up with a lousy hundred and fifty dollars to help me pay for the camp, and I told him about it months ago. If he'd sent the money like he promised…"

Roarke's biceps tensed under the force of his tightening fists.

"Which camp?" he asked, to distract himself from the foolish idea of gathering her close to comfort her.

"The one at Fernbank Museum. She really likes science, learning about animals and rocks and everything in between. I thought she would enjoy it."

"I'm familiar with the program. I volunteered there as part of my community service requirements for tenure. You're right, they have a good program."

"Yeah, well, it's too late now," Celeste said despondently.

Her eyes strayed to the water. The forlorn look on her face cut through him, and he wanted to take the weight of worry from her shoulders, protect her from the storm buffeting her emotions.

"Go ahead and get your feet wet," he encouraged. "The water's cool and refreshing."

"I think I will," she said, arranging a semblance of a smile on her face. She made her way across the yard down to the sand.

Go inside, Roarke.

If only his feet would obey the command from his brain. Instead, they followed her down to the water, away from the house, where darkness hovered more closely.

"Ooh, it's cold." The temperature didn't stop her from splashing through the shallow waves like a child. She laughed, glancing back at him over her shoulder. "You're so lucky to have this place," she said, her eyes aglow with newfound pleasure.

He stood there, entranced, as she swished the water around with her feet. He liked watching her. She had a beautiful mouth, for one. Whenever a smile played across the lavish symmetry of her lips, a stab of pleasure filled him. In the moonlight, her skin looked as smooth as it felt—like satin.

Without thinking, past caring, he walked into the ocean near her and kicked water at her calves.

"Hey!" With a look of surprise and brimming with laughter, she turned on him.

His chest swelled, and he treaded on dangerous ground. But now he'd heard it, her laughter was a drug. Like a drug fiend, he wanted to prod and tease her so he could hear the melodious tones continue to drift from her throat and watch her eyes dance with merriment.

She returned the splash, and before long, the game got out of hand. "Wait! Wait!" Celeste squeaked, rushing away from him to escape getting doused when he bent down and scooped up two handfuls of salt water.

"Where do you think you're going? Come back here and take your punishment."

He abandoned the terrible deed to race after her. With little effort he closed the gap between them and caught up to her on the grass, grabbing her around the waist.

"You started it!" Celeste squirmed, forcing him to tighten his hold.

Grabbing and holding her was the first mistake. Her soft buttocks pressed against his pelvis. For her part, Celeste suddenly stilled, though her breathing remained labored. Slender fingers clutched his wrists, but not to remove his hands. Her hold on him was tight, as if she were binding herself to him.

"You gonna behave now?" he asked in a low voice.

His body filled with the unbearable pain of wanting and the knowledge that every thought and touch was wrong. His conscience warred with his body and was losing ground fast. Even though guilt ate at him, it wasn't enough to stop him from lusting after her.

The second mistake was looking into her eyes as she tilted her head back. Her dark gaze lowered, and her sweet breath touched his chin from her parted lips.

The third mistake was telling himself all he wanted was a taste. Just one little taste of her soft mouth, and he would stop. Somehow he would find a way to pull back and fight down the agonizing erection pressed against the crease of her butt cheeks.

Liar.

His hand slid under the loose-fitting shirt and covered her breast. Her eyes closed on a moan as she made a sensual little movement in his arms, and he was lost. The other hand reached up and circled the back of her neck so he could hold her in place. A rush of consuming hunger, like nothing he'd ever known before, enveloped him, and he crushed his mouth onto hers. No teasing kisses, only desire, plain and raw.

She melted, pliant, pushing her hips back against him. His arousal pressed harder against his jeans, welcoming the exquisite pleasure of her cushiony backside. When he tweaked her nipple, he felt the shudder that blasted through her body. Through the cotton shirt, she squeezed the hand palming her breast, and soft, throaty moans fell on his ears and tore through him.

"You're gonna make me have an accident," he teased in a shaky voice. His teeth nipped at her ear.

"I want you so much."

The aching in her voice almost undid him. "You want me?" he asked, slipping his hand down the waistband of her shorts. "Let me see how much." She gasped when he made contact with the moisture between her thighs. "Oh yeah," he groaned, his lips now at her bare shoulder, punctuating his words with hard kisses. "You want me."

When he tried to remove his hand, she made a desperate grab to hold it in place.

"No. Please," she pleaded. "Please don't stop, Roarke. Please, don't stop."

Roarke resolved to oblige her request. He worked his fingers through the slick moisture, listening to her pants next to his ear where her head rested on his shoulder.

He inserted one, then a second finger inside her. With long strokes he glided in and out, simultaneously rubbing his warm hand against the tightened nub.

"I wish this was me," he whispered in her ear.

When the climax hit, she shuddered, biting down on her lip to keep from crying out. She grabbed his wrist in a viselike grip and pumped faster, riding out the release. When she came down off her high, her body pressed back against him.

With ease, he scooped her up in his arms and took her onto the grass beneath one of the trees away from the porch lights. When he lowered her weakened body to the ground, she reached for the button on his jeans, and his abdominal muscles tightened.

"What are you doing?"

"I want to touch you."

"Not a good idea," he said, bracing himself above her. She didn't listen, and he was powerless to stop her. She pulled down the zipper and freed him into her hand.

"Celeste…I can't…baby…" He cursed, tearing at the grass with curled fingers. "*You're killing me.*"

She dragged his head down to hers, opening her mouth for his tongue. The kiss was hungry, wet, devouring. She continued to stroke his hard length, each caress bringing him closer and closer to the brink.

A guttural sound left his throat when he pulled her hand away. He couldn't wait anymore. He undid her shorts and yanked them and her panties off. Then he pushed her shirt up and lowered his head to one stiff, toffee-colored peak. She arched upward, running her hand along his bare back. He grabbed her buttocks, lifted her lower body off the grass, and sank into her—deep—their mutual groans drifting on the night air.

Sweet mother…she felt so good…No woman should feel this good. He rocked into her, guiding her to take his rhythm. With each thrust he buried himself deep into the sleek wetness of her body as if his life depended on it.

Celeste wrapped her legs around his waist, a feeling of completion coming over her as he filled her. She matched each stroke with the upward tilt of her hips, but he controlled their movements. His big hands held her off the ground while his mouth continued to shower kisses on her breasts and lave her nipples with his tongue. Each possessive thrust tightened the spring of tension in her loins.

Her movements became more frantic, and his grip tightened, signaling he neared the limits of self-restraint.

She strained against him, mindless, sinking her fingers into the powerful muscles of his arms. Never, ever had she known such passion like she did with him. Never had she imagined she could feel this level of awareness, as if their bodies literally became one.

"I can't get enough of you," he whispered roughly.

The words were a match that lit the bomb inside her. She exploded, shattering. Spasms crashed over her like the waves at the shore. Her mouth fell open in a silent scream, her nails digging into his firm flesh. With a groan, he surged forward, burying himself to the hilt. He convulsed inside her, and didn't draw back, remaining frozen, as if he wanted to savor every blissful second.

Gradually, their breathing returned to normal, their tight, tense bodies relaxed, and he eased back.

"I'll never get enough."

He slowly ran his fingertips along the length of her collarbone. Celeste reached up and stroked his bearded face with the back of her hand. She wanted to tell him she loved him. After such explosive lovemaking, it seemed appropriate. The words burned the back of her throat, but she couldn't say them. He wanted her, and they were certainly compatible sexually, but love? She couldn't bear to experience his rejection once she said the words.

Roarke rolled onto his back in the grass and pulled her on top of him. Spent, she rested her head on his chest. He picked grass out of her hair, and she suspected her shirt would be grass-stained.

He spoke first. "We didn't use any protection."

"It's okay, I'm on the Pill. And I don't have anything."

"I don't, either, but I never…" His voice trailed off. He caressed the skin of her back, ran his hand over her bare bottom, and stroked down to her thighs. Instead of inciting erotic feelings, his touch soothed this time, comforting instead of urgent. "You drive me crazy, make me do things I wouldn't normally do. I don't know who the hell I am when I'm with you."

"Is that such a bad thing?" She kissed the indentation at the base of his throat.

He cupped her chin and lifted her face so he could look into her eyes. "It's not a good thing, and you know why."

She didn't want to talk about Derrick. Not so soon after. It would take her down off the high. "I don't want to do this now," she whispered.

"Celeste, I'm not the kind of man who sneaks around, and you're that kind of woman, either. I don't think I misread you when we met. We have to tell him, no matter what the fallout."

"My relationship with Derrick isn't what you think. It's hard to explain."

"Try."

"It's complicated." He allowed her to pull away, and she stood up and slipped on her underwear and shorts.

By betraying Derrick, she had effectively forced a deeper wedge between the two brothers. Derrick would never forgive her or Roarke. She could feel him watching her, his eyes boring into her back.

"Celeste." She stiffened. His arms crossed around her, and he nudged her hair from the back of her neck to place his lips in its place. "He's my brother. We have to tell him."

"I know." She turned and looped her arms around him and pressed a tender kiss to his mouth.

"I'm sleeping in your bed tonight."

Her eyes widened. "What about the house rules?"

"You make me want to break the rules." He drew her closer and kissed her. "I'll be out before anyone gets up. But there's no way I'm letting you spend the rest of the night alone in your bed."

Anticipation boiled her blood.

"I'm taking my Aunt Iris and grandmother to Savannah tomorrow morning. When I get back, you and I need to talk, and then we're going to have a talk with Derrick. Agreed?"

Celeste nodded. "Agreed."

CHAPTER ELEVEN

Celeste swung her legs off the side of the bed.

Although she and Roarke had agreed they would talk to Derrick together, she decided it would be better if she spoke to him alone. Once she explained the situation to Derrick, he would have to understand. Her feelings for Roarke weren't going away. If anything, they deepened after he held her in his arms all night. No lovemaking. Just the repose of two people comfortable enough to lie in bed together and enjoy a fitful sleep.

The drive to Savannah would take Roarke approximately three hours round trip. In the meantime, she would swallow her pride, tell Derrick everything, and make sure he didn't take out his anger on Roarke.

****

Roarke ran up the steps of the front porch. He'd broken every speed limit on his way back. If a cop had pulled him over, he would have been slapped with a reckless driving ticket for sure.

Up the stairs he went to the second floor and knocked on Celeste's bedroom door. No response. He knocked again.

When she still didn't answer, he went in. The bed was unmade, but with a cursory glance, he noted none of her personal belongings were in the room. Last night her toiletry bag sat on the antique dresser, but it was gone. Her suitcase had rested in the corner. Gone.

He strode over to the window and looked down at the beach. Uncle Reese, Lorena, Matthew, other family members and guests were down on the beach with umbrellas and chairs, enjoying the nice weather. No sign of Celeste.

Unease settled over him.

He rushed out the door and almost slammed into Derrick. The minute he saw his brother's face, he knew.

"Where is she?"

The sly smile grated on his nerves. "Who?"

"You know who." Roarke advanced on him. "Where is she?"

"Wouldn't you like to know?" Derrick laughed. He actually had the nerve to laugh and then turned his back to walk down the hall.

Roarke grabbed him from behind and shoved him against the wall. His fingers clenched around Derrick's lapels. "What did you say to her? Tell me where she is!"

Derrick looked pointedly down at his hands. "Are you going to beat me up?"

Roarke stepped back immediately, shocked at his own behavior. He took a calming breath. "Fine, don't tell me," he said. "I'll find her myself. If I have to call every Celeste Burton in Decatur, then I will." Hardening his jaw, he swung away from his brother.

"Did you get a good laugh at my expense?" Derrick's words halted him at the top of the staircase. "Did you enjoy keeping your little secret from me, knowing I'd brought her here and asked her to pretend to be my girlfriend?"

"Pretend? What are you talking about?"

Derrick's haughty smile faltered. His eyes narrowed. "You mean she didn't tell you?"

"Tell me what?"

"This gets even better. You slept with her thinking she was my girlfriend. Wow. You really are your father's son."

The words had been meant to cause pain, and they did. Roarke's conscience had already taken a beating, and this last lash only served to deepen the guilt.

"I'm not proud of what I did, but we had no intention of sneaking around behind your back. But now you're telling me you two weren't even involved?"

Celeste's comments came back to him. "My relationship with Derrick isn't what you think. It's complicated."

"Yep." His arrogance was really getting on Roarke's nerves. "But it didn't make any difference to you. You saw something you wanted, and you took it. Roarke Hawthorne always gets whatever he wants."

He bristled at the words. "It always comes back to our father. You can't let it go."

Derrick took two steps forward. "You wouldn't either if you had been the one rejected."

"I didn't have a choice, Derrick!" Roarke snarled. "None of us did. It's not like I told him not to have anything to do with you. I was a toddler, like you. But you know what, I'm done. For fifteen years I've tried to create a relationship between us, be a brother to you, but you'd rather hate me and wallow in self-pity. I've had it up to here." He brought his hand up to his forehead. "You want to hate me, hate me. Obviously, nothing I do will change your mind."

"Damn straight."

Roarke chuckled. "You have serious issues. The crazy thing is, you had a father, and still do. Maybe he's not the one you wanted, and you don't have the same DNA, but anybody can see how much Phineas loves you. Anybody but you. Somehow you even managed to mess up that relationship and convince yourself your stepfather only adopted you because your mother made him do it." With a shake of his head, Roarke continued. "That sits right up there with hating me because our father chose to stay with my mother. And while we're at it, do I get to hate you because your mother stole my father from my mother? Do I get to hate you because our parents' affair eventually caused me to lose my own mother? How exactly does this hate thing work? I'm new at it."

"This isn't funny!"

"I never said it was, but I'm tired of putting up with your nonsense. I'm tired of tiptoeing around your feelings. If I'd known fifteen years ago your anger and bitterness would still be so strong, I wouldn't have told the family to contact you." He started down the stairs.

"What? What do you mean you told the family to contact me?" Derrick had moved to the head of the staircase, his face a mask of confusion.

"Exactly what I said. I was the one who told Aunt Iris and Uncle Reese to find you. You'd lost two parents, like us. I thought, as family, we could help each other through a difficult time."

Silence.

Finally, Derrick said, "No one ever told me."

"It doesn't matter whose idea it was. You've been so busy hating me you can't see how much we care about you. We don't care about the private plane and the models you always bring around, obviously trying to impress us. We want you in our lives because you're family. You always held back—except with Cassidy."

"It was the pigtails," Derrick said softly. "The first time I met her she was eight years old. She wore pigtails and was so freaking bubbly. She's been under my skin ever since."

"Yeah, that's Cassidy."

Roarke watched emotions flit across Derrick's face. He didn't have time to decipher them or reminisce. He needed to find Celeste, and since he didn't know if Derrick had thawed enough to share her whereabouts with him, he took off.

Outside on the lawn, he paused. Chances are, she would be at the airport. But which one? Did Derrick take her to the airfield where they'd flown in on the private plane, or was she at the Brunswick Golden Isles Airport, to take a commercial flight?

"Roarke." Derrick stood on the porch with one hand shoved into his pocket. "I took her to the Golden Isles Airport." He glanced down at his Rolex. "If you hurry, you can catch her before she boards the eleven-forty-nine flight to Atlanta." Roarke nodded his thanks and whipped around toward the car. "And Roarke, tell her I'm sorry. I said some things to her I shouldn't have."

Roarke stood next to the car with the door open. "Tell her yourself when I bring her back."

Twenty minutes later, he pulled up with a screech of tires in front of the airport. He jumped out of the car and ran toward the door.

"Sir! Sir! You can't leave your car there."

"Tow it!" Roarke tossed over his shoulder.

Inside, his eyes searched the small terminal for Celeste. She must have already gone through security.

He got in line at the ticket counter. "I need to get on your next flight to Atlanta," he said, handing over his identification and credit card.

"Any luggage?" the woman asked, eying him warily.

"No." He knew that could be seen as a red flag, but he had to take his chances.

Once he received his boarding pass, he went through security with ease. He walked toward the gate, and then he saw her, leaving the restroom, dragging her wheeled carry-on behind her.

He went toward her. A bookmark, hanging precariously from the magazine she had tucked under her arm, fluttered to the floor without her noticing.

He bent to pick it up.

"You dropped something."

Celeste stopped dead in her tracks. She would recognize the whiskey warmth of his voice anywhere.

Turning slowly, she saw Roarke, wearing the most irresistible, bone-melting smile she'd ever seen. Without a second thought, she released the handle of her suitcase and let it clatter to the floor. The magazine tucked under her arm followed suit, and she dashed across the few feet into his arms.

"Trying to sneak off again?" he teased.

She shook her head, too choked up to speak.

They stayed pressed against each other for a while. At last, Roarke drew back to look into her eyes. "I almost lost my mind when I realized you'd left. I've had enough of you leaving me without a word."

"I didn't want to leave like that, but things got messy with Derrick. I swear I would have called you when I got back to Atlanta."

"I couldn't take the chance that you wouldn't." The teasing smile left his face. "Derrick told me the truth about your so-called relationship. Why didn't you tell me?"

"I didn't want to embarrass him, and we had a deal. I thought if I talked to him alone first, I could get him to come around, and then I could explain everything to you. I just thought it would be better than both of us approaching him at the same time, and maybe he wouldn't be mad at you. But I was wrong. He became livid and took out his anger on me. He called me names and said the only reason you wanted me was because of the competition between the two of you—because you thought I was his girlfriend. He hates you so much." She sighed. "After he told me I was no longer needed, he made me leave with him and brought me here."

"I figured he'd forced you out. I was so furious, I was two seconds away from hitting him." He took her hands in his. "I don't expect we'll be best friends anytime soon, but I suspect our relationship will go through some changes in the near future." At her questioning look, he continued. "We yelled, we talked—and we have a lot more talking to do—but I think I finally got through to him. We might finally be able to live as brothers instead of enemies."

"I'm so happy to hear that!"

"We'll have to take it one day at a time." The smile reappeared. "And I'm ready to tell the world how crazy I am about you."

Taken aback, Celeste titled her head sideways. "Crazy, huh?"

"Mhmm." He drew her closer so she could feel the hard length of his body. "It's the only adjective I can think of to describe my actions the past couple of days. I've gone against my conscience, slept in your bed against the house rules, and broken speed limits twice today just so I could get to you."

"You are crazy," Celeste said with a mischievous smile. She reached up and stroked his bearded chin with her fingertips.

"The craziest thing of all is…I think I've fallen in love with you. I know it's a lot to digest, but—"

"No, no, I completely understand." Celeste felt as if her heart would burst from joy. She never imagined he would have the same feelings. "I've never, ever felt this way, either…so…crazy…so in love…as if I've known you forever."

"Yeah?"

"Yeah." Celeste bit her lower lip. "But Roarke, my life is a mess right now. Now that I'm finished with school, I'm trying to find a job in my field and make more money so I won't have to work at…Sig's Cigar Bar anymore."

Roarke frowned. "Sig's Cigar Bar? Is that why you never told me where you work? Those outfits are questionable, and I've heard the food and drinks aren't the only thing for sale there."

"It's honest work," Celeste said defensively, "but I know how people feel about Sig's, and that's why I never mentioned it. I didn't want you to judge me. I don't envision myself working there much longer."

"I hope not," Roarke muttered, still frowning.

"The tip money is good, but I have to admit, not enough. I need to create a better life for me and my daughter. My ex isn't dependable, so I'm basically a single mom, and I'm struggling. On top of all of that, my mother lives with me." She looked down at the floor.

Using his finger, Roarke raised her gaze back to his. "Are you trying to talk me out of loving you, because if you are, it isn't going to work. I'm not going anywhere."

She shook her head in disbelief. "I swear to God you're too good to be true, you know that?"

"Have you missed the mess that my life is? My half brother hates me—although that may be changing—my aunt and grandmother are always in my business, trying to marry me off so I can hurry up and have kids, my sister's a drama queen—"

"It was her wedding. She's allowed to be dramatic."

"No. That's Cassidy all the time. I won't even tell you about my rowdy friends. Can you handle all that?"

"Is that the worst of it?"

"Yeah, that's pretty much it."

She pressed closer. "Then I think we're going to be fine."

She wrapped her arms around his neck, and they kissed for long moments before withdrawing.

"We better get out of here before we do something else crazy," Roarke said huskily, reluctantly pulling away from her.

"Like have sex in the middle of an airport?" Celeste asked.

"Yes. I'm not responsible for my actions when I'm around you." He picked up her luggage and handed her the magazine. She hooked her arm around his. "I just remembered another crazy thing I did," he said, picking up the pace. "I parked in a no-parking zone in front of an airport. We better hurry before our ride back gets towed, or before Homeland Security adds me to the no-fly watch list!"

EPILOGUE

"Mommy, hurry! You're gonna miss it!" Arianna yelled impatiently.

"I'm coming, I'm coming!" Celeste stacked the last of the glasses on the tray. On her way out of the kitchen, she stopped for a moment and looked at the picture Roarke had pinned to the refrigerator with a magnet—one of Arianna's drawings of herself, him, and Celeste watching the fireworks on the beach. A foreshadowing of tonight.

Smiling, she walked through the back door. Arianna had already raced back out onto the beach and staked her claim to Roarke's lap, even though an empty seat next to him was available for her use. At first she'd been shy around Roarke, but he'd charmed her the same way he'd charmed Celeste, and now the two were practically inseparable. Their love of science helped the bond between them develop quickly.

Her mother, Matthew, Cassidy and Antonio, Uncle Reese, and Aunt Iris were also on the beach, sitting with their chairs facing Pier Village so they could see the Fourth of July fireworks. Celeste handed out the drinks and took her seat next to Roarke.

"Love you," he mouthed before taking her hand and lifting it to his lips.

"Love you, too," Celeste mouthed back.

Melding their lives together within such a short time frame wasn't easy. She and her mother were in the process of packing up their two-bedroom apartment so they could move to Athens. In a couple of weeks they would be married, and in less than thirty days, she and Roarke would close on the new house, which would accommodate the four of them better than his condo.

Since they wanted to expand their family right away, they agreed Celeste could put off finding a job for a few years. In the meantime, Roarke handled the role of future stepfather well. Her ex had given her a hard time about it initially, but after he and Roarke had a man-to-man talk—which she had not been privy to—they no longer had any arguments about Roarke.

People couldn't understand why she and Roarke chose to get married so soon after they'd met. Celeste settled back into the chair. She had no reservations. Sometimes you just knew.

And this time, she knew she'd found a good man.

THE END

A Hard Man to Love

PROLOGUE

It was a day like any other day, but it wasn't an ordinary day. Today, Derrick Hoffman became a very rich man.

Twenty-six hours ago, his stepfather—Phineas Hoffman—had been placed in the family mausoleum. Two hours ago, his will had been read and he'd left everything to Derrick, his adopted son. The family was *not* happy.

The smoke from a Cuban cigar snaked upward and dispersed in the night air as Derrick stood outside on the concrete balcony of the mansion he had called home since he was a child. He stared out across the wooded acreage of the property that now belonged to him.

"What were you thinking, Phineas?"

Even though they'd always had a good rapport, Derrick was grateful that in the last days of his father's life, they had grown closer. He regretted the years he'd spent not appreciating the father-son relationship, skeptical of Phineas's love for him, even while he longed for his acceptance.

Derrick shook his head and continued the conversation with himself. "You had to know this would cause major problems for me. Why not leave me a nice little inheritance to live off of, instead of everything?"

If he felt like the odd man out in his adopted family before, it was even worse now after the bombshell dropped. His cousins, his uncles, and their wives had stared back at him with stricken looks at the end of the attorney's reading of the will.

Then the tears fell. Before the tears dried, indignation filled the room as Phineas's younger brothers rose to their feet and started yelling words like "preposterous," "not of sound mind," and "this must be some kind of joke."

But it wasn't a joke, and they all knew it. This was Phineas Hoffman's last will and testament, and his instructions were very clear. After the distribution of the charitable donations, the rest of his estate, which included the mansion in Atlanta, his homes around the world, his cash reserves and investments, and his highly profitable international logistics company, would all go to Derrick.

Derrick was now worth almost a billion dollars, and he had no idea why his father had made such a decision.

"I don't know why you did this," he muttered, "but you were a smart businessman. I have to assume you must have had a good reason."

He stepped back into the first-floor study and stuck one hand in his pocket. He took a deep draw on the cigar and let the smoke ooze slowly past his lips.

A wave of deep sadness washed over him when he looked up at the portrait of his mother and father over the fireplace. Both of them had been taken suddenly from him. His mother died in a plane crash fifteen years ago, and Phineas died from heart failure. His real father, the man he'd never cared to know because he'd never cared to know Derrick, died in the same crash with his mother.

He closed his eyes. Life was short, and death could come at any moment. Time to make some changes in his life.

CHAPTER ONE

As Eva Jacob left the house to go to work, she said a silent prayer of thanks that she hadn't thrown up her breakfast of buttered toast and ginger tea this morning. At almost four months pregnant, she was finally getting a bit of relief. Less than a month ago, she could hardly keep down any of her food.

Before her passing, her mother had told her stories about her own pregnancy with Eva, and she had worried she'd find her pregnancy equally as difficult. She was relieved her doctor's prediction she would feel better soon had finally panned out.

The drive to the clothing and accessories store in Pier Village on St. Simons Island, the largest of the Golden Isles off the coast of Georgia, took ten minutes. The village was the central location for cultural activities and commercial businesses on the island. Antique stores, souvenir shops, clothing stores, and restaurants lined the main street and the waterfront.

As Eva entered the store, the manager, Ms. Elsie, greeted her with a smile.

"How are you feeling today?" the older woman asked.

Eva started working for Ms. Elsie in February, after the hotel chain she'd worked for laid her off at the beginning of the year. As regional events coordinator, Eva had overseen all their special events in the southern part of the state of Georgia. Now she earned a fraction of her previous salary, and because she worked part-time, she didn't have any benefits. Ms. Elsie wanted to bring her on full-time, but the business didn't support such a move.

Eva walked behind the display case and placed her purse under the counter. "Better than usual. I think I might actually keep food in my stomach this morning. That's three days in a row."

"Bless your heart. It'll get better, sugar." Her sympathetic gaze lowered to Eva's stomach.

"She's not making it easy on me, that's for sure." Eva rubbed her belly, which didn't show any signs of her pregnancy.

Ms. Elsie laughed. "They never do. Just think, this is only the beginning. You still have the toddler stage, puberty, and the dreaded teen years to look forward to."

Her exaggerated shudder brought a smile to Eva's lips. "Don't rush me. I already have my hands full."

They chatted amicably as they went through their morning routine, preparing for the annual end-of-summer sale. Eva was in the midst of writing sale signs in a neat script to place throughout the store when the wind chime on the door tinkled an alert that a customer had entered.

She noticed the shift immediately as an intangible force stirred the air. The next stroke of the black marker in her hand remained suspended as she lifted her eyes toward the direction of the sound. A tall male figure stood in the doorway.

Derrick Hoffman.

She became a bundle of nerves as soon as she saw him.

Ridiculously beautiful, he had full lips and deep-set eyes that didn't miss a thing, and that *je ne sais quoi* all men wanted but most lacked. It oozed from his pores and had the ability to surmount the halfhearted objections of any woman. Make her forget her upbringing and drop her panties without a second thought and deal with the consequences later. She'd been one of those women.

The smoky blue-gray of his eyes, inherited from his white mother, found her brown ones. After putting down the marker, she rested her hands on the glass of the display case and asked, "What are you doing here?" at the same time Ms. Elsie inquired, "May I help you?"

For a moment, his eyes shifted to the older woman several feet away, but they slid back to Eva almost immediately. "You know why I'm here."

Eva willed her trembling fingers to remain still as she squared off against him behind the safety of the case. "No, I don't. Even if I did, right now isn't a good time. I'm working. Can we talk later?"

Eva could feel her manager's gaze and wondered what she thought. If Ms. Elsie guessed this was the father of her child, then she was correct. The last conversation with Derrick hadn't gone well, and she could only imagine why he'd decided to show up unannounced.

Derrick walked further into the store, his stride confident and sure. He planted himself in the middle of the dark carpet, feet set apart, as if he owned the place. He looked polished, elegant, and wore one of his pricey suits from London's famous Savile Row, hand-stitched to fit his muscle-packed body. The light complexion of his skin contrasted sharply against the black curls on his head.

His sharp eyes remained on her. "This is important. I'm sure your supervisor won't mind if you step out for a few minutes before the store gets busy."

His luscious mouth curved upward into a disarming smile, exposing a set of flawless white teeth. She knew from experience his warm smile concealed a cold heart, a point her quivering belly had forgotten. It only remembered how those same lips had kissed a path from her navel and lower, how for hours at a time he could make her forget the outside world and live only for the moments in his arms.

"I have no problem with it at all," Ms. Elsie confirmed. Her admiring glance remained riveted on Derrick's profile. Even Ms. Elsie had easily fallen under his spell.

Eva swallowed. "I'll only be a few minutes," she said to her boss, though the words were more for him than Ms. Elsie. She wanted him to know she had no intention of wasting a lot of time talking to him. They'd said everything they needed to on the phone.

She rounded the display case and self-consciously smoothed both hands down her dress. Derrick's eyes followed the movement, but his face remained expressionless. He was a master at the art of concealing his thoughts.

They last saw each other in May, when he came into town for his sister's wedding. He hadn't invited her to go, and the lack of invitation made her realize she had to accept the true nature of their relationship, no matter how much she longed for more. They would never have the kind of relationship she wanted, because Derrick didn't want a serious one. Even now the pain tore through her, the same as it had when she realized his feelings were nowhere near the extent of hers, and she'd made the foolish mistake of falling in love with him.

Eva swept past him, holding her head high and getting a good dose of expensive cologne. The citrus scent hurtled her back to more pleasurable times they'd spent together holed up in a villa on the beach during his visits to town. What a fool she'd been, holding on to the thought that somehow she was special, when she wasn't even worthy enough to meet his family when they visited the island. He'd kept her hidden, like some kind of terrible secret. It was her own fault for agreeing to a nonexclusive relationship, but it still hurt like hell.

The town hadn't fully stirred awake yet. Some of the shops were open, but most would remain closed for at least another hour. Eva stepped in front of the closed store next door so her boss couldn't see them as they talked.

Derrick squinted down at her. "Are you all right?"

"I'm fine."

"You don't look fine."

"Thank you."

As if she didn't feel bad enough, he had to insult her. She ran her fingers over her slicked-back hair. Her go-to hairstyle nowadays was a ponytail. It made life easier since she no longer had any disposable income to go to a hairdresser regularly. Had she known he would be coming today, she may have tried to look more presentable by fixing her hair and putting on a more attractive outfit.

"I didn't mean it as an insult. You…Are you taking care of yourself?"

"Of course I am." She stared out at the street and did her best to harden her heart because the sound of his voice did strange things to her insides, filling her with a raw, basic need that always surfaced whenever he came within ten feet of her. His concern tugged at her heart, and she felt weak, but she didn't want to feel weak because Derrick was strong, and she needed all her strength to handle him.

Whatever had brought him here, it couldn't be good for her. "It's been hard, that's all."

"Hard how?"

"I haven't been able to keep down much food for the past couple of months. I actually lost weight."

He made a noncommittal sound of frustration. "You need to take care of yourself. You're pregnant."

"I'm shocked at your concern." She leveled an angry glare up at him. Her head came only to his shoulder. "I didn't know you cared since you didn't even believe I'm carrying your baby. The first words out of your mouth when I told you were 'Whose baby is it?' Followed up by my favorite, 'So I'm supposed to believe it's mine?'"

He rolled his neck, something he did whenever he wanted to alleviate tension. "It's not the first time a woman's tried to pin a baby on me, Eva. It comes with the territory when you have money."

"Oh, poor Derrick. Is this the part where I feel sorry for you because you've been victimized by my gender? Well, I don't. If you think everybody's out to get you, that's your problem, not mine." She clenched her fingers into a fist. "What do you want? You must want something because like I told you over the phone, I never wanted to see you again, and I don't want anything from you. My baby and I will be fine."

"It's my baby, too." He spoke quietly, but his thinned lips showed his aggravation.

"And when did you come to that conclusion?"

He didn't answer right away. "Once I had time to think, about you, about us."

Us. Her short nails curled into her palm, shutting down the pain of her lost dreams. She'd learned the hard way the kind of pain loving a man like Derrick could cause.

"I realized you're not the kind of person who would try to pass off another man's baby as mine."

"Lucky me, more than two weeks after you insulted me, you came to the realization that I told the truth. What took you so long?"

A sorrowful look entered his eyes. Within seconds, it disappeared. "I had to bury my father."

Eva's fingers flew to her mouth. "Phineas?" His father was the only member of his family she'd ever met. She'd met him once when she visited Derrick in Atlanta. He'd told her how Phineas had adopted him and raised him as his own after he married his mother, a woman thirty years younger than him. "I'm sorry." The mumbled words seemed inadequate, especially when she wanted to reach out and put her arms around him in a comforting gesture.

He would never accept it anyway. In fact, the day after he'd told her the whole sordid story about Phineas, his mother, and his biological father, she tried to broach the subject again. He'd shut her down swiftly, letting her know the topic was off-limits, erecting the invisible walls again.

"That's why I'm here," Derrick continued.

Confused, Eva stared at him. "I don't understand."

"The past couple of weeks have been crazy since his death, but I finally feel like I'm getting my head above water. One lesson his passing has taught me is that life's too short. I don't want my child out there in the world, not knowing how much I want them."

"Derrick, I would never keep the two of you apart," Eva said in an earnest voice. "I told you as soon as I knew I was pregnant."

Eva had thought she couldn't have children, and coupled with irregular periods since puberty, she didn't even suspect she was pregnant for the first three months.

Only after she went to the doctor, complaining about tiredness and nausea, did she learn she was having a baby.

"Good, I'm glad to hear it. So you shouldn't have any problem with my suggestion." He stepped closer, eyes filled with purpose. Eva inhaled sharply, overwhelmed by his commanding presence. "I want my child to be with me at all times. I want us to get married right away."

She gaped at him, thinking her hearing must be going bad. If she didn't know better, she'd say he just asked her to marry him, but that would be ludicrous. A chuckle of disbelief broke past her lips, and she clamped her hand over her mouth when his face hardened.

"Did I say something funny?"

"I'm sorry, I could have sworn you asked me to marry you—sort of."

"I did." His solemn expression swiped the smile from her face.

"You—you can't be serious. People don't get married nowadays because they're having a baby."

"In case you didn't notice, I'm not 'people.' No kid of mine is going to grow up without knowing me."

"I agree, but I don't see why we have to get married to ensure it."

"Because I'm not satisfied with occasional visits. I want my son or daughter in my house, and I want to see them every day—not when it's convenient for you."

Eva stepped back, putting her hands up in a defensive motion against him. "Wait a minute. You're serious about this?"

"I've had plenty of time to think, and it could work."

"No, it can't!" She swallowed to calm her frayed nerves. She sounded hysterical, while he remained as cool as a tall glass of iced tea. Before she would have welcomed a proposal—such that it was—but a wedding because of her pregnancy was the last option she'd ever considered.

Lowering her voice, she said, "We don't have to get married. Besides, we don't even—" She stopped, finding it difficult to say the words, but managing to muddle through. "We don't love each other. We were already broken up when I told you I was pregnant. I don't want to marry you, and you don't want to marry me. Having a baby is not a good enough reason." She took a deep breath and gradually released it. "We need to come to another arrangement."

"All right," he said, which only unsettled her nerves even more. She had a feeling she wouldn't like his next words. "Then would you be willing to let me have the baby after it's born?"

Her eyes widened, and she recoiled from him. "You really are insane, aren't you?"

"What's so insane about a man wanting his child?"

"Nothing, but—"

"Let me guess, a father's not as important as a mother, right?"

"I never said that. I know how you feel because I never knew my father, either." A common thread between the two of them, but whereas she'd seen it as a pain they could share, he never wanted to discuss it. "But a child needs its mother."

"*And* its father."

His implacable expression worried her, and she tried to mollify him. "And you'll have all the access you want."

"I don't want *access*."

"Well, if you think I'm going to hand my daughter over to you after she's born, you are sadly mistaken."

He froze, staring at her. "Daughter? You know for sure it's a girl?"

Eva paused and nodded. "Yes. This week I found out I'm having a girl." She'd chosen to get a 3-D ultrasound done to determine the gender of the baby.

His gaze lowered to her stomach. "A girl."

He seemed stunned, as if hearing the sex of the baby really brought home the fact that a life was growing inside her. He ran his hand down the back of his head, across the black silk of his hair—hair she'd lovingly caressed with her own fingertips. She could almost feel the texture of it.

Eva's voice gentled. "Derrick, I know why you're saying these things, but you never have to worry about me cutting you out of your daughter's life. She'll know you love her. The relationship you didn't have with your biological father has no bearing on your relationship with our daughter."

He lifted his cool gaze to her face. "How much?" He pulled out his phone.

She frowned. "How much what?"

"How much will it take for you to give her up once she's born? I can be very generous. I have my accountant on speed dial, and with one phone call, I can have any dollar amount you request transferred into the account you choose within minutes."

He couldn't be serious. "Wait, *what*?" Eva shook her head in confusion. "Did I hear you correctly? Did you just offer to *buy* my baby?"

CHAPTER TWO

He didn't seem a bit perturbed, as if she'd overreacted—
as if he'd offered to purchase a cup of coffee instead of a
human being.

"I wouldn't use those words."

"What words would you use?"

"I'm offering you another option, freeing you from the
responsibility—"

"*Are you out of your mind?* You think you can pay me off
and I'll walk away? My baby is not for sale."

"Calm down."

She tried, but couldn't. Her head felt as if a five-piece
band, made up entirely of percussionists, pounded out a
constant beat inside her skull.

"What kind of woman do you think I am? You can't
seriously think I would agree to something like that."

"Everything has a price, Eva."

His matter-of-fact tone pushed her toward hysteria
again. "Not me, and not my child. You don't have enough
money to make me hand her over to someone like you!"

His face hardened at the insult, the ensuing silence only disturbed by the sound of a few cars passing by. A small family with laughing children descended from an SUV to have breakfast at the restaurant across the street.

"Do you really want to do this?" he asked quietly. Too quietly.

Alarm bells sounded in her head at the determined set of his jaw. When she'd called him to tell him about her pregnancy, she had never considered he would want his child so much he would do anything to get her.

"Do you really want to battle with me? Because I'm willing to do whatever it takes to get what I want."

Her heart raced at an alarming speed. This calmer Derrick frightened her more than the one who had withstood her hysterical outbursts moments before.

"I didn't want to do this," he continued. "But you've left me no choice." He reached inside his jacket and removed an envelope, thrusting it in her face.

Eva took it. Apprehension caused goose pimples to spring up on her arms despite the morning's warmth. "What is this?"

"Open it."

Filled with nervous tension, she tore open the unmarked envelope. It contained a letter, typed on ornate tan stationery with the name of a well-known law firm in embossed letters across the top. Her fingers tightened on the paper as she scanned the contents.

"If you don't change your answer, you'll receive a certified copy in the mail within the next day or two," Derrick said. "I brought along a copy in case I needed it, and clearly I do."

The gist of the letter expressed the attorneys' intention to file for sole custody of the unborn child on behalf of their client, Derrick Hoffman, as soon as the baby was born.

Eva frowned, shaking her head emphatically. She suddenly felt ill. "No, no. You won't get away with this."

"Try me."

"Courts don't separate babies from their mothers."

"If you want to take the chance, go right ahead. But here's something you should know. My father left everything to me. That means I have almost unlimited funds to fight you as long and as hard as I need to. How difficult do you think it would be for my attorneys to prove I'm the better option for our daughter, hmm?" He held up his thumb to start counting. "One, you haven't had a full-time job since January. Two, at the job you have now, you only earn minimum wage, and you work part-time. Three, you don't have insurance, so your access to adequate health care is questionable. Four—"

"Enough!" Eva crushed the paper in her hand. She stared down at the sidewalk, fighting back the tears of helplessness. Her heart felt swollen and heavy in her chest. He couldn't be this cruel. What had she ever seen in him? "Please don't do this."

"I gave you two other options," he said. "If you marry me, you'll live a comfortable lifestyle, and we can raise our daughter together. If marriage to me is so unappealing, I'm willing to take on the responsibility of being a single parent. You can give her to me willingly, and I'll compensate you for it."

She wrapped protective arms around her midsection. "I only have to choose, huh? Door A or door B. Or I'm stuck with door C."

"It doesn't have to be this way." An odd note in his voice caused her to lift her head, but his face didn't show the same emotion she knew openly displayed on hers.

"What about love, Derrick? Does that even matter to you?"

"Why do you think I'm doing this? You expect me to walk away from my own flesh and blood?"

"I thought we could come to a workable agreement. We need a middle ground. Our relationship is finished, but the only other real option you've given me is to pack up my life and come live with you."

His eyes glittered down at her. "Our relationship may have ended, but I wasn't done with you."

The quietly spoken words rocked her. Her heart stuttered in her chest. "Is that what this is about?" she asked in a soft voice. "You're angry because I ended the relationship?"

She'd stopped seeing him as an act of self-preservation. Whenever the phone rang, she ran for it, her heart beating fast in the hope it was him saying he was on his way to see her. What was she supposed to do, with her feelings for him growing stronger and stronger, knowing when they weren't together, other women slept in his bed? Knowing some other woman's lips trailed kisses across his golden skin? If she could flip a switch and stop caring about him, life would be easier.

She'd already grown disgusted with herself at the way she'd gladly accepted the open relationship he tossed at her. She couldn't continue to see him when she knew she wanted more than he could give her. If there had been any doubt before, his actions today left no room for doubt that her feelings for him were completely one-sided.

"Don't be ridiculous," he said scathingly. "I wouldn't give up my freedom to get back at you, and if I only wanted sex, I could get it anytime of the day or night I want. But what I want is my child, with me, at all times."

The callously spoken words crushed her. Of course she knew he could have any woman anytime he wanted. He was wealthy, good-looking, and charming when he wanted to be. What woman could resist such a combination?

She lifted her chin, refusing to be bullied. "Then I guess we're deadlocked."

The muscle in his left cheek flexed as he tried to rein in his temper. "You're making a mistake."

Tears stung her eyes, and she didn't care if he saw them. "*You're* making a mistake. Please leave. I don't want to see you."

"Don't be foolish and make an emotional decision. Think about what I'm offering you."

"Get out of here, Derrick, and don't come back."

Unfazed, he continued to talk in the same calm voice. "I'm staying in the beach villa I always rented for us when I came here. I don't leave until noon tomorrow. You know how to get in touch with me. If you give me your answer by noon, it'll be like this conversation never took place."

"I already gave you my answer."

His emotionless eyes stared down into hers. "I'll excuse your behavior because I realize your hormones are all messed up and you're not thinking straight—"

"Excuse my behavior?" She laughed, her tone shrill. "Don't do me any favors!"

"My offer is only good until tomorrow, so you need to spend the rest of the day thinking long and hard about this decision and everything you're giving up. If you marry me, you'll live a very comfortable life."

"Are you deaf? I don't want to marry you, Derrick. I couldn't care less about your money or your lifestyle. They mean nothing to me. I don't care enough about any of it to want to put up with marriage to *you*."

She hated getting so riled up, so emotional, she didn't even know herself. Her mother, originally from the South, had been a genteel woman and would turn over in her grave if she saw Eva's behavior. But even her mother would have to understand how Derrick pushed her buttons. Derrick could test the patience of Job. His dogged determination to get his way may be a plus in business, but it was a less than admirable trait on a personal level.

"Stop and think," he said through clenched teeth.

"No, you stop and think—about what you're doing. You and your fancy Atlanta lawyers can go to hell."

She walked by him.

"Eva!"

She swung around and hurled the crumpled letter at him, watching it float to the ground. "I said go to hell!"

Her voice quivered, and she hated herself for it. She could barely see through the cloudy screen of tears as she left him standing on the sidewalk. Before she broke down completely in front of him, she fumbled for the handle on the door. Once inside, she rushed to the back of the store and cried.

CHAPTER THREE

"The art of intimidation, my boy, is to make your opponent believe every word you say. Look them dead in the eye and never flinch. Never let them see weakness."

Phineas's words repeated in Derrick's head as he eased the rented sports car into the line of traffic and headed toward the two-bedroom beach villa he'd rented. Phineas had always doled out advice, and it turned out much of it could be applied just as easily to personal relationships as to business ones.

He hadn't intended to make Eva angry. He didn't know a whole lot about pregnant women, but he was pretty sure they shouldn't get upset. Unfortunately, her reaction to his suggestion of marriage had stymied him and forced him to reveal his intention to take the baby if she didn't go along with his plans.

After he let himself in and dropped his overnight bag in one of the bedrooms, he stepped out onto the patio to look out at the Atlantic Ocean, stretched out to the horizon as far as the eye could see. He shouldn't have come here, because of the memories of all the times he'd stayed here with her. He could have told his personal assistant to book him into another location, but old habits die hard.

The soothing sound of the waves and familiar salty scent of the blue water didn't have the same appeal this time. He pulled out his smartphone, trying not to think about her, but finding it impossible.

Damn. He really should have picked somewhere else to stay, because there were too many memories here—buying groceries at the local store and cooking together in the kitchen, splashing around in the villa's private pool, and, entwined in each other's arms, making love until they grew exhausted.

He turned on the ringer on the phone, which he'd switched off earlier so there would be no interruption during his conversation with Eva. He scrolled through the list of missed calls and saw one had come from the attorneys. Hopefully they had good news concerning the legal battle between him and his family. They'd pooled their resources and dragged him into court to contest Phineas's will. The attorneys had warned him to expect a long and dirty fight.

In the midst of all this, he had also become the CEO of Phineas's international logistics firm, Hoffman Logistics Company, also known as HLC in the industry. At his father's insistence, he'd worked at the company, in various positions, off and on over the years. Since his father's death, his most important task had been to calm employees and business associates and reassure them the company remained a viable player in the industry, even though its beloved leader was no longer at the helm. All the more reason to get a quick answer from Eva, so he could head back to Atlanta and deal with the issues he'd left behind to come down here and talk to her in person.

He spent every day and night reading reports, in meetings, doing everything he could to maintain a sense of order and keep the company from falling apart. Three senior executives had already bailed and gone over to the competition. Keeping up company morale was a priority to stop any further migrations.

He thought about Eva again. Today she'd looked so fragile as he'd looked down at her slender frame. He'd wanted to pick her up and take her away from her low-paying job and give her the care she needed because she obviously wasn't taking care of herself.

To think she carried his child, and he'd almost missed out because of his pride. He'd still been angry and tending to a bruised ego over their breakup when she called to tell him the news. Despite his response, deep down he'd known the truth. Unlike some of the mercenary women he'd come to know over the years, she'd been one of the few who'd never asked for anything from him. Not once had she ever asked him to pay her bills or buy her an expensive piece of jewelry.

What he couldn't figure out was what he'd done to make her hate him so much. The anger in her eyes had been almost enough to laser him in two. Did she have any idea how many other women would love to be in her position— to be offered marriage? Instead of being appreciative, she acted as if she'd been offered an all-expenses-paid trip to the depths of hell.

And why had she ended their relationship in the first place? He'd come to the island for his sister's wedding, and even though they'd made plans to see each other, she'd refused to see him until he showed up at her job on Saturday morning and gave her no choice. Her only explanation for why she no longer wanted to see him had been that their relationship had run its course and she wanted to move on.

He swore.

Sauntering back into the room, he loosened his tie. He hadn't been ready to move on. Women didn't end relationships with him; it usually happened the other way around. Her rejection had bothered him for weeks as he pondered her words, trying to find some hidden meaning in the things she'd said, but couldn't. Then, out of the blue, she'd called him to say she was pregnant.

Maybe he hadn't given her the best response, but he couldn't be blamed. Their relationship hadn't been exclusive. For all he knew, she could have broken up with him because of another man and was trying to trap him with that other man's child. But he had to be truthful and admit his role in this. The last time they'd made love, he hadn't used any protection. He'd been riled up by the thought of her seeing someone else.

They had an agreement: don't ask, don't tell. But he'd asked. And she'd told.

One day in April, he'd had to cancel his weekend plans to see her, and when he'd called a few days later to see what she was doing, she told him she planned to go out with a "friend"—a *male* friend. He'd been so jealous, he'd driven almost five hours straight without stopping because Phineas had taken the private plane out of town on business and he couldn't get a commercial flight. When he'd shown up at her apartment, she'd been surprised to see him, and he'd made up something about his plans changing yet again. All he really cared about, though, was making sure she didn't go out with this other guy.

She canceled her plans, and he'd stayed until the middle of the following week like a simpering idiot. He had conducted his business from the villa and rearranged his appointments until later in the week. When he returned to Atlanta, he found a real estate agent to put a newly formulated plan into action. The agent found a condo for her a few miles from his own place downtown. He planned to move her in and pay for it to have her close by, and if she wanted to work, he'd get her a job at his father's company.

He decided to tell her about the condo the weekend of his sister's wedding. He was ready to move their relationship to the next level and invite her up to see the place. But everything had changed. Their arrangement wasn't working out. So she'd said. In the back of his mind, he'd wondered if her *friend* had anything to do with it.

He never told a soul about his plans. Certainly not her. He wasn't about to beg. If she wanted out of the relationship, she could have her freedom.

When she'd told him about her pregnancy, he'd been purposely cold and cruel to her, but once he'd thought about it, he realized Eva would never tell him she carried his child if she wasn't one hundred percent certain. Another woman, yes. Eva, no. Even now she made it plain she didn't want anything from him.

He tossed the tie on the bed and dialed the number for his attorneys.

He'd given her until noon tomorrow, and now he would wait. He had rights, and he intended to exercise them, no matter how helpless she looked. This wasn't only about him; this was about his daughter, too. His daughter would never experience what he had. His daughter would never have reason to doubt he loved her.

****

"So what are you going to do?"

Back at her apartment, Eva sat in the cushiony armchair positioned across from the sofa where her best friend and roommate sat. Kallie tucked a lock of brunette hair behind her ear and screwed up her face into a concerned frown. Kallie's first roommate had moved in with her boyfriend, paving the way for her and Eva to move in together to save money after Eva lost her full-time job.

After Derrick left, Eva worked a six-hour shift with Ms. Elsie, automatically performing her duties of putting up the sales displays, ringing up customers, and folding and refolding clothes on the tables. The monotony of the tasks provided the type of familiarity she needed to get her through the day, but she had left the store in a semi-dazed state.

"I don't know," Eva said wearily. "I can't believe I got myself into such a mess."

Kallie folded her feet under her on the sofa. "You didn't get pregnant on your own. It takes two."

"I know, but still…"

"It could be worse."

She looked at her roommate. "How could it possibly be worse?"

"He could be completely uninterested in your child, which is what you originally thought. Now we know the truth. Or, he could be some loser who has nothing to offer. Derrick has money, and he wants to take care of this baby." She shrugged.

"He doesn't just want to take care of her, Kal. He wants to take her from me if I don't agree to marry him." She rubbed her hand across her brow. "I didn't see this coming. He's not going to budge, either. You should have seen him."

Kallie leaned forward. "Before you ended the relationship, you said you had fallen in love with him. What

141

if you could make a go of it? You know, have a real marriage."

Eva laughed shortly. "Yeah, right. I romanticized the situation, trying to make our...relationship...into something it wasn't."

She'd willingly accepted the terms of an open relationship even though she had reservations about it. She didn't see the harm, especially when they first started seeing each other. Too late, she learned she wasn't the type of woman who could handle it. In fact, she should have known right from the start, because she fell for him almost immediately, and the night they met remained burned in her memory...

****

Eva and her three girlfriends were having their annual New Year's Day dinner at their favorite restaurant on the waterfront. Every year they met and shared their goals for the new year and talked each other out of feeling sad about bad decisions from the year before.

Halfway through the meal, the waitress came over and said, "Ladies, the gentleman over there sent you this bottle of champagne with a wish for you to have a happy new year."

They all turned toward the bar, to the man sitting smoking a cigar. He smiled in their general direction, but Eva noticed his eyes lingered on her a fraction longer than the others. Feeling her cheeks get hot, she quickly looked away.

The waitress started pouring the expensive sparkling wine into glasses. "Let him know we said thank you," cooed one of her friends, Bev.

"He's hot," Kallie murmured. "Maybe we should invite him over."

Their animated conversation changed to whispered speculation about the man at the bar. A few minutes later, the waitress returned.

"He said he would love it if you come thank him yourself."

"Really?" Bev smoothed her fingers over her hair while her girlfriends gasped and whispered in excitement.

A pang of jealousy worked its way through Eva's stomach at the thought her friend would get to meet him. His cool stare had intrigued her, and his handsome face had made her heart thump a faster beat.

"Not you," the waitress said. "You."

It took a minute for Eva to realize she had spoken to her. She'd been focused on her plate. "Me?" she asked in shock. "I didn't say anything."

The waitress shrugged. "He asked specifically for you, honey."

He'd asked for her. Her belly flipped over itself.

She cast a glance over at the bar again, but he wasn't looking in their direction. He and the man next to him were engrossed in conversation. He nodded, and then tipped a tumbler toward his mouth. Even from this distance she could tell he had nice lips.

Kallie's excited voice broke through her shock. "Eva, go!"

"All right. Shush."

At the urging of her friends, Eva walked over to where he sat, wiping her sweaty palms on the skirt of her dress. "Hi."

His eyes drew her in. Blue, but not blue, gray, but not gray—an interesting combination of the two. His skin, the color of sand, had golden undertones, and the thick, wavy hair on his head made her fingers tingle with the desire to play in the strands. Like she'd noticed from afar, he had inviting lips that curved upward in a most seductive way when he smiled. She could tell he had money, despite being casually sexy in a black turtleneck and black jeans. He had an air about him.

"Hi yourself." His warm voice sent a shiver down her spine.

"Thank you for the champagne. That was very nice of you." She groaned inwardly at the sound of her voice. She sounded nervous, and her stomach muscles trembled in response to her heightened awareness of him.

He lifted one shoulder as if it were no big deal. "I saw a beautiful woman having dinner with her friends and wanted to impress her."

His open flirtation made her feel out of her depth. He reeked of confidence, and she found it both sexy and unnerving. "Mission accomplished."

He smiled. "Good to know. By the way, I'm Derrick Hoffman. What's your name?"

"I'm Eva. Eva Jacob."

She extended her hand for a handshake, but instead of shaking it, he lifted her fingers to his mouth and kissed the back of her hand. Tremors shot through her body, and she suddenly had the burning desire to remove all her clothing so he'd have the opportunity to place the same type of kiss on every inch of her skin.

Once he'd lowered her hand, he didn't let go. He rubbed his thumb across the back of her knuckles, which caused heat to suffuse her skin. Her instantaneous attraction to him overwhelmed and excited her. With her heart racing, she felt on the verge of a new adventure, unlike anything she'd ever experienced.

"Eva, I'm about to leave, but before I go, I'm going to give you my number. I hope you use it."

He released her hand to pull out a card containing his name and phone number, then handed it to her.

He stubbed out his cigar and rose from the barstool. Even though she wore heels, his broad-shouldered body towered over her. "It was nice meeting you, Derrick."

"Hopefully, it won't be our last meeting. I want to see you again."

He soon left, leaving the ball in her court. If he'd tried, she would have willingly gone to bed with him the same night, but he hadn't. Instead, he'd handed her his card, and she and her girlfriends found out later he'd picked up the tab for the entire table.

She didn't last one day before she called him.

****

Eva couldn't blame Derrick for his attitude about their relationship because he'd been up front with her from the beginning. They had an understanding. Whenever he came into town, she would be available to him. It was her fault for developing feelings for him. He had every right to see other women, as she did to see other men. Except she'd fallen for him and didn't exercise her rights, and it killed her to think he might be exercising his.

"He came down here all the time to see you. Maybe…"

"Kal, I know what you're trying to do." Eva turned grateful eyes on her friend. "But the truth is it was never serious between us. I was never his girlfriend." Fresh pain seized up her vocal cords. She should be past this by now, but the longing for more still hurt. "He didn't ask me to marry him because he's madly in love with me. He asked me because I'm pregnant. No matter what I may think about him, he definitely wants to be a father to this baby."

"Do you think you could buy more time?"

Eva shook her head in resignation. "You don't know Derrick. He won't budge, which means the noon deadline is final."

Once, she'd heard him on the phone using a commanding tone of voice to express his displeasure at something or the other someone had done. The way he spoke, the inflection in his voice, had made her climb on top of him the minute he hung up the phone. That tone of voice wasn't quite as sexy with the anger and the commands directed at her.

"Sounds like you know what you have to do."

In a few months, she would be twenty-nine, and like many women her age, she had envisioned her wedding day a certain way, after meeting and falling in love with a modern-day Prince Charming. Only she had met a prince in the financial sense, minus the charming part.

"I'll make my final decision in the morning. Maybe there's some way out I haven't thought about yet."

Even though she said those words to her roommate, inside, Eva resigned herself to the inevitable. She would never forgive herself if she didn't do everything possible to secure a safe birth and good future for her child—*their* child. Derrick could ensure that happened.

She shouldn't have gotten pregnant, or so doctors had led her to believe. Scarring left over from an appendectomy she had as a teenager blocked her reproductive system. For years she thought she would never become a mother, but they had been wrong. She looked forward to all the changes her body would take on because it meant her child was growing safely just under her heart. Her baby was a miracle, and for that reason alone, she could never give her up.

She knew what she needed to do, but she didn't look forward to it.

CHAPTER FOUR

The following morning, Derrick dined on a late breakfast of scrambled eggs, pancakes, and a side of cheese grits in the resort's restaurant. The floor-to-ceiling windows offered a stunning view of the ocean. Outside, the waves rolled up and spattered into white foam against the rocks that created a natural boundary between the resort and the thin strip of sand at this end of the beach.

To keep his mind off the pending noon deadline, he perused the financial section of the paper while he ate. Sleep had evaded him for much of the night, making way for plans and strategies he imagined implementing at HLC. In the early morning, he'd finally fallen asleep, only to awaken with a stiff erection, which further mocked his decision to stay at the villa. An erotic dream about Eva had been the culprit.

Once he'd eaten and had a couple cups of strong coffee, he should be able to tackle anything that came his way, including Eva's decision. She still had time to make the right one.

A motion beside the table made him look up. When he did, he saw Eva standing there. For a split second, his fingers tightened around the fork to counteract the involuntary jolt seeing her caused to his body.

"I went by the villa, but you weren't there, so I came here to look for you." She spoke quietly and looked as if she wasn't sure she'd be welcomed.

This morning her appearance had improved. Her hair brushed her shoulders in a neat style around her face. The makeup was no substitute for the glow he was accustomed to seeing on her chestnut-colored skin, but compared to her drawn appearance yesterday, it was an improvement. It added an attractive color to her cheeks and lips and emphasized her long lashes.

"May I sit down?"

"Of course."

Right away he stood and went over to her. As he reached out to help her into the chair, she withdrew from him and seated herself across the table from where he'd been sitting. The small act of rejection created a twinge in his chest.

In the past, she would have pressed her soft body against his with a warm smile on her face. She loved to tease him in public, flirting and batting those incredibly long lashes at him. He remembered several times rushing through a meal so he could get her alone to make love. On her back, on her stomach, it didn't matter the position—

Derrick slammed the brakes on his out-of-control thoughts and dropped into the chair across from her.

Don't go there.

Eyeing her across the table, he noticed how the green top accentuated her dark coloring, just as he couldn't help but notice how good she smelled. Because of mild allergies, she was very picky about fragrances and seldom wore perfume. She used organic soaps with ingredients like carrot and honey or peppermint and oatmeal. Today was a carrot-and-honey day. She smelled so good he wanted to lick her.

A sip of the black, bitter coffee redirected the path of his thoughts.

"I thought about our conversation yesterday, and I brought something for you," she said. She offered him a large manila envelope. He reached for it and pulled out the contents: a few grainy, yellow-toned photos. "Those are the pictures of an ultrasound I had this week." He didn't need an explanation to understand what he looked at. "That's your daughter."

Daughter. His gut tightened into a knot at the word. *His* daughter. *His* flesh and blood.

He flipped from one image to the next in silence. The detail was remarkable. Though slightly distorted, there were distinguishable features in the ghostly-looking photos. "Is she healthy?" he asked.

"They haven't detected any problems," Eva answered. "So far, so good."

Derrick let his finger trace the outline of the figure's body in the 3-D image, over the closed eyes and the tiny hands, amazed he had been a part of creating another life. While being a father had always been a distant thought in his mind, the pending birth of his child became a reality he looked forward to with surprising anticipation.

"I shared these with you for two reasons."

He lifted his gaze to hers.

"I wanted you to understand what you were asking me to give up. But it also made me realize what I was asking you to give up, too. I know you feel strongly about being a good father. I don't want to keep you from doing that."

He anxiously awaited her next words, not daring to believe she would say what he wanted.

She swallowed. "I'll marry you."

He couldn't move for several seconds, stunned into disbelief and an overwhelming sense of relief. Remaining motionless, he withheld the true extent of his feelings.

With the icy calm he hadn't inherited, but had learned from his father, he carefully replaced the sonograms in the envelope and set them on the table. "It's the best decision for the three of us."

She averted her dark brown eyes to the scenery outside the window, but not before he saw the despair in them. He gritted his teeth as anger filled him. Did she have to act like a lamb being led to the slaughter? She wasn't the only one making a sacrifice.

"I know this isn't what either of us planned for our future, but we'll have to make adjustments," he said, his tone harsh. "It's not an ideal situation, but we're stuck with each other."

Her eyes held surprise at his tone as she landed her gaze back on his side of the table. "I guess so," she said carefully. "Are you sure this is what you want to do?"

"Are you?"

A wry twist lifted the corner of her lips. "I don't have a choice."

"Actually, I gave you a couple of options."

"Your generosity is unparalleled." She plucked at the cloth napkin on the table. "What now?"

Moving quickly was the only option. "I'll get my lawyers to draw up a prenup." Including a clause that if he found out after the child was born she wasn't his, he could divorce Eva without concern she would have rights to his millions. "It's a precautionary measure."

"I wouldn't expect anything less."

DELANEY DIAMOND

Her caustic tone wasn't lost on Derrick, but he chose to ignore it. He scrolled through his phone. "Let's plan to do this two weeks from today."

Eva fixed her eyes on his bent head. "T-Two weeks? So soon? I can't leave Kallie in the lurch without a roommate. And we can't possibly plan a wedding on such short notice. After all, I'd like to have my family and friends there."

"Two weeks is plenty of time," he said, still not looking at her. "I'll cover your portion of the lease until Kallie can find someone else to move in, and we'll get a couple of wedding coordinators to help you." He started typing into the phone.

It was all happening so fast, and she felt like someone being submerged underwater. "Can we please slow down? What's the rush? I'm only a few weeks into my second trimester. We have plenty of time."

"Time is relative." He set the phone on the table in a decisive manner. "I have a lot of responsibilities. The sooner we get this over with, the better."

The sting of his words inflamed her temper. "Let's do *this*. Let's get *this* over with. You're so romantic."

Pausing, he narrowed his eyes on her. "Okay, out with it. What's really bothering you? Because it's obvious something is bothering you. The sooner we get it out in the open, the better, because I don't have time to entertain your dramatic outbursts. I'm a busy man."

"Nothing's bothering me."

"Something's bothering you." He tapped his forefinger on the tabletop. "Let me guess, this is one of those games women like to play, where I have to figure it out?"

Eva crossed her arms and stared out at the roaring waves.

"Even better," he said, a mocking pitch to his voice. "The silent treatment. I love the silent treatment."

She glared at him. "You want to know what's bothering me? We're getting married. It's a big deal, and you're acting as if it's nothing. A wedding ceremony shouldn't be an event you squeeze in between a meeting and a presentation on your calendar."

The moment the words left her mouth, she regretted them. She didn't want him to think she placed any more importance on their future marriage than he did.

"This isn't any easier for me than it is for you. I didn't plan to get married anytime soon, if ever. I'm trying to make the best of a bad situation."

She flinched.

"I didn't mean that the way it came out...but neither one of us planned this. Right?"

The undertone in the question caught her attention. "Are you suggesting I planned to get pregnant?"

His eyes surveyed her thoughtfully. "You told me you couldn't get pregnant."

"After you had already—" She broke off midsentence. The memory of how he'd taken her flashed through her mind.

He'd shown up unannounced to her apartment late one night after he'd already told her he couldn't come to town. She'd been excited by his unexpected visit, and he'd been edgy and extra amorous. In their haste, they'd been careless. They discussed the fact they hadn't used a condom, and she bared her soul and told him she couldn't get pregnant.

To her surprise, he hadn't expressed any concern over her infertility. But then, why would he, when there was never the expectation of a future together?

"You showed up at my apartment without notice and practically tore my clothes off," Eva said.

"I didn't hear you complaining when it happened. Are you saying you didn't like it?" he asked, his tone soft and gravelly, spreading unwelcome warmth through every limb.

"I'm saying you didn't use a condom," Eva replied in a firm voice. "No matter what I said afterward, you have to at least accept partial blame."

The waitress appeared beside their table and provided a temporary reprieve from the intense conversation. "Ma'am, would you like to order from the menu, or will you have the buffet this morning?" She topped off Derrick's coffee.

Grateful for the interruption, Eva shook her head. "I won't be eating, thank you."

"Have you had any breakfast?" Derrick asked sharply.

"No, but I'm fine."

"You should have something. You're eating for two now."

As if she didn't know. "I'm fine."

"At least have a drink—coffee or tea. What do pregnant women drink?"

To quiet him, she turned to the waitress. "I'll have a glass of milk."

"Anything else?" the woman asked.

Eva shook her head.

Derrick sipped his coffee. "I guess we both got carried away that night," he said, replacing the cup in the saucer.

He remembered the night and the days afterward well. It was the last time she let him touch her. Here he sat only feet away and was still denied the luxury. He had set the rules for their relationship. They were the same ones he had lived by for years, yet it had driven him crazy to think she was spending time with someone else when he wasn't around. A completely irrational response he couldn't comprehend to this day.

"Considering we're no longer together," Eva began slowly, "what kind of marriage will we have?"

"What do you mean?"

"I mean, um...will the relationship dynamics still be the same?" She asked the question with difficulty, seeming ill at ease.

Derrick stiffened. She couldn't be asking what he thought. "You mean, will I allow another man to touch my wife and the mother of my child? Will I allow my wife to have sex with other men?" Tension coursed through his body as he practically snarled the questions in his fury. "What do you think?"

Her eyes grew wide in her face. "I didn't mean me. I was talking about you. I assumed..."

His eyebrows dipped low over his eyes. "Assumed what? I would want to have sex with other women after we're married?"

"I-I wasn't sure. We had an open relationship. I don't know what your expectations are, Derrick."

"My expectations," he said, underlining the words in an acerbic tone, "are that we both respect the covenant of our marriage once we say our vows. Marriage isn't something to enter into lightly, where you get to change your mind after a couple of years, or sleep with other people when you're in the mood to try something different."

As the product of an extramarital affair, he understood the devastation it could cause. His parents ended their affair once it was discovered and his biological father was forced to choose between his wife and family and his mistress and illegitimate son. He chose his wife and family, but eventually, he and Derrick's mother became involved again, the proof provided when, after the plane crash that claimed their lives, the passenger manifest showed they'd been seated next to each other.

"I never…" Eva's mouth clamped shut. "Are you saying you expect this to be a normal marriage?"

His gaze didn't waver. "In every way."

Comprehension dawned in her eyes as the meaning of his words sunk in. They took on a slumberous quality, as no doubt the same thoughts going through his mind went through hers. She lowered her gaze to the table, but he'd already seen the heated look she tried to hide.

He knew that look. He'd drawn it from her on many occasions.

"I can't believe you expect us to sleep together when we can barely tolerate each other at this point. I thought you'd want to continue the same as before—with the option to see other people. I have to admit, I'm surprised." The lowered, breathy sound of her voice stirred his loins into awareness.

"I don't see why. You didn't end up pregnant through Immaculate Conception. Are you sure you weren't interested in keeping your options open for yourself? Maybe you're seeing someone?" If she was, he would insist the relationship end today.

"No. Like I said, I assumed *you* would—"

"You assumed wrong, and you know what they say happens when you assume." Derrick lounged back in his chair. "Why should we deprive ourselves? Right from the beginning, it's been good between us."

"You have to admit, this will be a strange union." She paused, watching him intently, weighing the next words before she said them. "What if I say I'll need time to get used to the idea? You can't expect us to fall back into bed with each other just like that."

"Why not?" He lowered his gaze to the telltale pulse hammering at the base of her neck, and he shifted to alleviate the strain of an erection pressing on the fabric of his trousers. Carnal thoughts of her dark, naked body wriggling under him raced through his mind. He had to get this simmering need for her under control. The combined lure of her slender, agile body and her personality were a powerful aphrodisiac. He lifted his eyes back to her face. "I can tell you want me right now, even though you'd like to deny it."

"That's your ego talking."

Amused, he whispered, "Are you sure you'll be able to abstain? I know you, Eva. You enjoy sex too much." What an understatement. She was a tigress in bed, uninhibited, and willing to offer pleasure in the equal amounts she took.

"You make it sound like I'm sex crazed!" she said hotly.

He smiled knowingly, which only infuriated her more, because her lips pressed together in displeasure. "I know what you sound like when you're turned on, and I can hear a little bit of it in your voice right now."

"Maybe you're turned on and you're trying to deflect your feelings off on me." She pulled in a shaky breath. "I'm only asking for a little time. If we want this marriage to be successful, there has to be an equal amount of give-and-take on both sides."

Derrick sat up, speaking slowly for the sake of clarity. "There's no fifty-fifty in marriage, and you'd be a fool to try to keep score. Equality in marriage is a myth spread on talk shows and in relationship books. The truth is, husbands and wives should treat marriage like they're running a business. It's a negotiation, a give-and-take, yes, but not in equal amounts. Like in business, each person is always trying to get the upper hand."

"No, that's the world you live in, but most people see marriage as a partnership."

He laughed and shook his head. "No, sweetheart, that's the world *we* live in." A pause. "Here's the part where the give-and-take comes in. I'll give you time to get used to the idea of us being married, but I'm not waiting forever."

A guarded look filled her eyes. "How much time are you going to give me?"

"As little time as possible."

"Has anyone ever told you that you have a heart of stone?"

A smile broadened across his face. "I've heard it a time or two. Thanks for the compliment."

He admired her gumption, but she had no idea who she was dealing with. Her little insults didn't trouble him because he had the upper hand and would eventually get what he wanted.

She may have ended their relationship, but she craved him just as much as he craved her. He would go along with her wishes for now. His eyes moved lower to her beautiful breasts. He'd already waited four months, and work kept him fairly busy.

He could handle a few more weeks.

CHAPTER FIVE

Mrs. Derrick Hoffman.

Mrs. Eva Hoffman.

Mrs. Eva Jacob-Hoffman.

Eva twisted the platinum ring with its pear-shaped yellow diamond around and around on her finger. As promised, only two weeks after Derrick came to see her on St. Simons Island, she stood ready to get married. Her image reflected back to her from the full-length mirror in a suite at Chateau Élan, a thirty-five-hundred-acre winery and resort located forty minutes north of Atlanta in the Georgia foothills.

Putting together a wedding on such short notice was not an easy feat, but when you had plenty of money at your disposal, seemingly impossible feats could be surmounted with a phone call from skilled assistants. The chateau was usually booked years in advance, but the offhand comment she'd made to one of the coordinators about it being the idyllic setting for a wedding had magically resulted in an opening. Marrying Derrick Hoffman offered more privileges than she realized.

She and Derrick had hardly spoken since they met on St. Simons Island. He remained tied up in meetings and putting out fires at the company. Much of their communication existed as texts and voice mails. For the most part, he let her plan the wedding, but a few times he overrode her suggestions, insisting that she spend more money. Outside of those few times, the decisions were made with the help of the wedding planners and Kallie.

Their lack of contact didn't bode well for their marriage. While she should consider it a plus because it allowed her to build up a wall of protection against her feelings for him, one small part of her couldn't fathom them continuing in the same vein and having a healthy relationship. Especially since he expected them to have a real marriage.

Kallie appeared beside her in a strapless amber-colored bridesmaid dress, concern in her blue eyes. "You okay?"

Her friend wore that look often in the past couple of weeks, and she wanted to allay her fears. As she'd pointed out a couple of weeks ago, it could be worse. "Of course. I'm getting married today." She didn't quite accomplish the cheery voice she'd hoped to, and Kallie's eyes filled with sympathy.

Kallie rested her hands on Eva's bare shoulders. "This is it. Last chance to change your mind."

Eva smiled. They both knew she couldn't go back. To go back meant fighting Derrick in court and possibly losing her baby, and she couldn't take the risk.

Derrick had made sure movers had all her belongings packed up and in the house, where she would sort them out later. Her mother's family had been flown in on commercial flights to attend the wedding, and an uncle on her mother's side was to walk her down the aisle.

Her mother had been a teen parent and single mother who'd told her a long time ago her father hadn't wanted a child, so she didn't know who her father was or anyone from his side of the family. Unfortunately, her mother died with the information about her father and where he lived.

She only had a first name and an old photo found hidden away in her mother's personal items after her death. Although she hadn't planned to keep Derrick and his child apart in the same way, her familial circumstances provided another solid reason to submit to his wishes. Her conscience wouldn't allow her to keep them separated when she understood the empty ache she felt in her own life because she'd never known her father.

"We both know leaving isn't an option," she said, fondling the necklace cushioned against her bosom.

She'd chosen the bridesmaid dresses to match the amber stone in the pendant. The pendant and the necklace it hung from had been the first piece of jewelry she'd received as a little girl. They'd never had much, but her mother had always made sure she was comfortable, and every now and again, they splurged on little luxuries.

The necklace had been a luxury. When she'd received it, she'd felt so grown-up. After her mother's passing, she'd worn it more often in an effort to feel closer to her. Eva regretted her mother wasn't alive to see the birth of her grandchild, or to see her daughter get married, even if it wasn't for love.

A soft knock preceded one of the other two bridesmaids poking her head through the door. "It's time."

Eva took a deep breath and straightened her shoulders. She took one last look at herself as a single woman. The sweetheart neckline of the dress showed off her slender neck and collarbone. She smoothed her hand over the layered organza skirt and made a final adjustment to the amber-colored satin sash wound around her waist.

"Okay, I'm ready."

****

"I now pronounce you man and wife. You may kiss the bride." At Pastor Jamison's words, Derrick lifted Eva's veil.

The ceremony went by even faster than he'd anticipated. It never ceased to amaze him how a wedding caused so much stress, but the ceremony took less than thirty minutes to complete. Had it been up to him, they would have had a small civil ceremony, but he'd wanted to give Eva a little bit of what she undoubtedly had hoped for, and had instructed the coordinators to get her anything she wanted. No request was unreasonable.

Eva made the majority of the decisions, and he hadn't thought much about the wedding during the preceding days, too busy concentrating on the task of sorting out his father's business affairs. But when he'd seen her walking down the aisle on her uncle's arm, all extraneous thoughts fled his mind, and he concentrated solely on the vision coming toward him.

The sudden clenching of his stomach had taken him aback. A fierce possessiveness filled him as he watched her move slowly, bouquet in hand, smiling sweetly at their guests beneath the lace veil. Right then he'd decided he'd made the right decision to make her his wife, and any remnants of doubt left his mind. They may not be in love, but they had chemistry. Plenty of marriages survived on less.

With the sole intention of giving her a quick peck on the lips, he lowered his head. But his memory had failed him, because when had he ever been able to touch her and quickly distance himself? After months without her, today proved no different.

When he pressed his mouth to hers, a surge of hot hunger swept through him, heating his blood. He lifted his head a fraction, noting her closed eyes, and right away dipped again to taste her soft lips. His hands settled on her bare arms to hold her in place and allow him to prolong the kiss, his mouth lingering over hers. The soft sigh she whispered into his mouth caused the muscles in his body to tense in response, and his hands tightened on her soft flesh.

His tongue made a gentle foray into her mouth. When she allowed him entry, he swept in past her teeth and delved deeper to stroke with unerring skill along the inside of her cheeks and the roof of her mouth, making an erotic promise of future pleasures to come. Subconsciously he knew this wasn't the time or place, but she had cut him off abruptly and for so long. This was the first time in months he'd had a taste of her, and he couldn't get enough.

His loins pulsed and ached, and he felt her hands reach up between them, flattening against his chest as if to stave off the attack on her body he very nearly perpetrated in front of their guests.

The sound of knowing snickers and Pastor Jamison clearing his throat permeated Derrick's heated brain and brought him back to the present. Eva must have heard them, too, because she withdrew at almost the same instant he did and pressed the tips of her fingers to her mouth.

Derrick dragged his tongue across his lower lip, relishing the fading taste of her as she averted her eyes. Her uneven breaths drew his gaze to her full bosom. What he wouldn't give to get her alone right then.

What the hell was it about her that had him so strung out? He'd almost mounted her in front of hundreds of people.

The pastor cleared his throat again and made the customary announcement to all the guests. "Ladies and gentlemen, Mr. and Mrs. Derrick Hoffman!"

CHAPTER SIX

From his seat at the bar, Derrick watched his half brother, Roarke Hawthorne, walk up with his stepdaughter, Arianna, in his arms. An outsider would never guess he wasn't her biological father. They had become close in a short time.

The six-year-old had been running around with some of the other kids, but her sagging body and head on Roarke's shoulder indicated she was done for the night. She was cute, wearing a lavender dress and her hair in two big Afro puffs held in place with lavender and white ribbons.

He scanned the ballroom, filled with empty round tables because most of the guests had already left. The band played a sultry song, and a few couples swayed to the music on the dance floor. The wedding decorations included colorful floral arrangements in the middle of each table and amber and blue decorations throughout the room—not blue, teal, they'd told him, as if it mattered.

Each guest left with two bottles of wine from the Chateau Élan vineyard. The bottles, bearing a customized label with Derrick and Eva's names and the date of the wedding, were individually wrapped in mesh bags tied at the top with ribbon.

"Well, how does it feel?"

Derrick shrugged. "Feels the same."

He sipped some of the champagne in his glass. Over the years, Derrick had harbored bitter resentment against him because Roarke Sr. had chosen to stay with his wife and child and reject Derrick.

A lot had changed. A few months ago, they'd agreed to call a truce and work on establishing a better relationship. Despite the short notice, Roarke had agreed to be the best man, and their younger brother, Matthew, had agreed to be one of the groomsmen.

"Hi there. I thought I'd squeeze in a hug since I didn't get a chance to earlier." Celeste, Roarke's wife, walked up and wrapped her arms around Derrick. "I guess I've dropped to second most important woman in your life."

"You had your chance, but you chose to marry him." Derrick pointed his thumb at Roarke. He'd been friends with Celeste long before she met Roarke, and in fact, he told them if it hadn't been for him, they never would have gotten together.

Tall, with her short, wavy hair falling in loose strands around her face, Celeste smiled lovingly at her husband and stroked his bearded face. "I think I did all right."

"That's my baby," Roarke murmured, planting a kiss on her lips.

A groan sounded nearby. It came from Matthew. Although the youngest, he was taller and beefier than his older brothers. He sauntered up. "You guys are going to make me throw up. When is the honeymoon period over already?"

"We've been married less than two months," Celeste reminded him with a playful punch to the shoulder. "Can we enjoy it a little bit longer, if you don't mind?"

"Well, all right, I'll give you a few more months." He tugged on his tie. "Man, I can't wait to get out of this damn monkey suit."

Celeste frowned at Matthew and darted her eyes at her daughter.

"Oh, sorry," he said, looking embarrassed. "This doggone monkey suit."

Celeste turned to Derrick. "So, how does it feel?" she asked.

"Why does everybody keep asking me about how I feel?"

"Well, you didn't let us know you were seeing anyone seriously, and then the next thing we know, we get a call there's a wedding in less than two weeks."

"I didn't know I had to check in with everybody about my personal life."

"Not check in, but we're family. This was kind of unexpected."

"Unexpected for you," Matthew added pointedly, looking directly at Derrick. "She's not your usual type. And I mean that in a good way."

"I'm glad you approve."

Derrick didn't need any reminders about the other women he'd brought around his family. The worst incident had taken place New Year's Eve, when the woman he'd taken down to St. Simons Island, to the Hawthorne family vacation home, had gotten drunk and slipped into Roarke's bedroom.

She'd sworn Roarke had made a pass at her, and an argument had ensued between the two men. The next day he'd been so disgusted by her behavior he sent her packing, but not before she blamed him for her indiscretion. She claimed if he paid more attention to her and wasn't so distant, she wouldn't have given in to his brother's passes. He'd grown tired of her anyway, and her words held little to no importance to him. A long period passed before he admitted to himself that she had lied and, under false pretenses, helped to drive a deeper wedge between him and Roarke.

"Does she have any family in town?" Celeste asked. "Maybe Cassidy and I could take her out to lunch one day."

"That's not a bad idea," Derrick said. "All of her close friends are on the island, and most of her family lives there and out west."

"Are you sure you want Cassidy to be her first extended introduction to the family?" Matthew asked. He enjoyed making fun of his younger sister, even when she wasn't around. She and her husband had already left. "She might scare her off."

"Cassidy's not even here to defend herself," Celeste said with a shake of her head. "You're awful."

"I don't think he knows how to be any other way," Roarke said.

"Your fault, big brother. You helped raised me." Matthew grinned.

"Where did I go wrong?"

"All right, you two, simmer down." Celeste's eyes found Roarke's. "It's getting late, and I need to get missy to bed. We should head home soon."

"You two run along," Matthew said. "The rest of us grown folk will shut the place down. The band's still playing, the liquor's still pouring, and some of us have plans, which include getting some h-o-t sex."

"Matthew!" Celeste scolded him. "You spelled the wrong word. And anyway, she can spell. She's six, not two."

Derrick and Roarke had a good laugh at his expense. "Damn, I'm sorry, Celeste." He rolled his eyes when he realized he'd cursed again. "Cover her ears," he said in exasperation.

"Give me my baby." Celeste took the exhausted Arianna from Roarke. The little girl moaned softly and wrapped her little arms tightly around her mother's neck.

Derrick imagined one day he would be doing the same—whatever he could to protect his daughter and preserve her innocence for as long as possible.

"I'll leave you men to finish up your conversation in the absence of a *minor child*." She playfully cut her eyes at Matthew before walking away.

"I said I was sorry," he called after her. He propped his shoulder against the wall. "So where are you and the mystery woman headed for your honeymoon?" His gaze trained on the bridesmaids standing near the exit.

"She's not a mystery woman. You've met her." Derrick repositioned himself on the stool. "We're putting off the honeymoon for a while, until I can get things under control at work." He didn't bother to mention his family was in the process of contesting the will, another reason he couldn't risk taking off for an extended period.

"Hmm," Matthew said distractedly, his gaze still focused on the women at the front. One of the bridesmaids momentarily paused in her conversation and looked in their direction. She smiled coyly and then looked away. A lascivious grin crept across Matthew's face, and he pushed away from the wall. "Excuse me, gentlemen, some seeds I've planted have sprouted. I'll have to call it a night."

"Are you ever going to slow down?" Roarke asked.

"Slow down?" Matthew had a look on his face like Roarke had asked the most ridiculous question he'd ever heard. "Like you old married men? No way."

"Who're you calling old?" Derrick asked. "Thirty-three is not old."

Matthew touched his hand to his chest. "I'm only twenty-seven. I'm in my prime. You guys are old, so I understand why you felt the need to get married."

"Thirty-three isn't old, Matt," Roarke said. "One of these days you're going to meet a woman who knocks you off your feet, and then you'll be eating those words."

"Yeah, yeah, cry me a river." Matthew started backing away and patted his stomach. "Nice touch with the filet mignon, Derrick. Congratulations to you and the new missus. I'm out."

He strolled across the almost empty ballroom and stopped in front of the young women. He bent his head to the one who held his interest and whispered in her ear, which made her giggle. As they slipped out the door, he flashed the thumbs-up sign behind his back to his brothers.

Derrick lifted the glass of champagne to his lips. "I remember those days," he said before taking a sip.

"They weren't that long ago." Roarke seated himself two stools down.

True. Until he met Eva, he'd been as bad as Matthew. Women came easily, and because he came from money, it was even easier. He'd partied quite a bit in the VIP rooms of exclusive clubs, hanging with celebrities, and jetting around the world to various events—some known, others so secret invitations had to be hand delivered. He'd partied hard, but he'd worked hard, too. Whenever he worked on a business project, he gave it a hundred and ten percent. Phineas had insisted on it.

It had been nothing for him to drop thousands of dollars in a night to impress a woman, but he'd always gotten bored easily. The relationships never had any substance, and he'd been content to play the field—until her.

"Now we're alone, how about telling me the whole story about Eva? Matthew's right. She's not your type."

"You don't know what my type is."

"Actually, I do, and it's not her. And, considering this is your wedding day, the two of you haven't been acting like a happily married couple."

"This is the part where I tell you to mind your own business."

Roarke laughed softly, unconcerned by Derrick's ill-tempered response. From the corner of his eye, Derrick saw him stroke his jaw. "I can't figure this out."

"There's nothing to figure out," Derrick said irritably. "Why don't you go home with your wife and daughter? Like she said, it's late."

Roarke twisted in his direction on the stool. "Enough joking around. It's obvious the two of you have been avoiding each other almost all night. Maybe no one else has noticed, but I have. If it weren't for the kiss during the ceremony, I'd think you couldn't stand each other. Most newly married couples leave the guests partying at the reception. The two of you are among the last ones here. What's going on?"

Derrick's jaw tensed. "Nothing."

"Derrick, are we going to do this or not?"

He looked at his brother's solemn face. "Do what?"

"This." Roarke motioned from one to the other. "Be brothers. Be family. Be closer."

"If you think I'm going to start spilling my guts to you, you're wrong. It's only been a few months. I don't even know if I like you yet."

"Yet you asked me to be your best man."

"I was trying to be nice."

"I didn't think you knew how," Roarke grumbled. He swiveled in the chair and faced the open room again.

Derrick went back and forth internally about how much to share. Heart-to-heart conversations were not his forte. "You'll find out soon enough anyway."

"Find out what?"

"Why I married her."

"Well, why?"

In a flat voice, he said, "She's pregnant."

Roarke digested the news in silence. "That's the only reason?"

"What other reason would there be? We're not like you and Celeste." He waited before adding, "We're having a girl."

"Congratulations." Quiet. The band stopped playing, and the couples meandered off the dance floor. "I was thinking, you didn't have to marry her. You could have moved her up here to have them close."

"I could have, but I chose to do it this way. I want my daughter near me at all times."

They fell silent again. Of course, he should have known Roarke wasn't finished. He must have been mulling over the situation for a long time, his astute brain in analysis mode to make sense of what had happened—how Derrick had gone from single to married in a matter of weeks, without warning.

"Seems like a pretty drastic step to take just to have your kid. You're telling me you had no other alternative? I admit I don't know her well, but from what I've seen so far, Eva doesn't seem like the kind who would have kept you from your child."

Derrick tossed back the last of the champagne and set the flute on the bar with unwarranted force. He didn't answer to anyone, and he wasn't in the mood to explain himself to Roarke. He rose from the stool.

"It doesn't matter now, does it?"

Roarke cast a speculative look up at him. "No, I guess not. Except…I was thinking—"

"Stop thinking." He'd grown weary of this conversation real fast.

"If you hadn't married her, you would still be free."

If he hadn't married her, so would she.

Free to do whatever she wanted, with whomever she wanted. He could have set them up in a house, but the thought of other men coming there, sleeping there, weaseling their way into his daughter's life didn't appeal. If his daughter was going to love any man in her life, it would be him, not some random man Eva picked to be her stepfather. He wanted to be there for every moment, from the time she was born. He couldn't stomach the thought of her growing attached to another man or calling someone else "Daddy."

"Freedom is a small price to pay to have my daughter with me at all times."

Roarke fell silent again, but not for long. "What happened between your mother and our father happened years ago. I hope you're not going to make Eva pay for what they did. She seems like a nice person."

"The nice ones are the ones you have to watch." He took note of Roarke's frown. "Don't worry, big brother," he said, even though only three months separated them. "I've learned from the mistakes my parents made so I won't repeat them."

He glanced at the Panerai watch on his wrist, wondering about Eva's present location. She'd excused herself fifteen minutes ago and hadn't reappeared. As the thought crossed his mind, he saw her in the doorway.

She looked over at him, and he clenched his jaw to constrain the reaction he had to her. Every time he saw her, he had the same uncurbed reflexive response, like one of Pavlov's dogs. His body hardened, his senses heightened, and he damn near salivated.

Yes, he wanted his child, but part of him recognized he had wanted her, too, and he had wanted to have exclusive rights to her.

He hated the power she seemed to have over him, and that was part of why he'd agreed to give her a period to get used to the marriage and living together. He needed to prove to himself he wasn't weak for her and the unchecked lust he felt could be contained. In the time since they broke up, trying to prove any woman would do had been difficult. The physical ache that had encumbered his body since May was for this woman alone, and his efforts to prove otherwise had resulted in unsatisfactory hookups.

She walked toward them and smiled at Roarke, who rose to his feet.

"Welcome to the family. One more hug." Roarke embraced his new sister-in-law. "I promise that's the last one for a while." To Derrick, he said, "We'll talk later."

Derrick nodded, though he had no intention of discussing his marriage any further.

Within minutes, he and Eva sat in a hired limo, on their way to start their new life together.

CHAPTER SEVEN

The next day, Eva awoke after a surprisingly restful night. She turned over onto her back and stared up at the silk canopy above the bed. She must have been more tired than she realized because as soon as her head hit the pillow, she had fallen asleep.

The mansion was located in Buckhead, an affluent part of the city. Last night they had driven past a number of stately homes, with bright lights bringing attention to immaculate landscaping, as if they all competed for neighborhood bragging rights.

Some of the homes sat at the end of long driveways, so far back they were hidden from street view. The driver had stopped at one of those homes, and the black iron gates swung slowly inward. The car had crawled along the stretch of pavement that bisected acres and acres of the parklike wooded property of her new home. When they rounded a bend, the sprawling estate had come into full view.

She'd visited Derrick in Atlanta before, but they'd stayed at his condo in the middle of the city. This place was an enormous Georgian-style manor that bespoke the wealth

Derrick's father had accrued over the years. In the fountain out front, water poured from the open mouths of two stone fish.

The driver stopped the car in the circular cobblestoned driveway. To her surprise, Derrick had lifted her up and carried her across the threshold, claiming tradition as the reason for doing so. For a moment she forgot how ruthless he could be and enjoyed being held by him. Too much, in fact, practically melting against the sturdiness of his chest. His unique male scent and cologne had surrounded her, making her dizzy with unexpected longing.

Inside, he had made the introductions to the team of staff members present at that hour: Saunders, the property manager, an older black man with a kind face; Svana, the tall, portly Icelandic housekeeper; and a weekend cook who was available any time of the day or night. The personnel not present included the family driver, head landscaper and the gardeners, maids, a chef on call during the week, and two personal assistants—one for Derrick and one for her.

Then they'd made their way up to their suite of rooms, and he'd taken her to her bedroom. *Her* bedroom.

Bemused, Eva had looked at him. "I don't understand. Why do we have separate rooms? We're married." Was this how rich people lived?

"My parents had separate rooms when they were both alive. I think it's a good idea for us to do the same. Sometimes I work late, and I don't want to disturb you when I come in. Plus, I like my own space."

She'd swallowed the bitter pill of disappointment and a few minutes later watched him walk through the connecting door to his own room.

She had told Derrick she wanted time to get used to being married, yet this development surprised her. If they slept in different rooms, it appeared his idea of a normal marriage meant living separate lives and perhaps having the occasional conjugal visit.

Coming back to the present, Eva yawned and stretched, then slipped from beneath the floral linens in the four-poster bed and walked over to the three windows that covered one wall. She drew aside the heavy drapes and squinted against the glare of the bright sun. Outside, the gardeners stayed busy pruning, cutting, and mowing.

After washing up and changing into comfortable clothes, Eva exited her bedroom and walked through the sitting area of their suite of rooms, filled with antique furniture and expensive-looking Impressionist paintings on the walls. The rest of the house she walked through was tastefully decorated in a similar way, with expensive art and traditional furnishings.

After a few tries, Eva found the kitchen. In a house this big, a GPS device would come in handy.

"Good morning, Mrs. Hoffman," Svana said in a heavily accented voice. "What would you like for breakfast?"

"Don't go to too much trouble," Eva replied. She couldn't wrap her head around the idea of having servants and staff who waited on her hand and foot. Derrick had called this lifestyle comfortable, but living in a mansion in Buckhead was more than comfortable, and she still had to get accustomed to such a swanky style of living. With a shrug, she said, "I'll be fine with some orange juice and toast."

"Are you sure, ma'am?" Svana looked disappointed. "How about some scrambled eggs or an omelet to go with your toast?"

"An omelet sounds good. Ham and cheese?"

"Coming right up." The housekeeper looked so happy, she realized that perhaps part of Svana's concern had been about pleasing her, the new woman of the house. "Would you like to have breakfast on the terrace?"

Outside the French doors was a table set up on the stone terrace that looked out onto the grounds. "Yes. That sounds like a good idea."

Once outside, Eva saw the terrace also had a sitting area with couches and a coffee table, perfect for a relaxing day while surveying the gardens.

Svana served her fresh-squeezed orange juice with her meal and beamed when Eva whispered, "Delicious," after swallowing a morsel of the fluffy omelet.

This became her routine over the next couple of days. If Derrick intended to show her his life wouldn't change now that they'd married, he did a good job of it. Their interaction was minimal, like roommates who had different work schedules.

While he worked in the study, she filled out thank-you cards for the wedding gifts and unpacked her clothes and other belongings rather than have one of the maids or her personal assistant complete the tasks for her.

Exploring the estate took a lot of time, as well. Saunders and Svana lived in the main house and each had their own self-contained private quarters with a small kitchen and living room. The entire compound consisted of the three-level house, a gazebo, a tennis court, and a guesthouse with a pool. The main house included a gym, a heated indoor swimming pool, home theater, and a recreation space with a ping-pong table and arcade games.

The grounds were her favorite part of the estate, and she delighted in watching the squirrels hop from tree limb to tree limb, and the birds take advantage of the bird feeders dotted across the property. Flowers lined the cobblestoned pathways. Black-eyed Susans and twenty-inch columbine flowers in shades of purple and pink greeted her on her walks.

The in-ground pool Derrick had told her about turned out to be a free-form pool, specially designed to look like a lake and fit into the landscape, with rock projections jutting out of it. Only a short walk from the house, it was a man-made oasis enclosed by bushes and flowers, with comfortable chairs, two cabanas, and a bar.

Her lifestyle had certainly changed.

****

Wrapped in a silk robe, Eva descended the stairs in search of a piece of Svana's chocolate cake. She hoped there was at least one slice left. If Saunders could help it, there wouldn't be. He'd wolfed down two humungous pieces earlier, and she wouldn't be surprised if he came back for more.

The kitchen lights were on, and she thought they'd been left on by mistake until she found Derrick, still dressed in his suit, sitting at the breakfast table in the corner with his head resting on his folded arms.

"Derrick?" She walked over and shook him.

Being a heavy sleeper, it took a minute for him to rouse. A frown marred his forehead as his eyes focused on her.

He scrubbed a hand over his face. "What time is it?"

"It's after one in the morning. You must have come in and sat down for a minute and fallen asleep."

With a shake of his head, he straightened in the chair. "That's exactly what happened."

The fatigue on his face tugged at something inside her. How deeply had Phineas's death affected him? Even though he wasn't his biological father, Phineas was the only father Derrick had known all his life.

Maybe taking over his father's affairs took a greater toll than she realized or he wanted to admit. Without much time to grieve his death, and the strain of keeping the business together resting on his shoulders, it was no surprise he had fallen asleep at the table.

"Are you feeling okay?" she asked.

"I'm fine."

The clipped response was meant to keep her from asking any more questions, but she couldn't help but be concerned. She loved—*had* loved him once. It was only natural to still care a little. But she had to remember that Derrick didn't do emotions, so asking him about his feelings was a waste of time.

"You don't look well. I know you're preoccupied with work, but you still have to take care of yourself."

Surprise lit up his eyes, and his voice held a hint of irony when he said, "If I didn't know better, I'd think you actually cared."

Stepping back, Eva cleared her throat self-consciously. "Of course I care, Derrick. You're the father of my child."

"What other reason would there be, right?"

She had the strange feeling he had expected her to say something else, and somehow she'd disappointed him.

"Don't worry about me," he continued. "You're the one who needs to take care." He looked at her stomach.

"I've been looking into doctors and have narrowed it down to three."

"You might as well start putting out feelers for a nanny, too. Your assistant can help you find one."

"I don't need a nanny."

He rose to his feet, intimidating at such close proximity. "You won't *need* a nanny, but it's a good idea. Managing this estate takes a lot of time, even with help from Saunders and Svana. There'll also be social engagements we have to

179

attend, and we can't leave our daughter with just anyone. Whether we hire someone full-time or part-time, it's good to have one."

"I want to raise my child myself." She wanted to be the kind of mother she'd had growing up and couldn't imagine letting someone else interfere with that special bond.

"Getting outside help is no reflection on the type of mother you'll be. I'm sure many more women would do it if they could afford to. We certainly can."

"I'll think about it." Eva's eyes scanned the room in search of the cake, needing a chocolate fix now more than ever.

"A nanny's role is to help you, not take your place."

"I said I'll think about it."

He fell silent. "It's not as bad as you think. I had a nanny growing up."

And look how good you turned out, Eva thought nastily.

"By the way, expect a call from Cassidy and Celeste. I forgot to mention it, but at the wedding, Celeste said something about taking you to lunch."

A lunch date sounded like a good idea, and her sisters-in-law had both been friendly and welcoming. "Did she say when?"

"No. She said she would give you a call." He pressed his fingers to the bridge of his nose and closed his eyes.

"What's wrong?"

"Didn't I tell you already that I'm fine?"

"I'm only asking because you look like death," Eva snapped. "Forgive me for showing some concern."

She swung on her heel and marched over to the counter where the rest of the cake sat on the cake stand. If he weren't in the room, she might have grabbed a handful and shoved it in her mouth. Of course, if he weren't here, she wouldn't be so upset that she felt the need to eat the cake in that manner.

"I have a headache," he mumbled, almost grudgingly. "If it doesn't go away in a little bit, I'll take something for it."

She glanced at him sideways. "Maybe you're working too hard. You're never here."

She yanked open the cutlery drawer.

"Don't tell me you miss me?" Derrick asked.

Focused on searching for a knife, Eva ignored the question. Behind her, the soles of his expensive leather shoes moved softly across the tile.

"Do you, Eva? Do you miss me?"

The outright question stilled her hands in the drawer. From his tone, she knew he stood right behind her. Closing her eyes, she bit back the words that would leave her vulnerable to him.

Yes, I miss you.

She missed him with a level of intensity she hadn't felt before moving into this house. On St. Simons Island, she could slowly recover from the breakup and had friends there to occupy her time so she didn't have to spend almost every waking minute thinking about him.

But here...here there was no escape from the thoughts. She tried to stay busy, but there was no way to dull the ache in the pit of her stomach. She couldn't even lie to herself any longer and pretend she felt nothing for him.

Not when she listened for him every night, longed for him to join her for dinner, and wished he would seek out her company just once.

Her fingers tightened around the knife. "You're fishing for compliments."

The biting sarcasm she hoped would fill her voice fell flat, but she still got her message across. It was one of the few defenses she had left, because her plan to shield her heart during the period he gave her to get used to married life had failed miserably.

She cared about him, no matter how much she didn't want to.

"Yeah," he said. "And I'm fishing for them in the wrong place."

A tight pain pulled at her stomach, and she turned around. "What do you mean by that? Are you going to cast your net somewhere else?"

He stopped midstride on the way out the door and turned to face her. "Why would I need to seek out other women when I have a beautiful wife at home?" he asked, his voice rife with sarcasm. With slow steps, he approached her, and her heart tripped with trepidation. "Which reminds me—I need to inform you that your time is almost up. And a word of advice…" His gaze swept the length of the robe, and she shivered at the hotness of his gaze.

The clothing seemed inadequate when before it had sufficed. She almost felt as if he could see right through the silk and the nightgown under it.

"Consider yourself lucky that I'm tired right now. In the future, I suggest you wear a potato sack or garbage bag when you walk around the house at night, because if I ever catch you in anything remotely close to what you're wearing again, your time to get used to the marriage will come to an end."

With those words hanging in the air, he left.

CHAPTER EIGHT

Bright and early Friday morning, both Cassidy and Celeste pulled up to the house at the same time in separate cars. Rather than a simple lunch, the three had decided to go shopping together. When Eva met them downstairs in the foyer, Cassidy—petite in contrast to her tall brothers—greeted her with a big smile and hug.

"Hi, sis!"

Cassidy's boisterous personality made Eva smile. She was the youngest of Derrick's siblings. She worked four ten-hour days, so she always had Fridays off, and with Celeste a stay-at-home wife, they had the entire day to hang out.

"Ready to go?" Celeste asked. She was model tall and more reserved, but Eva remembered she'd liked her right away when they met.

"Yes. Too bad your daughter's in school and couldn't come with us. She's so adorable."

"No, be thankful. She'll talk your ear off about this, that, and the other. Believe me, it can be exhausting. Right now

183

she wants to be an astronomer and can't stop talking about all the constellations."

"An astronomer? Constellations?" Eva closed the front door and followed the other two to the waiting car. "Sounds pretty advanced for a six-year-old."

The driver stood at rigid attention with the door open, dressed in black from the top of his cap to his shiny shoes. As they piled into the vehicle, the other two laughed at her surprise.

"Didn't Derrick tell you? Roarke is an astrophysicist. Arianna's always been interested in science. I don't know where she gets it from, because it certainly wasn't from me or her father. She and Roarke are as thick as thieves. He's been good for her, nurturing her interest. It helped them bond much faster than I would have expected."

"Believe me, Roarke loves it, too," Cassidy said. "No one else will listen to him drone on and on about stars, black holes, subatomic particles, and blah, blah, blah."

"Awww, that's one of the things I loved about him when I first met him." Celeste turned to Eva with love shining in her eyes. "He's so passionate about it. I'm interested in what he does—I really am—but I have to admit, sometimes it's so far over my head I space out."

"I knew it!" Cassidy said with satisfaction. She started handing them glasses from the minibar.

"Don't you dare tell him."

"I won't, but he probably knows already. Everybody gives him a hard time."

Celeste continued talking to Eva. "He's going to Europe next year to present his latest findings at a conference in Germany. I'm so proud of him."

"Roarke is smart," Cassidy agreed. "If he did oncology research, we'd probably have a cure for cancer by now." She poured champagne for herself and Celeste and sparkling cider for Eva. She held up her glass. "Okay, ladies, we're going to shop till we drop. You got your credit card?"

"I do," Eva replied, patting her purse.

Derrick had given her a credit card, and he set up a checking account for her, into which an obscene amount of money would be deposited the first business day of each month as her allowance.

When she'd protested and told him she couldn't fathom spending that much money every month, he'd shrugged and said if she didn't, that was fine, but it was available for her use. He reminded her that as his wife, she would need "a new wardrobe, dresses for various social engagements, maternity clothes, clothes for the baby, and we'll have to decorate the nursery. It'll be gone in no time. Trust me."

The three women clinked their glasses together. "Where are we headed first?" Eva asked. When Celeste had called to invite her out, she had been very secretive. She and Cassidy had planned the entire day for the three of them.

Celeste looked at Cassidy with a mischievous smile on her face. "Should we tell her now or wait?"

"Let's tell her now."

"We're going to New York."

"New York?" Eva looked from one to the other. "As in New York City?"

Cassidy nodded excitedly. "Your assistant worked with us on everything. We've got appointments at some of the most exclusive boutiques, and lunch and dinner plans are all set. Derrick let us use the corporate jet for the day, which means no horrible airport security lines. It's gassed up and ready for us."

"And here I was thinking we'd just visit some of the shops in the Atlanta area. It must be awfully expensive."

Cassidy crossed her legs and reclined against the black leather seats. "It is, but Derrick doesn't care, and neither should you. You're married to my brother. Relax and enjoy the ride."

"This is typical Derrick," Celeste added. "He does everything with style."

And what style it was.

They were greeted at the private airstrip by a smiling flight attendant who escorted them up the stairs into the cabin, which divided into three compartments. A small boardroom could be enclosed behind sliding doors covered in frosted glass. The second compartment was made up of tan, extra-large leather chairs that swiveled 360 degrees and reclined all the way back to accommodate sleeping. They were grouped in fours, separated by polished wood tables. This area led into a small, open lounge that contained sofas made of cushiony soft nylon in the same color as the leather chairs. In front of each were two narrow tables with space in between them to pass through to the third compartment, the bedroom. It contained a shower and queen-size bed.

Once they reached cruising altitude, they took off their seat belts, and the flight attendant served hors d'oeuvres and drinks. Individual itineraries, which had been waiting for them on the plane, listed each store and appointment. The entire day had been planned with military precision, and the excitement generated by her sisters-in-law carried over to Eva. Because the situation between her and Derrick hadn't improved, today's outing boosted her morale.

In New York, a car service took them to each of the appointments where personal shoppers laid out designer gowns and chic outfits befitting the wife of a multimillionaire. Eva had to admit she enjoyed all the fuss, and once she relaxed about how much the clothes cost, the day became less stressful.

It boggled her mind to think she didn't need to look at the price tag. If she wanted it, she could have it, along with all the accessories and shoes to match. By lunch, they were ready for a break and stopped at a trendy Manhattan restaurant where they counted three celebrities seated at tables around them.

"I can't eat another bite," Cassidy groaned, pushing her empty dessert plate to the edge of the table.

Celeste snorted. "Now that your plate is empty, you can't eat another bite?"

"Don't judge me. That cheesecake was delicious."

Eva nodded her head vigorously in agreement as the last bite of her slice melted on her tongue. "Mmmm. I may have to get one to go."

"Me, too. And one of those chocolate cakes Celeste had. Antonio has a weakness for anything chocolate—brownies, cake, you name it. I'll have to get one for him."

"Is that the way you get whatever you want out of your husband?" Eva teased. "Bake him some brownies and you're good to go, huh?"

Cassidy shook her head. "I can't cook a thing. I even burn water." Eva and Celeste giggled. "I'm serious. He doesn't care about that, which is shocking, because his mom and sister, who's my best friend, can get in the kitchen and whip up a yummy meal in two seconds flat. Lucky for me, I've found other ways to keep him happy." She winked.

"Don't start," Celeste warned.

"Don't start what?" Eva asked, on the verge of laughing already. Cassidy was quite a character.

"People get uncomfortable when I talk about sex," she said, rolling her eyes. "It's natural, and I don't talk about it with everybody—only the people I feel comfortable discussing it with."

"Except the people you feel comfortable discussing it with don't want to discuss it with you."

"Whatever." She took a sip of her water. "Can I just say one little thing?" She leaned over the table and lowered her voice. "Sometimes, when we're making love, he talks to me in Spanish. It's so sexy. Ohmigod."

"Do you know what he's saying?" Eva asked.

"Yeah, he might be saying, 'Oh, my back, my back.'" Celeste laughed at her own joke.

"Ha ha. Very funny." Cassidy shook her head with a smile. "No, I don't know what he's saying, but I've started taking a Spanish course. When we went to see his *abuela*—that's *grandmother* in Spanish—in Puerto Rico for her ninetieth birthday last month, I couldn't communicate with her and some of the other family members. I thought it would be nice for me to learn some words and phrases to ease communication."

"Good idea. I'm sure Antonio will appreciate it." Celeste signaled for the waiter. "We better get moving if we want to get to the next store in time for our appointment. I can't wait to see all the cute little baby outfits."

"Let me run to the bathroom," Eva said, rising from the chair. She placed the credit card on the table to cover the meals. "I swear my bladder's down to the size of a pea. Go ahead and get the chocolate dessert for your husband."

"You don't have to tell me twice," Cassidy said.

After Eva used the bathroom, she pulled out her lipstick to touch up her lips. As she stood there, a woman came in, but instead of going into one of the stalls, she walked over and stood next to her.

"Hi," the woman said. Her dark brown eyes gave Eva a once-over, as if she were checking her out.

"Hi," Eva said cautiously. A knot of unease settled in her gut.

The other woman was much taller, and her hair was cut very low in a short Afro. The haircut complemented the strong bone structure of her face. Her polished, stylish appearance made Eva think she came from a wealthy background.

"You're Eva, right? Derrick Hoffman's new wife."

The knot grew larger. "Yes, that's right. Were you at the wedding?"

"No. I'm an old friend of Derrick's."

The way she said the words, Eva knew immediately there had been nothing friendly about their acquaintance. She practically licked her lips when she said his name.

"My name's Johnnie. When you passed by my table, I wasn't sure at first if you were Derrick's wife. I'm in Atlanta almost as much as I'm in New York because I have a place there. I saw the announcement in the society pages."

Eva nodded, not sure what to say. "Oh, okay. Well, it was nice to meet you."

As she turned to go, Johnnie said, "Well played, by the way."

Against her better judgment, Eva stopped and turned around. "Excuse me? What does that mean?"

"It means exactly what I said. Getting pregnant was genius. The ratio of women to eligible men in Atlanta is something outrageous, isn't it, like ten to one or something? At least that's what I keep hearing, but who knows if those statistics are true? I've always been able to find a man." She laughed softly with the confidence of someone who understood her appeal and capitalized on it. "Whether those numbers are true or not, you hit the jackpot by scooping up one of the most eligible bachelors in the city off the market, and right after his daddy left him

189

all…that…money." Johnnie proceeded to pat her short hair, though it didn't need it.

Eva suddenly felt hot all over. How many people knew about the pregnancy? How many other people thought the same thing? She felt the need to defend herself.

"Not that my marriage is any of your business, but I didn't plan to get pregnant to nab Derrick."

Johnnie's eyes looked back at her from the mirror. "Please don't take what I said the wrong way. I'm not mad at you; I'm jealous. Wish I'd thought of it first. He was always so careful, though. He always wore a condom, and he only used condoms *he* bought, as if he didn't trust me."

Eva swallowed down the nausea creeping up her throat. She didn't want to hear about any of Derrick's past sexual exploits, and she certainly didn't want to talk to one of his previous lovers about his habits in bed.

"Maybe he had reason not to."

The comment came out before she could censor it, but in all honesty, she didn't want to. This woman had no right to approach her with this type of conversation. It was insulting, and she sure as hell wasn't going to let her or anyone else make her feel guilty or embarrassed about something she didn't do.

Johnnie stopped admiring herself in the mirror and faced Eva head-on. She placed one hand on her hip and smiled like someone who relished knowing a secret no one else was privy to. "It doesn't seem like I'm the one he had to worry about, now does it?"

Somehow Eva restrained herself from slapping the smirk off of Johnnie's face.

The bathroom door opened, and in walked Cassidy.

Johnnie smiled. "Hi, Cassidy. Good to see you again."

"The pleasure's all yours," Cassidy said loud enough to be heard as Johnnie took leave of the bathroom. She walked over to Eva. "What did that catty bitch want? I saw her come in after you and thought she might be up to something."

Instead of answering, Eva asked, "How do you know her?"

Cassidy sighed. "She's someone from Derrick's past and the daughter of one of Phineas's old business associates. No one important.

"Our family got together for New Year's, and he brought her with him. I didn't like her in the first place, but then she got drunk and tried to seduce Roarke. Believe me, it created major problems. We didn't see her again after New Year's Eve. I guess he got rid of her." She touched Eva's arm. "Hey, whatever she said, don't let it get to you. She's probably jealous. Derrick has a really good business sense—I guess that's why Phineas left him everything—but he didn't have the best judgment when it came to women. We're all trying to figure out how he ended up with someone like you. You're so normal."

Eva laughed shortly. "Yeah, I'm normal."

Apparently, normal didn't cut it for Derrick. Even though Johnnie may not have been liked by his family, she was the one he chose to introduce to them.

Not her.

CHAPTER NINE

Eva refused to let the unexpected conversation after lunch spoil her day out. Growing up as an only child, she'd always longed to have siblings. By marrying Derrick, she felt as if she'd gained two new sisters and intended to enjoy the time in their company.

Their trip ended on a positive note when they entered FAO Schwarz and shopped for items for the baby. Eva bought a few stuffed animals and other toys. She picked up items for Arianna, too, and insisted Celeste accept the gifts when she tried to protest.

Just after seven, they were on the plane and being served a gourmet meal. They then migrated over to the lounge after dinner.

Cassidy lay down on one sofa, using a cushion as a pillow. She yawned. "I ate too much, I need a nap, and my feet hurt. I wish my hubby was here to rub my feet for me."

Celeste curled her legs up under her. "We'll get there soon enough."

"I'm so spoiled, aren't I? He's so good to me."

Eva felt a pang of jealousy—a common occurrence throughout the day. Celeste and Cassidy were so happy in their marriages, with husbands who loved them and whom they loved. All day she'd listened to their cute stories and had nothing to contribute because she and Derrick didn't have the same kind of relationship.

He seemed further away now than ever before, even though in reality he slept only a few feet from her. He was giving her what she'd said she wanted, but she didn't really want this. She wanted to feel special, the way Antonio made Cassidy feel.

Derrick provided the basic needs of food and shelter, but there was one other need she had that he couldn't fulfill, the need for love, and he had no interest in fulfilling it, either. He wanted her sexually, but otherwise, he couldn't summon enough of an interest to spend any time with her.

Their marriage was a joke. They barely spoke, they slept in separate bedrooms, and whenever their paths crossed, they spoke in monosyllables to each other.

"I'm exhausted, but I had a good time," Eva said. "Thank you both so much for spending the day with me."

"Our pleasure," Cassidy said. She yawned again and closed her eyes. "Plus, we got some goodies. Thank you for the jewelry."

"You're welcome. It was the least I could do since you took the time to plan the day and spend it with me."

Within a few minutes, Cassidy was dozing on the sofa, and Celeste and Eva talked quietly. Celeste shared her advice about pregnancy and told Eva what to expect in the coming months.

"I can't wait until I start showing more," Eva confessed. She patted her stomach.

"You're so lucky. You know that show where they feature women who go into labor and didn't even know they were pregnant? I was the complete opposite. I had a baby bump early on. At six months pregnant, everyone thought I was full term. By the time I was full term, I could barely get around, my hips and thighs were ten times this size"—she waved her hand in the general direction of her hips and thighs—"if you could believe that—and my face, oh, don't get me started on my fat face and neck." She smiled wistfully. "But I love my baby girl. I wouldn't trade her for the world."

"From what I understand, you and Roarke got married very quickly…?"

"Mhmm. I'll spare you the details. Here's a quick summary. I met him the week before Cassidy's wedding, but nothing came of it. I went to the wedding with Derrick, and we met again and realized we wanted to be together. It was crazy and spontaneous."

"I didn't know you went to Cassidy's wedding…with Derrick?"

Celeste looked slightly embarrassed when she realized her slip. "Not *with* Derrick. I mean…well, he needed a date, and I agreed to go with him, but we've always only been friends."

"Oh."

"I'm sorry, Eva, I wasn't thinking. Believe me, it was nothing. Derrick covered the costs of the trip as a favor because I couldn't afford to miss work." Then she added with a wince, "You and Derrick were together at the time, weren't you?"

"Well…" Eva hedged. She didn't want Celeste to feel bad. Derrick chose to go with her because he wanted to. Eva's feelings on the matter were irrelevant, and Celeste's disclosure proved once again that she had not been as important to him as he had been to her. "Actually, we stopped seeing each other around that time, so really, it's not even an issue."

"Oh, that's why he said his plans fell through and he had to find another date."

The words caused a sharp stab of pain in her chest. Even before Celeste, there had been someone else he planned to take?

"Good, because this conversation was about to get awkward. And I'm glad the two of you worked out your differences and found your way back to each other."

"Thanks."

Eva put on a brave front for Celeste, but inside, her heart seized up with pain. What reason could there be for him to share his life with other women in such an intimate way, but not with her?

Over an hour later, Celeste and Cassidy drove away in their respective cars. With Svana's help, Eva trudged upstairs with all her purchases. Derrick wasn't home yet, so she took a shower and donned a peach nightgown.

By now, her hurt had transformed into anger. The more she thought about the conversation with Celeste, the more upset she became. She walked over to the door leading into the sitting room of their suite and cracked it open so she could hear Derrick when he came in.

He would not ignore her tonight.

****

Derrick rose from behind the desk he'd been practically fastened to all day. Across from him sat his vice president of operations and his CFO, both of whom he had come to rely on heavily in recent weeks. With their help, he expected to distribute a package about the financial health of the company to all the firm's employees and leak key elements to the top business outlets in print and digital media.

The purpose was to show the stability of HLC as they moved toward expanding their reach by entering a strategic alliance with a key player in the Greek shipping industry. If he could ink the deal, a negotiation his father had been working on before his death, it would expand HLC's interests abroad and capture a significant percentage of the international logistics market.

"All right," he said. "That's enough for today."

"Do you need us this weekend?" his VP of operations asked.

Derrick stuck the pages he'd been writing notes and figures on into a file. He couldn't tell if the tone of her voice was hopeful because of the hefty additional wages she earned for working on the weekend, or because she looked forward to getting a break.

"No, I'm good. Let's take the weekend to think about what we discussed today. We'll meet in here first thing on Monday morning and tweak our plans if necessary."

After they left, he dropped the files in his briefcase and snapped it shut.

He didn't relish going home and sleeping next door to a wife he couldn't touch. Before Eva moved in, he never stayed this late at the office. He took the work home and finished up there.

Derrick shook his head. He was running from a woman half his size, and all because he'd agreed to give her time. It was just as well. He got plenty of work done and felt a lot better about the direction the company was going in than he did when he first took over.

In the outer office, his administrative assistant was logging off her computer. Her head snapped up when she heard him.

"Do you need anything else, Mr. Hoffman?"

She'd been his father's admin, too. Since she was young and attractive, he'd had his doubts about his father's decision to hire her, but having worked closely with her, he grew to appreciate her work ethic and professionalism. He'd been tempted to sleep with her when his father was alive, but now he was glad he hadn't. He would have jeopardized a relationship with a great assistant.

"No. Have a great weekend. I'll see you next week."

When he arrived home, he didn't go upstairs right away. He entered the study, which had been his father's. Two of the dark walls were filled with books on built-in shelves. File cabinets took up half of one wall. In the center of the room sat a heavy wooden desk, directly across from the fireplace, above which hung portraits of his mother and father.

Set off by itself sat a cabinet humidor, polished until the wood gleamed. Phineas had been a cigar aficionado, and Derrick had given him the large piece of custom-made furniture as a gift for the storage and preservation of his cigar collection.

He removed a cigar from the cabinet and lit it, then stepped out onto the terrace. Holding it between his index finger and thumb, he took a puff and let the smoke ease past his lips.

What would Phineas think of his progress so far? Would he be proud? Was he on the right track? He hoped so. The success of the company depended on his ability to think and strategize in the same way his father had when he was alive.

If all went well with the Greeks, the only other major item on his plate would be the court battle with his family.

When he finished smoking, he went upstairs to get ready for bed. He looked forward to a shower and a night of rest.

CHAPTER TEN

With the door cracked open, Eva heard Derrick the minute he entered their suite. Her heart started into a sprint like a racehorse jumping forward at the crack of a gun. She hopped from the bed, where she'd been rereading the same page for the past half hour, and clicked the door shut. Pacing the floor, she decided to give him time to get settled before approaching him.

When she felt enough time had passed, she pulled on the lace-edged robe that matched her nightgown, knotted the band around her waist, and went to the connecting door and knocked. The absurdity of having to knock on her husband's bedroom door infuriated her. No response came from his side, so she knocked again, louder this time. Still no answer. Couldn't he hear her?

She twisted the doorknob and stormed in, but came to a halt in the middle of the room when she found it empty. As the door clicked close behind her, she took a look around. It was decorated in masculine tones, dark, heavy wood and varying hues of the colors brown and black. Without a single flower or soft color in sight, no one could mistake this for anything but the room of a driven, potent male.

Her eyes strayed to the huge, perfectly made bed with a wrought iron frame. It was custom-made and sat high off the floor. To get in, she'd have to climb up…Her thoughts screeched to a halt, and she tore her eyes away, noting the clothes tossed carelessly across one of the armchairs near the window. Where the hell was he?

In answer to her question, the bathroom door opened, and Derrick emerged in an unexpected way. He strolled out, naked as the day he was born, rubbing a towel across his wet skin.

It had been so long, she'd forgotten the type of sensual power the sight of his bare skin wielded. For a moment, she couldn't remember why she'd gone there in the first place, reason vanishing as her eyes drank in every piece of sinewy flesh.

Breathing, normally an instinctive process, became a chore that needed a heightened level of coordination she became incapable of performing. A sheen of water remained layered over his golden skin. He paused at the sight of her, and she shamelessly focused on the muscles of his arms, his hair-sprinkled chest, and rock-hard abdomen.

Her thighs clenched as her gaze traveled further south to the thick shaft hanging between his muscular legs. A long time passed before she was able to tear her eyes away, and only because it made a show of rising halfway in a slow salute to her.

Eva's gaze met Derrick's, and a gradual smile transformed his face. Guilty heat blazed across her cheeks at his knowing look.

"Would you please cover yourself?" She cleared her throat to take the attention off her tremor-filled voice, but she knew he heard it.

He took his sweet time blotting his skin with the towel. "It's not my fault you came into my room without asking and got an eyeful. Although I don't see why you're acting like such a prude. You've seen all of this before."

What he said was true, but in the past, she'd also been able to touch him at will. Right now she couldn't, and her greedy gaze lingered about his hips as he wrapped the towel around his narrow waist.

"I need to talk to you." She curled her fingers around the loop of the knot in her belt in an attempt to fight back the ache pounding between her legs.

He walked by her, and she smelled the minty freshness of toothpaste or mouthwash and the clean scent of pine from his shower. She had to close her eyes for a moment to keep her bearings. Her body, jolted into sexual awareness, was acutely cognizant of his. Beneath the layers of satin, her nipples grew tight and strained against the fabric in appreciation of his hard physique.

Maybe this wasn't such a good idea.

"What about?"

She turned around to look at him. He stood before the dresser and picked up a bottle of deodorant.

"I had an interesting conversation with Celeste today."

He raised a brow at her reflection in the mirror. "Why would this interest me?"

"Because we talked about you. She mentioned accompanying you to your sister's wedding in May."

"And?" he asked, rolling the deodorant under his arm.

"You and I were seeing each other then, and we had an agreement that when you were in town, you spent your time with me."

"If you recall," he said, "that was the same weekend you told me you wanted to end our relationship because it wasn't working out. I don't see the relevance now."

"That's not the point. We weren't finished yet." She stopped, afraid to ask the next question. "Why didn't you ask me to go to the wedding with you?"

He set down the bottle. "Because I asked Celeste."

The droll answer angered and hurt all at once. She pressed on, though, because she needed to know if she'd really meant so little to him.

"She said you even invited someone else before you invited her." Her voice sounded steady, even though pain twisted in her and made it difficult to talk. "She thought it was me, but it wasn't. Why didn't you ask me? You owe me an answer."

With a sigh, Derrick turned from the mirror. "No, actually, I don't. I went to my sister's wedding with a friend, and that's all you need to know. Celeste and I have always had a platonic relationship, and she's married to my brother now. I'm sure she explained we went as *friends*."

"She did, and she also explained that you took care of her costs for the entire trip. You went through all that expense when I was already there."

"What do you want me to say? I never lied to you, Eva. This is a ridiculous conversation. I told you from the beginning I would see other people."

"Not when you came to town. You promised. And what about the other woman you chose before Celeste? Who was she?" She didn't want to be one of those women— whiny and needy—yet here she was, being whiny, being needy, and hating herself for it.

He pinned her with a withering stare that probably caused others to shake in their boots but bounced off of her because of her determination to get answers. "We're not going to talk about this anymore. I have my reasons for doing what I did, but it's in the past now. Let it go. I'm surprised you're even asking me these questions when that was the same weekend you told me you no longer wanted to see me."

"Would you have been okay with me coming to Atlanta and seeing another man while I was here?"

His gaze narrowed. "Don't be ridiculous."

"Just as I thought," she said bitterly. "You had a different set of rules for yourself."

"I don't need this right now." He rolled his neck. "When you go to see the doctor next week, see if they can prescribe something to get your hormones back into balance."

Eva trembled with rage at his condescending tone. "There is nothing wrong with my hormones. You just don't like being called out for the hypocrite you are. Since you didn't even respect our agreement, I can only imagine how many women you slept with during the short period we were together. Oh, by the way, I ran into one of your exes—Johnnie, the one you spent New Year's Eve with. Charming."

His mouth settled into a disapproving line, but otherwise, he didn't react. She'd thought, hoped, she could get through to him, but that wasn't the case. No closer to getting answers than when she walked in, Eva's frustration mounted.

Derrick folded his arms across his bare chest. "I don't have to explain myself, but Johnnie was before you. Even if she wasn't, my seeing other women didn't affect what we had. You don't hear me demanding to hear all the juicy details about your other male friends, like the schmuck you planned to go out with the weekend I canceled my trip to the island. Spare me the jealous act. I don't question the men you slept with when we were together, so don't question what I did."

But there hadn't been anyone else for her. Because she'd waited around for him to grace her with his presence whenever he was in town, happy for the crumbs from the table of his time.

"You don't even know him. James isn't a schmuck. He's a nice guy."

He became very still. "His name is James?" His eyes locked on to hers, and she saw the anger simmering in them. The smoky blue-gray darkened to slate. She'd never seen that look on his face before. "Don't ever mention his name in this house again," he said quietly.

A little piece of her thrilled at the command, even as she understood the gravity of his words.

"We shouldn't have gotten married," she said in a quiet voice. "This whole thing was a huge mistake. We don't see each other. We don't talk. We don't do anything."

With a sardonic lift to his eyebrow, he said, "I figured you'd be happy to be alone."

"Normal people don't like being alone."

"I take it you're implying I'm abnormal?"

She let her silence be the answer.

"What you see is what you get. What more do you want?"

She thought about the day spent with Cassidy and Celeste and the life they shared with their husbands.

"I want a real marriage—"

"We have a real marriage."

"With affection and…love."

"Love wasn't on the table."

Her throat tightened.

"You can't live off of love," he continued. "It doesn't pay the bills. Ask your girlfriends what they would rather have: love or money. The realistic ones will say money. The

Pollyanna ones looking at the world through rose-colored glasses, like you, will say love."

"I'm not Pollyanna," Eva said defensively. "Is it so hard for you to understand a woman would want to marry for love? This—this marriage won't last."

"It has as much of a chance of survival as any other marriage. Fifty-fifty. Those are the odds. I promised you fidelity, and I promised to take care of you. That's a hell of a lot more than most women can say they receive. You should be on your knees thanking me."

He moved restlessly, pushing away from the dresser, and took a few steps in her direction. "This conversation is over. I've had a long day, and I'm ready for bed."

His gaze wandered down her body, and prickly longing oozed into her again. Why couldn't she stop wanting him? Even when he angered her, the heat of desire stirred her blood.

"Unless you plan to join me, I suggest you head to your own room."

Eva pulled the robe tighter around her body. "I wouldn't let you touch me if you begged."

"Beg? You must think you have kryptonite between your legs."

"No, because that would make you Superman. And we both know there's nothing super about you."

"Ouch, you're really pulling out the big guns tonight."

"You make me sick."

His mouth lifted at the corner. "You're so sick you come up in here like a jealous wife. If I didn't know better, I'd think you were purposely trying to piss me off. Is that what's going on?"

Was it true? Had she come here to goad him into some type of response, to get a reaction—anything—instead of him being so cold all the time? She certainly wanted more contact, and ached for the way they used to be before they broke up, even if it had been one-sided. Nothing would please her more than to get just a little bit of affection from him, a touch...*anything*.

"I'm riled up because of your dishonesty, and I wish I'd never agreed to this sham marriage," she said instead.

"Too late to back out now, sweetheart."

"You'll never change, will you?"

His smile came slow. "Why should I?"

"God, I hate you."

This entire episode had been a wasted effort. Nothing could penetrate the ice around his heart. With nothing left to say, Eva stepped wide around him toward the connecting door.

Derrick drew his fingers into a fist, watching her as she moved past him.

He was going to let her walk away. He really was. The random tantrum tossed at him at the end of another long day had irritated him, and he wasn't in the mood to deal with her accusations. But when she flounced by him in a whisper of satin and lace, he caught a whiff of carrot and honey. The scent grabbed him and shattered his good intentions. Hunger assailed him like miniature daggers attacking his groin. It reminded him that she was his wife. He had every right to her body, and he would no longer deprive himself.

When she swung open the connecting door, he was already behind her, and his palm collided with the wood above her head, slamming it hard against the frame.

She froze.

"You're sleeping in here tonight."

CHAPTER ELEVEN

Only seconds passed before she responded, but it seemed longer. He waited patiently, his jaw aching as he fought the tension taking over every cell of his body.

"I'm going to sleep in the other room."

He bent to her ear, dragging another breath of her provocative scent into his lungs. She smelled so good he couldn't wait to lick every inch of her body. "Is that what you think?"

She edged sideways, refusing to turn and look at him, and he brought up his other hand to the door, imprisoning her in the wide circle of his arms. Stepping closer, he wedged a knee between her legs and pressed his erection into her buttocks, the urgent pounding of his hard flesh leaving no doubt as to his intentions.

His actions were demanding, but he didn't have a choice. The choice had been wrenched from him the minute she walked in and he saw the heated look in her eyes when she caught sight of his nakedness. Their argument had only delayed the inevitable.

He continued to whisper in her ear. "We haven't consummated our marriage yet, which is interesting, considering before we were married, we couldn't keep our hands off of each other. You want us to get it over with, don't you, Eva? Isn't that why you came in here so angry, all worked up with jealousy? And you got me worked up, too."

"You're wrong. I'm not jealous," she said unconvincingly.

"Oh, you're jealous, all right."

She pressed closer to the door to evade him, but he followed, drawn like a bear to a honeycomb, unable to resist the primal urges of his body. A soft laugh drifted across his lips as he closed in, trapping her in a tight cage made of skin and muscle.

"You said you were tired." She could pretend if she wanted to, but the tightness in her voice laid bare the truth for his ears to hear.

"Not anymore." He reached around in front of her and tugged the knotted belt loose. "I warned you about what you should wear walking around this house at night. Turn around. Let me look at you."

Slowly, Eva turned to face him, so close in proximity the soft satin dragged across the skin of his chest. He grabbed the edges of the robe and pushed it from her shoulders, allowing it to fall in a puddle at her feet.

He lowered his head and tasted the fullness of her mouth, setting off a spark of fire that blazed through his blood. "You taste so good," he murmured, nipping at her lips. "I could just eat you up."

Seizing her lips again, he devoured them with a demanding kiss. She half moaned, half whimpered as she collapsed into him, opening her mouth for the erotic twirl of his tongue. He crushed her, flattening her soft breasts against the hard plane of his chest and grinding his hips into hers to alleviate the pressure in his loins.

Eva whimpered softly, splaying her hands across Derrick's back, delighting in the velvety softness of his skin over the rigid muscles of steel. Her hands drifted lower and loosened the towel, discarding it to the floor so she could drag her nails up his hair-dusted thighs, feeling the muscles tense beneath her touch. He groaned and shoved one hand into her hair to anchor her mouth even harder to his. Slowly, she moved her hands higher up the back of his legs to grip his tight buttocks.

Tearing his mouth away, he lowered his head and dropped kisses down her neck—sucking the sensitive flesh there—and moved across her collarbone, then to her breasts covered by the sheer material.

The pressure of his lips made her ache unbearably. It had been so long since he'd touched her, since she'd felt his mouth on her body, that she grabbed him by the back of his head and pulled his head tight to her breast, forgoing gentleness and silently making her demands. His mouth opened over the turgid peak of one nipple and sucked it through the peach-colored satin, the sharp pain of pleasure landing like a lightning bolt between her thighs.

He soaked the material with his fervent sucking, and her knees buckled, so that the only reason she stood upright was because of her arms entwined around his neck. Her fingers combed through the curls at his nape, holding him tight, her voice vibrating with need as she whispered, "Yes, yes."

When he lifted his head, she greedily sought his mouth to tug on his lower lip, then nibbled his chin and rubbed her nose along the crook in his neck. His heavy pants matched her own.

"Take off your panties."

The rough texture of his voice as he whispered the command almost made her come right then. What could she do but obey? Primed as she was, they were of little use to her now, soaked with the evidence of her voracious need for him.

She slipped the underwear past her hips, stepping out of them as he gathered the end of the gown and proceeded to pull it over her head. Once she was naked, they reached for each other at the same time, their mouths fusing in a hungry kiss. He backed her across the room until her thighs hit the edge of the bed.

When he released her lips, he gave her direction without saying a word by turning her around and then patting her bottom to urge her up onto the bed. She climbed up and crawled to the middle on her knees. Eyes closed, she felt the mattress depress as he joined her. Anticipation raced through her body, and she bit her lip to stop from begging him to hurry.

He edged closer, and she wobbled in her position on all fours. One hand smoothed over her right butt cheek, and his moist lips pressed a kiss to the hot flesh. Biting down harder on her bottom lip, Eva lowered her shoulders and arched her back, pushing her bottom toward his mouth.

He sucked his breath between his teeth and swore softly. "Look at you."

He treated the outer edge of the crack of her backside to the slow, intimate trail of his tongue, all the way up to the base of her spine, where he pressed a solitary kiss. She couldn't take much more, certain she'd lose her mind if he didn't hurry and enter her soon.

The palm of his hand landed on her butt cheek. "On your back. I have something else in mind for you first."

Eva rolled onto her back.

"Now open those pretty legs for me, sweetheart."

Her legs fell apart immediately. She watched him through half-closed eyes, anxiously awaiting his next move.

The breath hitched in her throat when he lowered his head between her legs and became reacquainted with her in the most intimate way. With her legs opened the span of his powerful shoulders, he had unrestricted access. His tongue stroked across the sensitive flesh, pulling her closer to heaven on earth. With each lick, more moisture oozed from her body, coating his tongue and mouth. The rumbling sound of his groans confirmed the pleasure he took in the carnal act.

His hand glided up the heated flesh of her stomach to cup one breast. He stroked and caressed, adding to the inferno of pleasure that threatened to explode within her at any moment.

Lick. Kiss.

All of a sudden, the strokes grew firmer. His tongue lashed across the damp, aching folds, his lips pressed hard between her legs as if he'd suddenly grown angry he'd been denied for so long.

Lick. Kiss.

Eva moaned, tossing her head from side to side, pressing her heels into the bed to resist the urge to crush his head between her thighs. Because even though the pleasurable sensations were too much, she felt she would die if he stopped.

Lick. Kiss. Suck.

A hoarse cry exploded from her throat as she filled with ripples of ecstasy. Her thighs trembled, her back arched, and her toes curled into tight, painful knots. Clutching his head, she undulated her hips in a fevered attempt to ride out the storm.

As her heart rate slowed, Derrick lifted his head, licking his mouth to clear her body's dew from coating his lips. He slowly began to kiss his way up her rounded stomach, toward her breasts.

"Derrick, please, I c-can't," Eva whispered, begging for a short reprieve after the twister-like sensations that had just swirled through her. She was still so sensitive and emotional after that climax, but he wasn't listening.

Derrick made his way up to Eva's breasts, admiring the way the nipples strained up at him like perfect little chocolate berries. He curled his tongue around one dark tip and sucked it before moving to the other.

The demand for satisfaction beat through him insistently. He positioned himself at the drenched entrance to her body, cupped her hips with his long fingers, and with a slow, easy stroke, he slid into her inch by inch.

The sound of her long, low moan sent shivers down his spine. She quaked beneath him, but he took his time, using unhurried, steady movements. Canting her hips upward, he dug deeper but maintained the same slow pace, and she curled backward with her eyes closed and the hands on either side of her head curled into tight fists.

He lowered his head and kissed her breasts, flicking the walnut-colored tips with his tongue, sucking and kissing the soft underside of each one.

"Is this how you hate me?" he breathed as he moved in and out of her in slow motion. His lips migrated up to her neck. He nuzzled the sensitive spot below her ear. "I love how you hate. All hot and wet around me…driving me insane…*making me lose my damn mind.*"

Panting, she reached around to grab his buttocks and sink her nails into the taut flesh, encouraging him to dig deeper, prodding him to drive harder. She lifted her feet off the bed and drew her knees into her chest. "More...*more*."

Raw need clawed up his spine at her desperate pleas, even as he struggled to contain it. He wasn't ready to let go yet, but he could feel her internal muscles clamping down, drawing him further into the wet channel, clutching him as if she would never set him free.

He tightened the muscles of his buttocks to keep from ramming into her and prematurely ejaculating before she got her pleasure.

She constricted her internal muscles, effectively wrenching control away from him.

"Damn..." he groaned. "*Damn...you...*"

Sucking deep, shuddering breaths between his teeth, he accelerated his movements, going deeper, pounding harder. Her face contorted into lines of sensual agony as he pumped in and out of her. He loved to watch her. She held him enthralled and had complete control over his body at this moment.

He knew the exact minute she came. Her lips parted on a silent cry, and her nails dug deeper into the skin of his buttocks.

Watching her reaction and feeling her convulse around him shattered the last of his reserved strength. Finally, after months of deprivation, he released inside of her with a broken groan, his body tight as a quivering bow.

Blistering fulfillment followed, and he fell over onto his side and collapsed beside her.

****

Derrick reached for the remote control beside the bed and turned out the light.

His voice came to her in the darkness from a few inches away. "I'll have Svana move your things in here tomorrow. We're sharing a room from now on."

After handing down his edict, Derrick rolled onto his back and almost instantly fell asleep. He only needed a few hours to recharge. She should sleep, too, because when he awoke, he'd reach for her again, and she needed the rest to keep up with him.

Sleep escaped her, and she stayed awake for a while, listening to the sound of his even breathing. When her eyes grew accustomed to the dark, she studied his face. He looked so different when he slept, with the hard lines gone. He looked younger, almost boyish.

She grappled with conflicting feelings. Loving and hating him at the same time. Wanting nothing to do with him, but craving his touch. It hadn't taken much for him to disprove her words tonight. She hated being so weak, but her own body had called her out for the liar she was.

Even worse, she'd been ineffective in protecting her heart. The battle she'd waged against him had proven to be as effective as using a feather to beat back the advance of a boulder.

He still owned her heart, just as sure as if he'd emblazoned his initials on it with a hot iron.

She loved him. She'd never stopped.

And there was nothing she could do about it.

$$****$$

In the middle of the night, Derrick rolled onto his side and reached for Eva. His hand dragged across her skin, skimming her slightly rounded stomach and then pushing upward to squeeze her breast. She moaned in her sleep.

He brought her awake with featherlight kisses to her neck and breasts. The soft, feminine sounds she made provoked an urgent response inside him. He guided her leg across his hip and inserted his hard flesh between her legs.

Wrapped around each other, their bodies moved together as one, chest to chest, stomach to stomach, and hip to hip. Rapid thrusting quickly brought them to the edge. She panted her sweet breath into the cords of his neck. Derrick's fast pumping silently coaxed her forward until, with a shuddering groan, he tumbled headlong into ecstasy behind her.

With a little sigh, she went back to sleep.

In the dark, he watched her and brushed her hair back from her cheek. It seemed nothing could temper his lust for her.

He preferred his own space in bed, but tonight he made an exception. He might as well, anyway. Other women had understood his need for space, but not Eva. No matter the position they fell asleep in, she always migrated over to his side of the bed and curled into him at some point while they slept.

He closed his eyes and tightened his arms around her.

****

In the morning, Derrick awoke to Eva's soft bottom snug against his groin. He shifted slightly, and she wiggled closer, setting his loins on fire. His penis did what it always did when he woke up next to her—hardened like quick-setting concrete.

Last night he could tell she'd grown tired, partly due, no doubt, to the pregnancy. She used to have more stamina, but he had to remember, with a baby growing inside of her, he needed to ease up. In his current erect state, he found the prospect of lying next to her like a eunuch unappealing. Resisting the urge to wake her up, he freed his arm from under her body and, with a low groan of regret, rolled away.

"Down boy," he whispered to his erection.

While shaving in the bathroom, Derrick thought about how to proceed in the relationship. She was the affectionate type, always wanting to touch and snuggle. Having her in the master bedroom would mean waking up every morning like he did today, with her soft, warm body seared to his, and the scent of her tattooed into his skin.

He had to be careful because Eva dulled his instincts of self-preservation, making it easier for her to lead him around by the nose if he wasn't careful. He'd seen a similar result between Phineas and his mother.

Sometimes he wondered if Phineas had known that his mother resumed the affair with his biological father. Thinking back, there had been signs of her deceit. The frequent trips, the long periods during the day when she couldn't be reached at all, the hushed tones when she talked on the phone. Could he have known and simply ignored it, choosing to turn a blind eye in order to hold on to the trophy wife he'd fallen completely and irrevocably in love with?

Love. Derrick wouldn't wish it on his worst enemy.

Everyone talked about the beauty of it, but few ventured to discuss the damage the rejection of love produced. It destroyed marriages, made fools of intelligent men, and crushed the souls of innocent children.

He washed his face and slapped on aftershave, his movements jerky, trying but failing to expunge the memory that he'd never been able to rid himself of. The memory of the one and only time he'd ever met his biological father.

At nine years old, he'd found out where he worked, lied to the family driver, and convinced him to take him to the address. He'd thought that maybe if his father met him…maybe, just maybe he would realize he'd made a mistake and want him. After all, everyone said Derrick was good-looking and tall for his age. Surely that counted for something.

But it hadn't. He'd never forgotten the words Roarke Sr. said. "You have a father. And I already have a son." The devastating words had crushed him.

Of course his mother had been furious, but by then, he'd shut down. As she scolded him for sneaking off and going against her wishes, his only regret had been getting the driver into trouble.

From that moment on, he learned to maintain a certain emotional distance from those around him, including family. It was a protective mechanism that worked for years. Foolishly, he'd allowed Eva to penetrate that wall. He'd lowered his guard and let her get close, sharing pieces of his past with her he hadn't shared with anyone else. He didn't need to get burned twice to understand fire burned, and Eva was pure fire. Deceptively soft and with an angelic face, it made it easier for her to cut a man off at the knees if she were so inclined. That's why he had to be careful with her.

Ever since he'd seen her in that restaurant with her friends, she'd had an unbreakable hold on him he couldn't shake. He was starting to wonder if he even wanted to.

****

Eva yawned and stretched. An inordinate amount of contentment filled her body, and no wonder, after being made love to by Derrick.

He had accused her of purposely coming into his bedroom to force a response, and he'd been right, though she hadn't realized it until he called her out.

She rolled over into the spot on the bed he'd vacated. The sheets were cool, meaning he'd probably been up at the crack of dawn. The sheets and pillows smelled like him, and her body tingled with delicious sensations. She missed him already. Boy, she had it bad.

CHAPTER TWELVE

A few Saturdays later, Eva strolled into the kitchen.

"Good morning, Mrs. Hoffman," Svana said. "Breakfast on the terrace today?"

"Yes, that would be nice."

"What would you like?"

"Surprise me." On her way out the door, Eva asked, "Have you seen my husband this morning?" *My husband.* She never got tired of hearing the way those two words sounded together.

"He's in the garage with Saunders discussing a problem with one of the cars."

Svana started to prepare breakfast while Eva sat at the table on the terrace. Heat lamps kept the fall temperature at a comfortable degree, but soon it would become too cold to sit out there.

Saunders and Derrick walked up the stone steps, engrossed in deep conversation.

Her heart rate stepped up its pace. He really was beautiful. His features hard and masculine, his mouth—her body flushed with heat—sensuous and pleasure giving in a way she looked forward to on a regular basis. As her pregnancy became more apparent, Derrick limited their lovemaking out of concern for her and the baby. Once the doctor confirmed it was perfectly acceptable for them to continue having intercourse, he no longer denied himself, and they made love regularly, like two randy teenagers who'd recently discovered the joy of sex.

In the midst of explaining something to Saunders, Derrick gestured with his hands. The sight of his long, lean fingers reminded her of how they often caressed her skin and brought her trembling body to the edge before they joined together and he pushed her over into a climax.

She sighed. She loved him so much it hurt.

When he saw her seated at the table, he paused, and his features softened for a fraction before he returned to his explanation.

A sign. A little one, but a sign nonetheless that the closeness she felt to him was mutual. Optimism flickered in her chest. She saw those signs often nowadays. They were growing closer, or as close as Derrick allowed anyone to get to him.

Their changed relationship nurtured the love she already had, but she didn't know for certain how he felt about her. He cared for her, but how much?

The larger her waistline grew, the more protective he became by constantly following up and making sure she was eating well and getting enough exercise. He even got involved in her nightly sessions of rubbing cocoa butter on her skin to prevent stretch marks. On more than one occasion, she'd reminded him she wouldn't be the first woman to give birth, and millions of women did it every day. Although she complained about him being overprotective, she enjoyed the attention he lavished on her.

"Did you sleep well?" Derrick asked after Saunders disappeared into the house.

Eva nodded. "Did you?"

"Like a baby." He smiled. He looked relaxed and seemed in a good mood. His demeanor reminded her of the good times they used to share on St. Simons Island. "How'd the shopping go yesterday?"

"It went well. I found the cutest little outfits and a few more stuffed animals."

Derrick's lips quirked upward. "She's not even born yet, and she's got more clothes than I do and more toys than Toys 'R' Us."

"They were so cute, though. I couldn't resist."

She was used to his teasing, even though he encouraged her to get whatever she thought best for the baby. In another week, the nursery would be finished. A local artist was coming to paint a mural of purple dinosaurs dancing in a field of marigolds on the wall. Derrick thought the design looked wacky. She thought it was adorable, and since he'd given her carte blanche over the nursery, her baby would awaken every morning to the sight of polka-dot curtains and purple dinosaurs in a field of marigolds.

"I'd like to see them after breakfast. Did you buy anything for yourself?"

"A couple of outfits for the charity events, like you suggested."

"I'd like to see those, too."

They had attended a few business dinners, but he'd informed her to expect the invitations to increase as people grew accustomed to him as the head of HLC. Most they wouldn't attend, but some—like the upcoming charity events—were a must.

"How is the court case going?"

"The whole thing is ridiculous," he said with frustration. "They're throwing everything at us in court, from fraud to claiming that my mother somehow influenced him or threatened him into changing his will. Never mind she's been dead for fifteen years. Even if she had some influence over him when she was alive, I think that influence would have waned considerably in recent years.

"They're all so used to Phineas taking care of them, they're in panic mode. He bought them homes, paid for their children's educations, and each of his brothers got a substantial monthly allowance."

"I understand why they're panicked, don't you? He's taken care of them for years, and now they have to fend for themselves. Seems strange he cut them off like that."

"Yeah. Unless…" Derrick frowned. "Maybe that wasn't the intention. He used to say all the time if you don't work for it, you won't appreciate it. None of his brothers worked in the business, and he only has one niece who expressed any interest in working for HLC, and she's in the New York office." He paused, the wheels in his head turning. "Maybe he didn't cut them off. The reason he left everything to me was so that I could continue to mete out the allowances and disbursements. If he gave them a chunk of the estate, they'd squander their inheritance in no time."

"So…what are you going to do?"

He sat back, a thoughtful frown on his face. "I'll call the attorneys on Monday and tell them to talk to the other side and see if we can mediate an agreement. I'll be able to head up the business according to Phineas's wishes, and they'll continue to receive income and the other perks they received just like when he was alive."

"Do you think it will work?"

"I hope so. It'll be a relief to get this behind me."

Svana came out with plates of food. Biscuits with redeye gravy and chunks of country ham on the side. She left and came back with bowls of fresh fruit drizzled with honey, tall glasses of orange juice, and coffee for Derrick.

Eva took a deep breath, bracing herself to tell Derrick her news. "I hired an investigator to search for my father."

After a split-second pause, Derrick continued to slice the ham on his plate. "When did you decide to look for him?"

"Right after we got married. You said I could use the money you put into my account in any way I want."

"You can. It's your money." He lifted a slice of ham into his mouth and chewed. "How much have you spent so far?" When she told him the amount, his eyebrows raised in shock.

The skepticism in his eyes made her respond defensively. "I know it's expensive, but the investigator feels like he's close."

"It's your money. I said you could spend it however you choose."

"I know, but I don't want you to think it's all a waste. He thinks my father could be in California, which makes sense because my mother lived out there for a while after she left school."

He set down his fork carefully. "Eva—"

"Don't say it." She gripped the fork and knife in her hands. "I know I'm taking a risk because he didn't want me when I was born. I know that. But people change, Derrick."

He looked steadily at her. "I don't want you to get your hopes up because you might get hurt. You're excited by the prospect of finding your father, but you have to be prepared for the fact that he might not be excited to be found."

Giving her head a vigorous shake, she swallowed down the lump of emotion filling her throat.

"I'm not trying to hurt you."

"Then why would you say something so cruel?"

"I'm not being cruel. Listen to me—"

"No, because you're wrong. I can't believe you'd be so negative."

"I'm not being negative. I'm being realistic. You can't keep looking at the world with this Pollyanna viewpoint—"

"I'm not Pollyanna! Stop saying that. The world is not all bad. And what is so wrong with me wanting to find my father? My mother's gone, and all I know about him is that he was a teenager, too, and he didn't want to be a father. The photo of him is so worn I can barely see his face. I could have brothers and sisters, and he'll be a grandfather soon."

They sat in tense silence for a few moments.

"He could be looking for me," Eva added, trying to make him understand. "From what I can tell, when my mother left California, she never tried to contact him again." She paused, her voice growing softer. "I'm not like you. I can't pretend he doesn't exist."

Derrick set his knife next to the fork. "My situation was different, but..." She saw how he struggled to get the words out. He unclenched and clenched his hand several times. "I understand the need to know him and meet him. Let me know if you need me to get involved."

"I won't. I can handle this on my own."

He looked steadily at her. "You're my wife. It's my job to protect you."

"I don't need protecting."

"I'm going to do it anyway."

She had to admit there was a certain level of comfort in knowing he'd be there if she needed him. He never talked about it, but he still bore the pain of his father's rejection from years ago. How unfortunate a good support system had not been available to him as a child.

"I don't want to fight. We've been getting along so well. Let's pretend I never brought up this topic, and if I need you, I'll let you know."

He picked up the silverware. "Fair enough."

CHAPTER THIRTEEN

Derrick sat at the head of the conference table at HLC headquarters. It was Thursday night, and he was ready to go home. He'd called Eva earlier to inform her to go ahead with dinner without him, but he now regretted the decision. If he hadn't insisted on having this meeting, he could be at home now. He'd decided the executive team needed an update on the merger with the Greek shipping company, and the CFO and VP of operations led the after-hours meeting with the details.

So far, so good. There had been a few hiccups, as were expected, but overall, the alliance was proving to be a good idea. With access to such a large fleet of ships, HLC had gobbled up even more market share and sat on the cusp of becoming the dominant force for the international movement of goods in Europe and the Americas. He already had his mind on expansion, having charged his team to research distribution channels and entry into the next target markets—Asia and Africa.

Despite all the success and the excitement of accomplishing the goals laid out before his father's passing,

Derrick acknowledged an equal amount of pleasure came from having Eva in his life. In the role of a wife, he couldn't imagine anyone else doing a better job. She adapted to any social environment. Initially, he could tell she'd felt out of place among the other wives, but gradually she'd relaxed and become the perfect hostess and the guest others looked forward to seeing.

She took over management of the household, which included overseeing the maintenance on the house, the grounds, and the cars. She also became involved in the charitable organizations the Hoffman estate supported. In addition to attending functions such as award ceremonies and fundraisers, she made sure that any funds dispersed from the estate were spent in accordance with the stipulations in Phineas's will.

Her experience in event coordination had also come in handy, making her a popular committee member of several organizations. Not only was she sought after for her ability to plan and coordinate large events with skill, but her knowledge of the industry enabled her to negotiate very favorable terms on events contracts that saved the organizations a lot of money.

And him...well, marriage had changed him. He looked forward to going home now, and while the thought of having a family used to scare him, it no longer seemed daunting. In fact, he liked the thought of having someone to go home to. He'd had to take a few business trips, but when he did, he seldom went a night without talking to Eva when he was out of town.

He always returned as soon as possible, even if it meant arriving in the middle of the night. When he did, as he eased into the bed, she would awaken and roll over toward him.

"You're home," she'd whisper.

"Yes, sweetheart, I'm home," he'd whisper back and pull her into his arms.

As the CFO droned on about the increased market share and showed graphs of the revenue HLC anticipated earning in the coming years, Derrick smiled to himself. He and Eva refrained from discussing the past, but that didn't stop them from arguing like an old married couple. For example, during their conversation at dinner a few nights ago, he broached the subject of hiring a nanny again. She'd insisted they didn't need one. An argument ensued from there.

Then there was the time when he climbed into bed and had the displeasure of rolling in crumbs. He'd told her for the umpteenth time not to eat in bed, and she'd yelled back she couldn't help it and was eating for two. Right afterward, she burst into tears, and he, feeling like a heel, had ended up apologizing.

Somehow all their arguments ended with him apologizing.

He chuckled, and eleven heads turned in his direction.

"Was there something you wanted to add, Derrick?" His CFO looked curiously at him from the other end of the table. A multicolored pie chart showed on the screen behind him.

Derrick had reviewed it all before he allowed the data to be presented to the entire team, so he had no concerns. "No, ah...you've been doing a good job. Continue."

The CFO smiled and turned back to the screen. Using a laser wand, he drew a circle around a slice of the chart. "So, based on our projections, in five years we expect market share to—"

"You know what?" Derrick interrupted. "It's late. Why don't you all go home? You've been working hard, and I think this could wait until the morning, don't you?"

They all looked around at each other, but no one had the courage to agree with him, as if they thought it was a setup.

Derrick stood, signaling the legitimacy of his comment. "How about we reconvene tomorrow at noon? We'll order in some food and make it a working lunch. Any objections?" He didn't expect any, nor did he plan to entertain any. "All right, then. Review the files carefully and come prepared to discuss and offer suggestions. Good night."

The executives had stunned expressions on their faces as he left the room. It didn't matter to him. As the boss, he could do whatever the hell he wanted, and right now he wanted to get home to see his wife.

On the way out, he stopped by his suite of offices to get his briefcase. Once he retrieved it, he exited to find his administrative assistant had returned to her post and was making copies.

She looked up and smiled. "Good night, Mr. Hoffman."

"Good night." Derrick's steps slowed. "How late are you scheduled to work every day?"

She looked confused. "I...I work as long as you need me to, sir."

He smiled. "But how late are you *scheduled* to work?"

"Until six."

Last he checked, it was almost nine o'clock. "I tell you what, why don't you go home? And from now on, leave at six. I'll let you know if I need you to work late."

Her mouth opened and closed a couple of times before she finally got any words out. "Oh, thank you. Thank you, Mr. Hoffman."

"One more thing. From now on, call me Derrick. Mr. Hoffman was my father."

With a smile of pure pleasure, she said, "Yes, sir. I mean Derrick."

"I'll see you in the morning."

****

At home, Derrick dropped his briefcase in the study and went upstairs. The bedroom was silent, and the television mounted on the wall was on, but had been turned down to mute. After a quick sweep of the other rooms and not finding Eva, he removed his jacket and tie and went in search of her. He found her downstairs in the kitchen.

Standing at the door, he watched her at the counter as she ate some combination of food to satisfy her strange cravings. Her belly was a little more than seven months swollen—looking like an oversized basketball. She'd never looked more beautiful, and he'd never wanted her more. The feelings rushing through him were so fierce, he remained glued to the floor.

In that moment, he accepted what he should have known all along, what he'd refused to accept for fear of leaving himself wide open for hurt and possible humiliation.

I'm in love with her.

His throat constricted, as if someone were choking the life out of him. To breathe, he had to undo the top button of his dress shirt. The last thing he ever expected or wanted to do was fall in love with her. He'd fallen prey to the very thing he'd hidden from all his life.

"Hey, you're home."

The warmth of her smile filled her brown eyes and heated his soul. He still couldn't move. He swallowed, exerting tremendous effort to clear the passageway in his closed throat.

I'm in love with her.

How could he not have seen it before?

Because he knew the danger of love—or the lack thereof. But it was too late. He was all in.

By loving her, he handed her the power to hurt him. The same as she'd done when she ended their relationship, though he hadn't wanted to admit it at the time. The same as his father had done when he rejected his nine-year-old self. The same as his mother had done by endorsing his biological father's decision to give up his paternal rights so another man could adopt him.

"Derrick, is something wrong?"

He shook his head and cleared his throat. "No. Ah, what are you eating?"

Her eyes lowered from his in embarrassment. "Raspberry jam and Nutella on crackers…with a sprinkling of salt."

Derrick approached, eyeing her spread on the counter. "Well, at least you left out the bananas this time."

"We're out of bananas," she said in a morose tone. She puckered her lips into a cute little moue of misery.

"That's 'cause you ate them all."

"You know I can't help it. It's the hormones." She slipped another cracker into her mouth. Her hair fell into loose waves onto her shoulders. He lifted and fingered a strand before letting it fall back into place.

Perfect. The perfect woman, right under his nose.

"So when you mention hormones, it's all good, but when I do, I get yelled at."

Eva arched an eyebrow. "Do I really need to explain to you why?" she asked around a mouthful of food.

"Have a seat." Derrick gathered up the two jars, the box of crackers, and the salt. He walked to the small table in the kitchen and took a seat beside Eva.

"You look tired," she remarked.

"Nah, I'm good. I just have a lot on my mind." Like how he'd managed to fall in love with a woman he'd blackmailed into marrying him. And how did she feel about him now that they'd been married for a while? "How are you feeling today?"

"Okay, although I felt a little pain around lunchtime."

Derrick frowned. "How long did it last?"

"Don't worry," she said, spreading Nutella on a cracker. "It didn't last long. Just a few minutes. If it happens again, I promise I'll call the doctor."

"You should have called the doctor today."

"I knew I shouldn't have mentioned it." She sighed. "Derrick, I can't make a big deal out of every little thing. I can tell they're getting tired of me already because I keep bugging them, and I still have almost two months to go. The last time we visited the doctor, he said the pregnancy is progressing normally. It was probably gas or something." She applied the raspberry jam over the hazelnut spread.

"I'd rather know for sure." He lifted both of her sock-covered feet onto his thighs. Outside of her belly, there wasn't much else to indicate Eva was pregnant. She hadn't gained much weight, but her feet had grown larger, and her ankles started swelling. He removed one sock and started to massage her feet. This is what being in love did to you. It made you sappy and considerate. "And for the record, that's what they get paid for. If it happens again, promise me you'll talk to the doctor."

She nodded. "I promise."

Using circular motions, Derrick dragged his fingers from the toe to the ankle of one foot.

"Mmm," Eva murmured. "That feels so good."

He continued the same movements, using his thumbs on the sole of her foot, gradually increasing the pressure.

She moaned. "Oh, that feels so good."

Fairly certain there was no need for that tone of voice, Derrick lifted his gaze to Eva's. The pupils of her eyes had darkened with desire to an even richer brown. "Eva," he warned, fingers paused on her ankle.

"We haven't made love in over a week. That's a long time."

Ten days to be exact. "I know, but I'm trying to ease up on you."

"I don't want you to ease up on me," she whispered.

His body tightened, and he suppressed a groan. The words roused his libido, as if it needed rousing. Looking at her pregnant body served as an adequate aphrodisiac on a day-to-day basis, and only through sheer willpower did he manage not to spread her legs at every opportunity.

"Remember on the last visit, the doctor said it's okay as long as I'm still comfortable."

"I know, but I can tell you don't have the stamina you used to."

With a coy smile, she said, "So we'll just do it one time."

"I don't want to hurt you," he murmured halfheartedly, feeling a rise in his pants already.

She lowered her feet and rose from the chair. "I'm okay. Really."

The red, long-sleeved maternity dress drew attention to her radiant dark skin, and the round neckline emphasized the size of her breasts, enlarged by the effects of her pregnancy. He couldn't wait to get his hands on them.

As their eyes met and held, he let his fingers travel lightly up her thighs. With the back of his hand, he stroked the damp material between her legs. A little tremor ran through her, and her eyes glazed over with passion. Slowly, he lowered her panties past her hips and let them fall to the floor.

"Come here," he said, patting his thighs.

With a sultry smile, she lowered onto his legs. Their lips connected instantly, moving gently over one another before becoming more frantic as desire flared between them. He wound his fingers in her hair and tipped her head back so he could pass heated kisses down the length of her neck.

He nibbled at the soft skin there and then moved to her ear, where he caught the fleshy lobe in his mouth and sucked. The uneven sound of her breath aroused him further, and he pressed his face to her soft throat.

Peppermint and oatmeal.

He cupped her full breasts in his hands, and she gasped with pleasure. "Yes," she whispered as he kneaded the soft mounds, rubbing the flats of his thumbs across the nipples until they came to rigid points.

He wanted to tell her how he felt. The need to do so built to such a pitch, he undid the buttons on her bodice and plucked one of her breasts from inside the dress, filling his mouth to curtail the urge.

He had never said the words "I love you" to anyone. Not once in his entire thirty-three years. But this was his woman, his wife, and even if he couldn't say the words right now, he could show her with his body how much he loved her.

He hurriedly undid the belt on his trousers and then unzipped his pants. Her fingers gripped his shoulders in an effort to remain steady. Under the dress, his hands helped guide her onto his erection.

"I love how wet you get for me," he said tightly.

"Only you. Only you," she breathed against his mouth.

His chest puffed with pride, and he pumped his hips, his hands cupping her backside. Her head fell back as she rocked against him, riding with abandon, clinging to him like a lifeline.

He lowered his head to the bare breast and plucked the swollen nipple back into his mouth, curling his tongue around it. Her hips moved with more frantic motions. It was hard as hell to hold back when she started getting so excited.

Their moans came in a synchronized cadence, bouncing off the kitchen walls in their mutual climb to satisfaction.

"I'm coming...I'm coming, Derrick."

Sweeter words had never been spoken. She came apart, clutching on to his shoulders with a mighty grip. Her brown eyes blazed down at him with passion. He bucked within her, the contractions of her body dragging him toward repletion. One arm fisted around her waist, while his other hand clamped down on the edge of the table to resist clutching her to him with undue force.

Afterward, when their breathing was back to normal and her breast tucked inside the bodice of the dress, Eva pressed a kiss to his cheek.

"I think you needed that as much as I did," she whispered. He could feel her smile.

"I guess so." He turned his head and kissed her mouth. She tasted like raspberry and sweet hazelnut.

"Ooh." Eva grabbed her stomach. "I think we woke her."

Derrick placed his hand beside Eva's and felt his baby's movements. "She's pissed at you. She must be doing karate chops in there. That's those Hawthorne genes."

"I think she is pissed. And this is Jacob all the way." She fell silent, and they sat for a while, their palms spread across her belly to track the movements of their unborn child. "She'll soon be here," Eva whispered. "I can't wait."

When she stopped moving around, they rose from the chair and fixed their clothes.

Derrick swooped her up in his arms and headed for the door.

"Oh, wait, my snack."

After a long sigh, Derrick walked back over to the table and bent his knees so she could gather up the items.

Walking through the house, he warned, "No crumbs in the bed."

"It happened one time."

"Twice. If you make a mess in our bed, I swear..."

They continued their argument all the way into the bedroom.

****

With a start, Eva awoke in the middle of the night. Sharp pains jabbed at her back and stomach, forcing her to clutch her round belly. They felt like the vicious swipes of a knife, ripping through her, so acute she couldn't breathe or make a sound for several seconds.

When she caught her breath, she looked over her shoulder at Derrick's sleeping form. "Derrick, wake up."

She whimpered at another slice of the hot, scraping claw inside of her. She must be going into labor. She curled into the fetal position, her eyes unfocused from the searing pain.

"Derrick, wake up," she panted, reaching back to grab his hand and squeeze with all her might.

He roused from sleep, his voice groggy when he said, "Eva? What is it?"

"I don't know. I think...I'm going into labor."

She cried out in agony as her uterus felt like it twisted inside out.

Derrick swore and bolted upright. He reached across her and grabbed the remote from the table beside the bed to turn on the lights.

"I don't know. This doesn't feel right," Eva said, her voice shaking in panic. Between her legs was wet, but if her water broke, was it supposed to feel so thick? "Something's wrong."

With trembling fingers, she pushed the comforter off of her. That's when she saw it.

Blood.

She screamed in horror. "No! No!" Her head fell back. A wave of nausea assaulted her from the pain and the sight of the garish red color staining her negligee. Her arms folded over her stomach in a protective gesture. "No. No."

Derrick sped into action, jumping off the bed and gathering her in arms. "Shh. I've got you, sweetheart. I've got you."

His voice remained calm, steady—the complete opposite to her panic-stricken cries seconds before. But she could feel his rapid heartbeat against her cheek as he lifted her in his arms and raced from the room.

"Saunders!" he bellowed down the hall.

The pain didn't subside. It was excruciating and relentless. Eva's arms tightened around Derrick's neck. Tears streamed down her cheeks. She was losing her baby.

"Saunders!" Derrick called again. "Help me!"

She sobbed because of the pain. Sobbed because of her fears. This wasn't supposed to happen. This was her miracle baby.

****

She must have passed out.

When she regained consciousness, she found herself bundled in a blanket in the back of one of the cars, cradled in Derrick's arms. Outside the tinted windows, the lights of the city sped past as they raced up the highway.

Derrick would take care of everything.

That was her last thought before she closed her eyes and passed out again.

CHAPTER FOURTEEN

Derrick rose from the chair beside Eva's bed when the doctor motioned him outside the VIP delivery suite at the hospital. She rested now, hooked up to beeping machines with an IV drip attached to one arm. The drugs had sedated her enough so she could get some relief from the pain.

In the hall, the doctor's sympathetic gaze behind horn-rimmed spectacles made his stomach twist uneasily.

"Derrick!" A female voice came down the hall. Matthew and Cassidy rushed toward him with concern etched in their faces. "How is she? How's the baby?"

"I don't know. The doctor's about to give me an update now." He didn't feel like himself. Maybe that's why his voice sounded like he'd chewed and swallowed a plateful of rocks. He'd never felt so helpless in his life.

"Mr. Hoffman," the doctor began in a soothing tone, "after examining your wife, we've determined there's been a placental abruption."

"A what?"

"A placental abruption. What that means is that the placenta has separated from the wall of the uterus. It doesn't happen very often, and usually when it does occur, the effects are not serious and can be contained. Unfortunately, that's not the case with your wife. Her condition is very problematic. She's lost a lot of blood and continues to bleed, and the baby is not getting the necessary oxygen and nutrients it needs."

"Violet," Derrick said, feeling dazed.

"Excuse me?"

"Violet," he repeated. "Her name is Violet. We named her after Eva's mother."

"Violet." The doctor directed his gaze at the three of them. "Violet is experiencing what we call fetal distress. It's too dangerous to induce labor. If we want to save her, we'll have to take her immediately."

A soft sound of dismay came from Cassidy. She brought her hand to her mouth, and her fear-filled eyes looked up at Derrick.

All of his senses seemed heightened and concentrated to form a stiffening tension from his neck up into his head. The lights were too bright, the air too thin, and the hospital sounds around him were too loud.

"Did we do something wrong?" he asked, thinking back to him and Eva in the kitchen.

"There are risk factors, none of which pertain to your wife. It's one of those things that can happen, and it can't be prevented. All we can do is limit the damage at this point."

"Is that safe to take Violet now? She's got almost two months left. Will she be all right?"

"Violet's gestated for more than seven months. The chances of survival are very good."

Very good was not good enough.

He needed to stay calm, but the doctor needed to understand what was at stake. Drawing on the steely restraint that had carried him through other difficulties, he laid his left hand on the doctor's shoulder.

"Derrick…" Matthew said.

He lifted his other hand toward his younger brother. "It's all right, Matt, I'm just talking to the man." He looked the doctor in the eye. "Listen, that's my wife and my daughter in there. I don't care what you have to do, who you have to call, but you make sure they both come out of this, you understand me?"

"Mr. Hoffman, I can't promise—"

He brought his face close to the doctor's. "*Do you understand me?*"

Matthew stepped forward. "Derrick, for God's sake—"

"Get back, Matt," he snarled through his teeth, keeping his gaze locked on the doctor. The man had backed up, but Derrick's hand tightened on his shoulder so he couldn't escape. "Do you understand me?"

The doctor nodded, gulping, and shoving his glasses further up on his nose.

When he hurried away, Derrick leaned against the wall with his palm flat on the surface. With his head bent, he closed his eyes, clenching his other hand into a fist, and did something he couldn't ever remember doing before. He prayed, no begged, for the health of his wife and safe delivery of his daughter, and that all the wrong he'd perpetrated over the years would not conspire against him to harm either one of them.

He felt Cassidy's little hand wriggle between his fingers and loosen his fist to hold tightly to him.

"It'll be okay," she said softly. "Go. She needs you. We'll be right here, okay? Waiting." She squeezed his hand.

****

Eva felt like she'd been run over by an eighteen-wheeler. When she shifted, pain cut through her, and she winced.

"Easy." Derrick's voice came from beside the bed. She opened her eyes to find him looking at her. The corners of his mouth lifted into a small smile. "Hey."

Snatches of memory came back. They'd had to perform a Caesarean section to deliver Violet because of complications. Violet!

Her gaze scoured the room. "How is she? Is she okay?"

"Shh. She's fine. They have her in the neonatal intensive care unit."

"I want to see her. Take me to her." She tried to get up, but the effects of the general anesthesia and dull ache from the incision in her abdomen forced her to plop back against the pillows.

He brushed the hair back from her face with a gentle hand. His touch soothed her racing heart. "You're not in any condition to move around right now. You'll see her later." He held his smartphone up for her to see. "I know you hate how I always have this phone with me, but it came in handy. I took pictures."

He scrolled through the images. She saw her daughter at birth, covered in blood and fluids. Then there were photos of her in the NICU, inside an incubator to keep her warm, tubes attached to her body to give nourishment and help her little lungs breathe. She was almost as pale as the sheet she slept on.

"She's going to be all right?"

"So far, so good. The doctor said she'll have to stay for a while—it could be a couple of weeks or longer—until she can do all the normal things on her own: breathing, sucking, swallowing. It depends on her progress."

The effects of the anesthesia made Eva feel groggy, and she closed her eyes. When she opened them again, Derrick

241

looked down at her with worry lines creasing his forehead. She reached up and cupped his jaw. The rough hairs of morning stubble scraped the palm of her hand. "You were wonderful. You took care of me." Her hand fell back to the bed.

"I promised you I would. I couldn't let anything happen to you or Violet."

If she told him her feelings, what would he say? What would he do?

She should tell him now, whisper it, because her chest hurt with the need to say the words of love she'd held back all these months. Despite the rocky start to their marriage, maybe they could make this work. The idea didn't seem far-fetched anymore, and Violet cemented their emotional bond.

"I'm glad I wasn't alone when it happened." Her voice trembled. "I knew you'd take care of everything." Tears filled her eyes. "I love you. I love you so much."

There. She'd said it.

She didn't know what she'd expected, but she hadn't expected the color to drain from his face. "Never mind. I don't know why I said that." She twisted her head away from him, squeezing her eyes shut in humiliation. "It's the anesthesia...I'm not myself right now. I don't know why...I don't know...I'm delirious."

"Eva—"

"Derrick, it's okay. I'm extremely emotional right now. I just had a baby, and I don't feel like myself. You don't have to say a word. I don't know why I said such a thing. It's okay. Really. It's okay. I'm sorry." She was babbling, and at the same time, she couldn't look at him for fear of what she'd see in his eyes.

She didn't want to hear him say this wasn't part of the deal, or some such nonsense he was fond of throwing at her. He'd been up front and honest with her about what to expect. He promised to take care of her and pledged his fidelity. Why couldn't it be enough? Why did she keep reaching for more than he could give?

"Are you saying you didn't mean it?" he asked.

She'd always done her crying over him in private, but this time she couldn't stop the tears from slipping beneath her lids.

"You said you love me." He took her hand. She tried to pull away, but he tightened his grip.

"I didn't mean it," she said in a broken whisper.

"I don't believe you."

"Please. I can't do this now. It's too hard." She opened her eyes and stared across at the closed curtains.

Derrick handed her a single tissue, which she used to wipe her nose. He still held on to her other hand. Sniffling, she lay there, wishing she could go back in time and stop the impulsive words from leaving her mouth.

"I've never told anyone," she heard him say. She listened, noting the somber tone of his voice, as if he were about to say something of great importance. "I never told anyone that I love them."

She turned her head slowly in his direction. "No one?"

He shook his head.

"Not even your mother?"

"No. Maybe I did when I was a kid, but I don't remember. We never said those kinds of things to each other. We didn't have that kind of relationship. She wasn't a bad mother. She was just...distant, I guess is the right word. When she married Phineas, they hired a nanny to watch over me, which made her life easier."

He swallowed, and she saw the difficulty it took to share his intimate feelings. She remained quiet so he could let it all out.

"I was a mistake. In a way, I messed everything up for her—at least for a while. Once I was born and my father's wife found out, he had to choose. My mother never wanted to have a child, so I guess I should be glad she didn't get rid of me." He rubbed his thumb across the back of her hand. "Phineas was a good man. He never told me he loved me, either, but when I think about it, I know he did. He told me on more than one occasion how proud he was of me."

"He trusted you, too. He left you everything."

Derrick nodded. "Crazy, but true." He looked down into her eyes. "I love you, Eva. It took a long time for me to figure it out because I didn't want to need anyone. But I need you." He brought her hand to his lips, and her eyes flooded with tears. "I hope you meant it when you said you love me."

Her bottom lip quivered. "I did." A tear glided out of the corner of her eye. "I was so afraid to tell you because I thought you didn't care. When we were seeing each other, I wanted so much more, but you told me up front that you didn't want a serious relationship."

"Yeah, that's what I said, but believe me, that was a rehearsed speech I'd given to other women. It didn't apply to you. I wanted you to myself almost from the beginning."

"Then why were you so distant? Why didn't you ever let me meet your family? How could you bring another woman to the island when we were together? I don't understand."

"It had nothing to do with you," he said earnestly. "The weekend of my sister's wedding, I planned to spend as much time with you as possible when I got to St. Simons Island. The truth is, I didn't want you to meet my family because my family life was so messed up. I didn't have a good relationship with anyone on my biological father's side of the family. I didn't want to introduce you into that mess. Our relationship was so good, I didn't want to spoil it. That's why I only let you meet Phineas. That was about the only normal family relationship I had at the time."

"So you weren't ashamed of me or something like that?"

"Ashamed of you? No! I thought if you knew how jacked up my family life was, you might not want to see me anymore." He squeezed her hand. "Sweetheart, you were the one good thing in my life. I wanted to keep you separate from all the ugliness." He lifted her hand to spread her fingers along his jaw. "I don't know what I did to deserve you."

"Maybe you're not as terrible as you think," she whispered.

"You make me want to be a better man."

"Oh, Derrick."

"It's true. And you have no idea how much I looked forward to our weekends together."

"Why didn't you say something?"

He shrugged. "I didn't know how. And I didn't know how you felt, either. When you mentioned that schmuck, James…"

"He's not a schmuck."

"When you mentioned that schmuck, James," he said again in a harder tone, obviously not liking that she defended the other man, "it drove me out of my mind. Up until then, I assumed you weren't seeing anyone because I wasn't."

"I wasn't 'seeing' James. He really was just a friend. But I'm surprised you weren't seeing anyone else."

"No one. I swear. In fact, the woman I planned to take to the wedding wasn't someone I was involved with. I just needed a date because I didn't want to show up alone, and she didn't mind accompanying me. My plan was to spend most of my time with you at the villa." He smiled slowly.

"For some reason, all I could think about was you, and no other woman had a chance."

Eva glowed from the inside out. "I didn't know I had so much power," she whispered.

"Don't take advantage too much. Go easy on me," he whispered back.

"I don't think anyone can take advantage of you." She sighed. "I do love you. With all my heart. Promise me we'll always talk to each other. Just like this."

"I promise. Anything you want."

"Anything?"

"Anything."

"Can I eat in bed?"

"Eva…"

"You said anything," she reminded him with an impish grin.

"All right." He shook his head. "You can have anything you want, sweetheart. All you have to do is ask."

****

The nurse came in later and gave Eva some pills for the pain. Derrick sat with her until she fell asleep, and then he quietly left the room.

Outside in the waiting area, two couples and what looked to be grandparents sat watching the television mounted in the corner. Cassidy sat flipping through a magazine. Roarke had arrived, and he sat next to her, while Matthew paced the floor restlessly. They all three looked up.

"Consider yourselves lucky to be here for this momentous occasion," he announced. "Your beautiful niece, Violet Hoffman, has arrived, weighing in at a whopping three pounds, three ounces."

A cheer of relief went up in the room. Even the other people in the waiting room clapped and smiled. Cassidy ran over and gave him a hug. "I knew it," she said. "I knew she'd be fine."

Since only parents were allowed in the NICU, they couldn't see Violet in person, but Derrick showed them the photos he'd taken with the camera phone.

Matthew offered to buy a box of "It's a Girl" cigars from the gift shop. "I know these aren't as good as what you're used to," he said to Derrick.

"It'll do for now," he replied.

The four of them went outside into the early morning. The sun was just beginning to rise on a new day. After a couple of puffs, Cassidy started coughing, followed by Matthew.

"I can't do this," Cassidy said, wheezing.

"Don't inhale," Derrick advised.

She put out the cigar and left the smoking to her brothers.

Derrick blew his smoke up into the early morning sky. He suddenly realized the most important people in his life were all here in the same place. His wife and daughter were safe upstairs, and his brothers and sister were lending their support beside him.

A wry smile lifted one corner of his mouth.

Life couldn't be better.

CHAPTER FIFTEEN

Derrick scrolled through Eva's account online, a frown creasing his forehead. He didn't like what he saw.

Large disbursements had been made over the past three months to the investigator searching for her father, and after their conversation last night, it didn't sound as if the so-called investigator was any closer to finding him since the last time they'd discussed his progress. Yet he needed more money. And Eva had come to Derrick to ask for more money—something she'd never done before.

He'd recognized the look in her eyes. The pleading desperation he acknowledged came from wanting something so much you'd do anything to get it.

He'd promised to have the funds transferred over after the weekend. Under normal circumstances, he would have done it right away, but a peculiar sensation in his gut made him want to look into this further. The negligible amount didn't concern him. What concerned him was that this "investigator" could be taking advantage of her desperation. That he couldn't tolerate.

Derrick understood the emotional need to connect with family and how it could cloud logic, and as he looked at the situation from the outside, he saw what Eva couldn't. Her explanation for why he needed more money sounded fishy. In emotional situations like this, normally intelligent persons could be swayed into unintelligent behavior. Coupled with a heart as big as Eva's, the detective had hit the jackpot.

Call it cynicism. Realism. But no one was going to take advantage of her.

He picked up the phone and called his assistant. "I need an address," he said. He gave her the name of the investigator, and within minutes, she called back with the address and the GPS coordinates.

A glance at the digital clock on his desk told him he had plenty of time to get over there before heading home. The day had been a bust anyway. He had spent the morning in the attorneys' office signing a multitude of paperwork.

Once his uncles understood their allowances and the other advantages of the Hoffman name weren't jeopardized, negotiations went a lot more smoothly. Knowing Phineas left his entire estate to a non-blood relative may have been a slap in the face, but common sense prevailed. After weighing the pros and cons, they decided forgoing the financial benefits in the short term for potential gain in the long term—which may not even come—was not worth it.

Derrick slipped into his coat and wished his assistant a good weekend. He certainly intended to have one. After four weeks, his baby girl was coming home from the hospital today. With Christmas around the corner, Eva decided to have a combined welcome home/Christmas party with the family. He intended to be there on time.

Right after he finished taking care of this little problem.

****

"Sorry for the mess. We just moved in and haven't had a chance to get organized yet."

The investigator, Danny Jackson, grinned at Derrick and guided him toward a chair in his private office after telling his secretary to hold all calls.

I bet, Derrick thought cynically, figuring the money he'd taken from Eva had helped to upgrade his offices.

A stack of boxes stood precariously in front of one wall between two file cabinets. The room smelled of fresh paint, and all the furniture looked shiny and new.

"Where'd you move from?" he asked in a conversational tone.

"We were up in the city of Lawrenceville, near the highway. Real convenient, but this is better."

"Much better," Derrick agreed, flashing a smile he knew would put the man at ease. "You can't beat a Buckhead address. It means better clientele, although the rent must be killer in a place like this."

Danny chuckled as he settled into the chair across from Derrick. His coffee-colored skin crinkled around the eyes. "Well, business has been good the past couple of months, and I expect it to get even better now that I have access to a certain 'clientele,' as you put it." He folded his hands together on the large desk. "How can I help you?"

"You can start by explaining what's going on with the investigation into finding my wife's father. Eva Hoffman."

"Ms. Hoffman! Yes." He frowned. "Does she know you're here?"

"Yes," Derrick lied.

The other man's smile faltered a bit. "I've always only dealt with her."

"I'm taking over." He crossed his legs. "I married an angel, but me—well, let's just say people have used some colorful terms to describe me." He pulled out a cigar and dragged it under his nose, inhaling the hint of vanilla and the aroma of the tobacco leaves. "Care for one?"

"I don't smoke."

Derrick cut off the tip. "Yeah, it's a bad habit. I picked it up from my father, but it's my one vice."

He lit the cigar. Completely rude, but it established he was in charge and didn't care what the other man thought. It was a calculated act to shift the power in his direction.

No more Mr. Nice Guy.

Danny recognized what was happening. The smile died on his face completely, and the radiance in his eyes dulled.

"As I was saying—my wife—she's a good woman. She sees the good in everyone, even me." He smiled, took a puff of the cigar, and blew the smoke out the side of his mouth. "I'm the complete opposite. I suspect everyone and everything. Trust no one, that's my motto. So I'm here because I don't trust you. Eva has paid you a lot of money, and you have yet to deliver any valuable information for her. Why is that?"

Danny laughed uneasily. "Well, I'm sure you can understand, Mr. Hoffman, that these things take time. I explained all this to your wife."

"Explain it to me so I can understand. Because here's the thing…For the amount of money my wife's paid you, I'm sure you could have found the remains of Amelia Earhart by now."

He swallowed. "I didn't have much to go on to begin with, but I'm very close to finding her father. As a matter of fact, I've learned he was in the military."

"Uh-huh. What else?" This time he blew the smoke across the desk.

Danny coughed and rolled back his chair. He snapped his fingers. "You know, you reminded me of something. I do have information for her. It recently came in. I completely forgot. I did happen to find…" His voice trailed off, and he bounced up from the chair. He unlocked one of the cabinets and withdrew a file.

With an anxious smile on his face, he walked over and handed it to Derrick.

"This is all of it?"

Derrick thumbed through the file. It held a few pictures, one of them an older, dark-skinned man dressed in an army uniform who bore a striking resemblance to Eva. A couple of newspaper clippings, a photocopied birth certificate, and typed pages rounded out the package.

"Yes. Everything." Danny stepped behind the desk. "Please let your wife know how happy I am she'll finally be able to meet her father. It was a pleasure meeting you."

"Wish I could say the same." Derrick stubbed out his cigar on the desk, leaving a burn mark on the wood. "You need to find a new line of business."

"A new line of business? This is my business."

"You're stealing people's money. I can't allow you to continue to do that. You have one week to close this place down."

"What? I gave you everything! Who do you think you are? You can't come in here and threaten me."

"The art of intimidation, my boy, is to make your opponent believe every word you say. Look them dead in the eye and never flinch. Never let them see weakness."

Derrick looked Danny in the eye without flinching. "I can, and I did. Trust me, you don't want to tangle with me."

After that pronouncement, Derrick rose to his feet and started toward the door. He stopped with his hand on the knob.

"If it means I have to buy this building and put you out, I will." His icy stare didn't waver, and even though he could tell by the rigid set of his mouth that Danny was furious, the other man didn't utter a word. "You have seven days."

****

Derrick entered the house to a flurry of activity. Eva had hired some help to decorate the house and grounds. Last count they had three Christmas trees, including a huge one out front. Other decorations included lights, holly, a couple of Santa Clauses, snow on the windows, and heaven only knew what else.

The scent of cinnamon and other delicious aromas filled the air, and the faint sound of Christmas carols came from the room in the back where he assumed the party would be taking place.

"There are my girls," he said when Eva made an appearance with Violet in her arms.

She wore an early Christmas present he'd given her. The simple necklace had a diamond pendant, and with her hair swept atop her head, the matching diamond studs twinkled like stars in her ears.

"She got through eating about ten minutes ago," Eva said, rising up on her toes for a kiss.

"Mmm." He dipped his tongue between her lips and got a taste of ginger. "You taste good," he said, going instantly hard. "How much longer?"

"We're supposed to wait at least six weeks, which means we have a couple more weeks," Eva reminded. He knew exactly how long the wait was. He had the date marked on his calendar.

"I don't know if she's worth all this trouble," Derrick teased, looking down at his daughter. She looked warm and comfortable while she slept, bundled like a little ball against

Eva in a pink outfit. Her skin had darkened to a golden hue over the past month.

"Stop." Eva dropped a kiss to Violet's cheek. "Roarke, Celeste, and Arianna are already here. They're spending the night."

"Okay." Derrick pulled the folder with the information from under his arm. "I went to see Danny Jackson today."

Eva grew still. "Derrick, what did you do?"

"Nothing. He gave me this file for you." He opened it and showed her the papers.

"Where did all this come from?"

"According to him, this information recently came in. He planned to get in touch with you, but since I was there, he gave it to me instead."

Eva stared down at the photo of her father in uniform. "I look exactly like him."

"I thought the same thing."

She looked up at Derrick with tear-filled eyes. "Oh my goodness. He found my father."

He nodded. "After the party, we'll review the file, okay?"

She nodded, too emotional to speak. "This is the best Christmas I've ever had," she finally said, her voice filled with emotion. "My baby's here, and she's safe, and I'll finally get to meet my father." She reached up and gently touched his face. "See, Derrick, I told you. The world's not all bad."

"I know," he replied. Then he said what he always did whenever she chided him about one thing or another. "Bear with me. I'm a work in progress."

"I love you anyway." She rose up on her toes again to give him a kiss.

"That's all that matters."

****

Within an hour, family filled the great room, everyone dressed in holiday colors of red, green, and gold. Hired servers circulated with hors d'oeuvres and drinks, and the instrumentals of Christmas carols poured from hidden speakers.

Derrick walked over to Roarke, who stood near the fireplace, watching the activity.

Roarke sipped his drink. "Well, how does it feel?"

He remembered being asked the same question months ago. "Pretty damn good." He smiled and held up his glass. Roarke touched his against it.

Lucas Baylor, a good friend of Roarke's, came toward them with Matthew following close behind.

"What's in this?" Matthew asked, holding up a cup of steaming glogg. The mulled wine contained aromatic spices and several different kinds of spirits. "I'm a big guy. I've only had two glasses, and I'm starting to buzz."

"Be careful. It's some kind of secret Icelandic recipe Svana makes every year around the holidays. Don't be surprised if you end up having to spend the night because you can't drive."

"I'll let you know if I need to."

Derrick looked at Lucas. "Who invited you to this family gathering?"

"Come on, I'm practically family," Lucas said with a laugh. "I hate I couldn't attend the wedding, but congratulations. Beautiful wife, beautiful baby. You're a lucky man."

"Thanks."

"I just want to know one thing."

"Oh boy. Here we go," Roarke groaned with a shake of his head.

"No, I'm serious. I've been thinking about it ever since I found out Derrick was getting married."

"What's that?" Derrick asked.

"What the hell is going on with you Hawthornes? Three weddings in less than six months? Is it something in the water? If so, who's next?"

All eyes turned to Matthew.

"*Hell* no!" he said.

Roarke threw his head back and laughed. "It's only a matter of time, little brother."

"There's nothing you can do about it," Derrick added. "One minute you're going through life minding your own business. The next..." His gaze settled on Eva across the room. She sat in a chair holding Violet, and three family members crowded around her, smiling and cooing at the baby. His chest filled almost to bursting. "The next minute you can't imagine your life any other way."

The four of them fell silent.

"Well, it won't be anytime soon," Matthew said after a long pause. "Not if I can help it. But I'm happy for you."

The sound of a fork hitting the side of a glass drew everyone's attention.

Cassidy stood in the middle of the room. "Can I have everyone's attention? I'd like to make a toast."

The room filled with groans.

"I'll be quick this time, I promise." Her mouth turned down in a hurt frown.

"Somebody wake me when she's done. I've heard that before," Matthew said. "Antonio, talk to your wife."

"Leave my baby alone," Antonio fired back.

Cassidy bestowed an appreciative grin on her husband. "I'm so happy that we're all here together like this. Derrick and Eva have a new baby, and Roarke and Celeste are pregnant."

Next to him, a startled Roarke started coughing. When he caught his breath, he looked at Celeste. "I thought we weren't going to say anything yet."

"I didn't." She looked equally stunned.

"She didn't," Cassidy confirmed. "But I'm not an idiot. She didn't have any glogg, and when I offered her some wine, she refused to have any. One plus one equals three."

Derrick shook his head. Laughing, he patted his brother on the shoulder and joined in with the rest of the room in congratulating him and Celeste.

"As I was saying…I'm so excited. Our family's growing. I want to make a toast to Derrick and Eva. Congratulations on having Violet. And keep 'em coming. I want more nieces and nephews!"

A chorus of "Hear, hear!" went through the room.

Derrick waited until the voices died down before stepping away from the fireplace and clearing his throat to get everyone's attention.

"I want to make a toast, too," he began. "To my wife, Eva, who loves me, despite my flaws. To my daughter, Violet, who will be on lockdown until she's thirty." The group chuckled. "And to my brothers and sister." His voice thickened on the last sentence, and he cleared his throat again. The group fell completely silent, with only the soft sound of a Christmas carol playing in the background. "I'm glad we've grown closer over the past six months, and I want you to know how much I appreciate your support. To family," he finished with a smile at them.

Everyone in the room raised their glasses. "To family."

THE END

MORE STORIES BY DELANEY DIAMOND

Hot Latin Men series
The Arrangement
Fight for Love
Private Acts
Second Chances
Hot Latin Men: Vol. I (print anthology)
Hot Latin Men: Vol. II (print anthology)

Hawthorne Family series
The Temptation of a Good Man
A Hard Man to Love
Here Comes Trouble
For Better or Worse
Hawthorne Family Series: Vol. I (print anthology)
Hawthorne Family Series: Vol. II (print anthology)

Love Unexpected series
The Blind Date
The Wrong Man

Bailar series (sweet/clean romance)
Worth Waiting For

Short Story
Subordinate Position
The Ultimate Merger

Free Stories
http://DelaneyDiamond.com

ABOUT THE AUTHOR

Delaney Diamond is the bestselling author of sweet and sensual romance novels. Originally from the U.S. Virgin Islands, she now lives in Atlanta, Georgia. She has been an avid reader for as long as she can remember and in her spare time reads romance novels, mysteries, thrillers, and a fair amount of non-fiction.

When she's not busy reading or writing, she's in the kitchen trying out new recipes, dining at one of her favorite restaurants, or traveling to an interesting locale. She speaks fluent conversational French and can get by in Spanish. You can enjoy free reads and the first chapter of all her novels on her website.

Join her distribution list to get notices about new releases.

http://DelaneyDiamond.com
https://www.facebook.com/DelaneyDiamond

Made in the USA
Lexington, KY
28 January 2015